Secrets of Like Souls

A Julie Madigan Thriller #4

Val Conrad

Black Rose Writing | Texas

ISBN: 978-1-61296-240-5
PUBLISHED BY BLACK ROSE WRITING
www.blackrosewriting.com

Printed in the United States of America
Suggested Retail Price (SRP) $19.95

Secrets of Like Souls is printed in Times New Roman

*As a planet-friendly publisher, Black Rose Writing does its best to eliminate unnecessary waste to reduce paper usage and energy costs, while never compromising the reading experience. As a result, the final word count vs. page count may not meet common expectations.

Other Novels in this Series

Blood of Like Souls

Tears of Like Souls

Promises of Like Souls

Secrets of Like Souls

CHAPTER 1

June 6, 1998

Never before had I believed that a sudden lack of stress in one's life could be as empty and disturbing as what I've experienced since I opened my eyes and found Zach standing in our kitchen, holding his gun to the head of a man who was there to kill me. I felt relief and overwhelming happiness that my husband was really alive, yes. Appreciative, of course, because he'd saved my life. But since that early morning, I sometimes feel like one of those odd creatures living many miles below in the ocean depths where sunshine does not illuminate the sea floor, so accustomed to the darkness and extreme pressure that when captured and brought to the surface, its body just explodes. Sort of like an unprotected human would in outer space.

Wouldn't a body freeze solid before becoming a pink mist of non-existence in the vacuum?

Gross as it was, that was the string of thoughts meandering through my brain as I lay sprawled on the bed, having slept late again because I could sleep. The sheet tangled around my body and my feet poked out. It wasn't really late, of course. The sun hadn't been up long, and my always-punctual and recently-back-from-the-dead husband had no doubt already been out to feed the horses and water the garden. Now he was the creator of those grand aromas of breakfast snaking their way from the kitchen up to our bedroom. So far, this had the makings of a glorious day.

A glorious day, indeed, I thought, closing my eyes again and smiling.

Until chaos erupted, starting with the sound of breaking glass followed immediately by a string of profanity-substituted words, and a barking dog, then the phone ringing.

Even in chaos, I was happy to have Zach and Amber home again.

"Julie?" my teenage stepdaughter yelled up the stairs. "Are you awake? It's for you!"

So much for glorious.

I rolled over and picked up the extension, croaking a greeting I had to clear my throat and attempt a second time.

"Julie, I'm sorry to wake you," Sheriff Wade Fordham said, so short of breath I could hear him wheezing. "Could I get you to go to Portland to talk with a woman who was transferred out of White Salmon early this morning? She went to the hospital late last night, saying she fell into a fire pit. Had burns severe enough to earn a helo ride to the burn unit," he said, then paused to take a deep breath. "When I dropped by her house this morning to make sure it was secure, I met up with the not-quite-sober boyfriend who wanted to fight. He'll be going to jail for drunk and disorderly, assault on a peace officer, and anything else I can think of."

In the background of the call, I heard some not-so-substituted profanity.

"Is she in any shape to talk?" I asked, sitting up. I turned toward the door to find Zach holding out a cup for me. I whispered a thank-you before taking my first sip of perfectly brewed, well-creamed and sugared coffee that made me close my eyes in a moment of bliss.

A girl could get used to this again.

"I don't know that medical stuff, Julie," Wade said, interrupting my reverie. "But there's something else you need to know." He paused, as if I needed to brace myself.

With everything I'd gone through and witnessed in the last few years, I doubted anything he said could shock me. "Yeah?" I finally said to get him to continue.

"This woman," he said, "it's Geo's sister."

"Our dispatcher, Georgia McAdams?" I asked, glad I hadn't taken another sip I'd have choked on. Not shocked, just surprised.

"Yep. She's probably in Portland by now. Sat at the hospital with Dana until the flight team came in." One more brief hesitation. "Geo doesn't think it's an accident."

CHAPTER
2

After learning a few more details, I dropped the phone back into the charging cradle.

Zach continued to lean on the doorframe, watching me, arms crossed as he patiently waited for details he knew I'd provide.

"I have to go to Portland," I explained, getting to my feet but not letting go of the coffee cup he'd brought me. I shuffled into the bathroom, knowing he'd follow as I talked. "Geo's sister was burned."

"Is she okay?" he asked.

"The sheriff didn't know," I replied. "But he says Geo doesn't think the injuries were an accident like her sister apparently told them."

"So your trip is not just support and good will, it's an investigation," he concluded for himself. "I'll make you a breakfast burrito to go."

Being married to someone in law enforcement makes these sorts of conversations about interruptions of plans much less complicated, I thought as I washed my face. But sometimes I wanted to talk through the details aloud to get things organized in my head. In this case, I had a long drive to focus on a new case.

I tied my hair back, put on my armored vest and then the uniform, and snapped my utility belt in place over the belt in my pants before loading it with the tools of the profession – holster, extra magazines, key clip, radio, and handcuffs. I also snugged my ankle holster on over my sock. I'd get my guns and boots downstairs

"Julie! Breakfast is ready!" Amber called from below.

Padding down the stairs in a hurry, my foot slid off the third to last riser, and I tumbled to the bottom. While the body armor saved my ribs, I thought, my hip and leg took the weight of the fall.

Zach rushed to me, asking if I was okay and helping me stand when I insisted I was fine, but the first step on my left ankle proved me wrong.

Amber scooted a dining room chair over so I could sit.

"Just bring me my boots before it swells so much I can't get my foot in," I stated, yanking off my ankle holster and sock to see, then more carefully pulling the sock back on. I put the holster on the outside of my right ankle, knowing it was much further out of my reach than if I'd took the time to reverse the holster.

Given my task for the morning, the second gun would be no more necessary than the bulletproof vest that I put on anyway.

"You need to go get x-rays," Zach said, then shook his head at me. "I know. When you get back."

"Maybe," I offered as a consolation.

Once I had my work boots on and zipped up, they provided enough support that I gathered my weapons from the locked box in the foyer closet to holster, then pocketed my keys and the rest of my stuff.

Zach held out the foil-wrapped burrito, an oversized tortilla stuffed with everything he'd been cooking for our breakfast – eggs scrambled with peppers, onions, mushrooms, bacon pieces, along with hash browns and shredded cheese. He'd poured a travel cup full of coffee for me, too.

"I think I told you once that you're way too good to me," I said before I kissed him.

"Yes, but I keep treating you like this anyway, don't I?" He laughed. "Be careful."

Limping only slightly because I didn't want Zach to worry, I exited the kitchen through to the garage. The double door stood open, but to get to my patrol car, I still had to walk through the collection of vehicles we had amassed – two Harley-Davidson motorcycles, a Ford Mustang, and two Chevy Suburbans. Someday soon, we'd need to add another vehicle for Amber.

Zach and Laser walked with me to the car. The human carried my breakfast, although the non-human had offered to take it, I think.

I could tell the dog wanted to go. Occasionally when I worked, if the weather was not too hot, I took him with me, but not today.

After I slid into the driver's seat and buckled up, Zach leaned in for a goodbye kiss. I was about to close the door when Amber came running out.

"I made you an ice pack big enough to drape over your foot while you drive," she told me, reaching in to put it in place across my boot. "There. That might help a little."

"Thanks. I can feel it already," I said, though I really couldn't sense the cold for the throbbing inside the leather, but I appreciated the effort. "I'll be back in a few hours, I hope."

Because my business was in Oregon, and I was most likely not going to be chasing down anyone on foot if I stayed in Washington anyway, I crossed the Columbia River at the Bridge of the Gods and headed west on I-84 toward Portland.

I like driving alone because I can talk out loud, spouting out all sorts of crazy stuff I'd never say in front anyone else. To ignore my ankle, I made a concerted effort not to think about Geo and her sister, which meant I sang to the radio, listened to a little news, and laughed at a few drivers who saw the light bar on my cruiser and slammed on their brakes. Finally, I changed my mental gears to the task at hand.

Geo doesn't think this is an accident, so did Dana do this to herself? Probably not. Burns are horrible, and I can't imagine anyone doing that to herself. But the sheriff had a physical altercation with the boyfriend this morning. Did the boyfriend do it? If so, why? Burning someone is either intensely sadistic or the result of gross intoxication and rage.

Still outside Troutdale, I picked up my cell phone and dialed the station, asking for the sheriff.

"He's not back yet," Bette Donovan said, her slow Carolina voice a perfect example of the calmness she radiated like perfume, even in crisis. "I'll have him call you when he gets back."

"That's okay," I replied. "I'll catch him when I'm done at the hospital."

"You tell Geo we're praying for her and her sister," Bette told me. "I'll be waiting for an update."

We disconnected, and I thought more about Geo.

She was in her mid-fifties, older than me but still slim and active. She'd offered more than once to teach me to play tennis, an invitation I turned down, knowing she'd wipe the court with me. I had shared a few meals with her when Zach was playing dead, had gone to her house a couple of times. She was upbeat, even when the situation was dire, like when Daphney Clinton had been injured. Always the first to volunteer to coordinate a food drive or a 'thon of some sort for a local cause.

I hated to see her and her family at the receiving end of needing.

With only one wrong turn, I made my way to the Oregon Burn Center at Legacy Emanuel Medical Center and parked in its expansive lot.

The sky was gray but dry for now, though it mimicked the mood I'd begun to slide down into for the morning. After growing up in Albuquerque, I never minded the rain here, but some days I really needed a good dose of sunshine to cheer me up.

Limping through the halls, turning this direction and that, I finally arrived at the waiting area for the burn unit.

Georgia McAdams sat in a corner, eyes closed but not asleep, I was sure.

I spoke her name as I walked toward her.

First she nodded, then when she looked up, her expression was something between relief and panic.

"Julie? Oh, I'm so glad it was you who came!" She stood and hugged me, squeezing hard.

We sat.

Glad to be off that foot.

"So tell me what happened to Dana," I said. "The long version."

Geo took a deep breath and began talking. "She has a trailer house west of White Salmon, set on a few acres. She got divorced about fifteen years ago, and since then, she's dated or lived with a dozen progressively worse losers. For the last two years, a man named Jack Browning has lived with her on and off. Apparently he gets mad and leaves, then he comes back and they make up." She stopped and took a drink from a bottle of water. "She ended up in the emergency room a year ago with a broken arm when he shoved her out the front door and she fell off the porch. I've seen the other bruises, but she always defends what he does to her. When I talked with her midweek, she said he'd been on a drinking binge."

"She tolerated him abusing her all this time?" I asked.

"Yeah," she answered, hanging her head. "There's just no talking any sense into her about it. I know – I've tried, and so have my folks."

"So what does she say happened last night?"

"Her story is that they had a bunch of people over and everyone was drinking, which really means they were all drunk," she said, wincing. "They had a fire – like a campfire, only about four feet across, ringed with bricks. She says she was clumsy and stumbled, falling into the fire pit. She insists her burns are so bad because everyone was so drunk, they had trouble getting her out."

"Okay," I said. "And what do you think happened?"

She pursed her lips a moment. "He's a mean son of a bitch, Jack is. I suspect that he caused this. Whether he pushed her into the fire or something else altogether, I'm sure in my heart he did it."

"Do you think he's a threat to anyone else in your family?"

"He's never been around any of us," she said. "Dana's always kept us away when he was there. But I suppose I'd have to say I'm afraid of him. I mean, if he'd do those sorts of things to her, then why not to anyone else?"

Why not, indeed?

"Do you think she's going to be willing to talk to me?" I asked.

"No. If she did, she'd only tell you the same thing as she told me and Wade."

"No way she'd press charges against him this time?"

Geo shook her head. "You haven't seen her, Julie. She has third-degree burns on her face, both arms and hands, a good portion of her torso, and down one thigh. She's lucky to still be alive, but she won't cross him."

"Then I won't bother her for now. She's safe for a few days, though," I said. "Jack Browning's in jail because he crossed Wade this morning."

❈

I didn't ask go in to see Dana, knowing it would be a lengthy process to change into sterile garb, only to find her swimming in painkillers and unwilling to tell me the truth. But her nurse allowed me to see a drawing of where Dana's burns were and their severity, and I had to agree with Geo, they didn't *look* like burns you'd get from falling into something hot. The burns to her knees and palms were not any worse than the others on her thighs, torso or face.

"Can I ask you a professional opinion question?"

The nurse looked up at me, surprised. "I guess."

"She says she fell into a fire. Based on what you see, does that sound right?"

"It's not my place to say."

"Look, I'm not asking for anything provable," I pushed. "But this isn't a dipping scald burn. It's not a pull-soup-from-the-stove burn. I just want an opinion, based on burns you've seen in the past, whether this could have been caused by a fall like she claims."

She stared at me for a moment, chewing her bottom lip. "The only opinion I'll offer is that I've never seen burns like this that were not inflicted by someone else." She turned and walked away.

CHAPTER
3

The drive to the burn unit had been worthless as far as gathering evidence of a crime, but Geo insisted that she was grateful I'd come. Still, without her sister's statement, there was little we could do as far as making a case against Jack Browning for any sort of involvement.

That infuriated me, knowing Dana Watson had put up with him hurting her.

Except I realized my first marriage had similar facets of domestic abuse, too. I had been almost as guilty of provoking David Wesley as he was of losing his explosive temper, but he never broke my arm or pushed me into a fire.

Okay, so he cut my throat. That was altogether different, thanks to Anthony Bock.

Limping to my car, I realized how far I'd come from those dark days after I'd survived what David had done. And he had died for it.

And I realized how much my ankle really, really hurt.

I took the Washington route back to Skamania County, crossing north into Vancouver before taking Highway 14 east. Once I'd passed through Camas, I called Wade Fordham again.

"Is there something that makes you think this wasn't an accident?" I asked when he came on the line.

"I got a look around the house when I went out there this morning in the daylight. First, it seems that Jack Browning is, as I've heard before, a major-league asshole even when he's sober, which he wasn't when he showed up," he said. "There had been a fire, leaning toward bonfire size, set well away from the house, but unless a dozen drunks picked her up out of it and then put all the pieces back where they belong in the fire pit, I can't believe that's what happened. When I peeked in at the hospital, she wasn't covered in ash and dirt like I'd expect if she fell. And none of the people at the gathering have told the same story so far today." He paused, taking a deep breath then blowing it out, almost deafening me. "I didn't go to four years of college without understanding that drunks may think two plus three equals two or seven or nineteen, but none of them can agree on five."

"Yeah, but you got a degree in phys-ed, Coach," I kidded him. "I have to conclude, after talking to Geo and a nurse who tried really hard to say nothing at all, that Dana wasn't burned by falling into a fire. Did you find anything else that might tell the story for her?"

"Maybe, but I'd like you to go look," he told me. "I know it's your day off, but you're really good at that sort of thing."

Flattery will get me to work a little while longer, I guess.

❁

Almost an hour later, I pulled the cruiser into the gravel driveway that circled behind Dana's house, hoping all the drunks had gone home after the sheriff took Jack away this morning. The place looked deserted, so I parked and got out, immediately regretting the lack of ice and elevation for my foot during the drive.

As Wade described, the fire pit was set away from the house. In it were several smaller pieces of partially burned wood, lots of ash, and one large log – a foot in diameter and more than two feet long – that had almost burned through its middle into two chunks. Regardless of how Dana might have ended up in the fire pit, I saw no evidence of any number of people trying to help her out. No shoeprints inside the brick ring, nothing kicked around except one brick out slightly out of place.

I scanned the area around me. A rusted rear axle and a haphazard pile of bald tires were stacked at the side of a rusty sagging shack –

trashy but unremarkable. When I turned back toward the house, I saw the one thing that made all the lies and cover-up meld into one ugly truth.

Taking another step, I reached into my pocket for my phone when I heard – a split second before it hit me in the back – an unmistakable growl of a large dog.

The attack from behind knocked me to my hands and knees, and the cell phone tumbled out of my reach.

Putting my left arm up around my neck as protection, I tried to roll to my left to reach my Glock on my right hip. But with the weight of the dog – seemingly a blur of teeth and fur attached to a writhing, growling animal intent on chewing through my left wrist – I couldn't pull my arm back far enough to reach my holster. So I did the next best thing – I grabbed my ankle for my backup weapon, drew it and pointed under my left arm and fired.

And fired again.

And finally the third bullet must have hit something vital, as the dog suddenly went limp and collapsed on top of me.

Relieved, I laid there, out of breath for a moment before gathering the strength to shove the dog's body off mine. My left forearm was bloody through my shirt, and it hurt.

Part of me said I should call for help, but the other part argued that the threat was over, so why bother everyone?

Three or four minutes later, when I was still unable to get up, I was left with no choice but to call dispatch to send someone to help me.

I tried to do it without sounding hurt, hoping not to start a panic, but as soon as Bette Donovan heard my voice, she determined I was in trouble.

Crap. Do I really sound that distressed?

Apparently so, as she immediately sent the closest available county and state units to the address, advising that the sheriff and an ambulance were on the way, too.

"No, I don't need all those people," I tried to insist, feeling more embarrassed by the minute. But honestly, starting with a bad ankle and ending with being mauled by a big dog, I supposed I could use some help.

By the time the first unit - a county cruiser, I was glad to see - came screeching up beside mine, I'd managed to get to a sitting position.

Doug Logan raced out of his car toward me, hand on his gun, ready for the next pack of wild dogs to race out from hiding.

"I'm fine," I said. "Please cancel the state troopers and everyone else responding."

"Ma'am, you're bleeding," he said, kneeling beside me.

"Yes, and I'll continue to bleed whether or not anyone else with a badge shows up, Doug." I'm sure I sounded grumpy. "Cancel everyone else, and then fetch your jump kit."

He looked at me with a blank expression.

"Doug?" I prompted.

"Yeah, okay," he finally said, talking into the mike clipped on his shoulder, telling the dispatcher that all further law enforcement units could cancel, but the ambulance should continue to the scene non-emergency.

Very good. Now for a bandage or two.

In the distance, I heard a siren, knowing it was Sheriff Fordham, who would not have been canceled under any circumstances.

Doug brought his orange kit from the trunk of the patrol car and opened it, revealing the sort of collection amassed by someone who volunteers as an EMT. I didn't need oropharyngeal airways or a bite stick, although the pain had almost become bad enough I felt like grinding my teeth. He dug for some saline to wash my wounds and gauze pads to dress them.

I stopped him. "Doug, get a pair of gloves on."

Bewildered, he replied, "Julie, I'm sure you don't have any –"

"No, I probably don't have any dreaded diseases," I said, "but I'm no different than any other patient, and I have no idea where your hands have been, either."

He looked rather sheepish, but gloved up anyway before cutting away the sleeve of my uniform shirt. While it crossed my mind that he'd ruined it, it was already ripped and bloody, thanks to the dog and the fall.

I tried to keep my thoughts focused on something else while Doug worked, and it occurred to me that I had been looking at something I thought was relevant to the case when the dog attacked.

What was it?

I looked around me, unable to see anything I remembered was important.

My wiggling and lack of direct attention to Doug and his efforts seemed to be disconcerting to him, but he continued rolling a gauze bandage around my forearm.

We both looked up when Wade Fordham's car pulled up beside the other two. The sheriff seemed to be in much less of a panic than Doug had been, but the news of cancellation of other responders had probably inferred the situation was under control.

"Julie, what happened?" he asked, kneeling down on my right side.

I told him about seeing something I'd thought needed investigation then about the dog. "This might have ended better had I not sprained my ankle this morning falling down the last few stairs at home," I confessed.

He didn't even turn away to hide when he rolled his eyes.

"But Geo was really glad I went to see her, and she appreciates that we're giving her suspicion a listen. Sounds like this isn't the first time Browning has assaulted her sister, so we need to check into prior injuries she received."

"And we will," Wade assured me. "After you go to the hospital. And don't even bother taking a breath to argue with me, young lady."

Who am I to argue with anyone old enough to call me a young lady?

CHAPTER
4

I had to explain what happened at least four more times before Zach and Amber got to the emergency room. Although it seemed pretty self-evident to me that four words should have been sufficient – *sprained ankle, dog bite* – everyone wanted more details. By the time Zach asked, I felt frazzled and impatient, but the pain medication had mellowed me out a bit.

"Doug had me just about bandaged, but when they stood me up at the scene," I explained to my husband, "I saw the red gas can – I mean it was plastic so it's really not a can, but –" I frowned, struggling for the right word.

Zach nodded that he understood what I meant, so I continued.

"It was over in a planter next to the house. I couldn't see it when I was sitting on the ground, but when I stood up, I saw it." And suddenly, though I had repeatedly described what I'd seen already, the meaning of the words and their subsequent conclusion hit me like, well, like the dog had – out of the blue.

Someone had thrown gasoline on Dana. And then ignited it.

"No, you don't think that's possible, do you?" I asked Wade after explaining my revelations to him. He'd come back to where I was being treated as we awaited the radiologist's long-distance interpretation of my ankle injury.

Wade nodded. "I took the container –"

"Yeah, that's the word I couldn't think of!" I blurted, interrupting him.

"I took the container for fingerprinting," he repeated. "It would have Browning's prints if he used it for the fire, but we might be able to make some other connection later." He hefted his belt, sagging a bit due because he'd lost some weight. "As for you, get fixed up then go home. Do not show up for work for a week. Do I make myself clear?"

Although I took a breath to start a debate, Zach nodded with grave conviction.

"You can pick up your take-home unit when you come back to work."

I'd forgotten all about it when I came in by ambulance, at Wade's unwavering insistence.

A doctor, whom I thought looked like maybe his mommy had to drive him to work because it was too far to ride his bicycle alone, pulled the curtain back to reveal the four of us.

"I'm told the dog had current rabies shots, which is good. I won't suture up those bites because of the risk of infection. Keep an eye on them for oozing, redness or increasing pain, and take all of your antibiotics," Dr. Gene Sanderson stated. "As for your leg, you don't have a fracture, but honestly, you might wish you did. Given the exam, the sprain appears to be significant, so healing may be more difficult than a simple break. I've arranged for you to see an orthopedic surgeon in Portland next week. Until then, stay off it completely, ice at least four or five times a day for twenty minutes, elevate it as much as possible, and take the anti-inflammatory medications regularly."

Pfthth! You're no fun.

I looked around, hoping I hadn't just said that out loud.

Damned drugs.

The doctor and the sheriff left at the same time, replaced by a nurse holding a pair of crutches and an elastic bandage.

"Have you ever used crutches before?" she asked.

Curtailing any further mental sarcastic remarks or lengthy explanations, I merely nodded my head.

She wrapped my ankle, explaining how I would need to rewrap it as swelling increased or decreased. When she was done, she had me stand on my good leg so she could adjust the aluminum crutches to the right height, extending the lower segment to the longest it would go before placing it under my right armpit. "No, a bit shorter." One more adjustment, then she did the same to the other.

By the time she was done setting the length, I began to feel nauseated and sweaty. Despite her plans to review how to ambulate, I sat down on the edge of the stretcher again.

Next thing I remember, I was back on the gurney looking up at the ceiling.

"Mrs. Samualson? Can you hear me?"

The nurse's face looked slightly concerned. Zach's more so. Amber's eyes were wide.

"I'm all right, really. Demerol makes my blood pressure drop sometimes."

Damned drugs.

❈

After much more discussion with the doctor about passing out, and because Zach had kept me from actually falling, I was allowed to go home. The nurse did come back and demonstrate the correct use of the crutches, making me promise not to attempt being up until my blood pressure stabilized.

At the cabin, Zach made the couch comfy with pillows and a blanket, helping me get situated. Amber disappeared into the kitchen, showing back up with crackers and slices of cheese.

"I'm not sure if she should eat this," Zach told her when she set the tray on the coffee table.

"Sure I can," I said, reaching for a cracker. "Can I have a ginger ale, too?"

Amber's face lit up, and she whirled back to the kitchen.

"Are you sure?" Zach whispered.

I nodded with a reassuring smile as Amber rushed to my side, pouring the contents of a can into a glass full of ice.

As I munched crackers and cheese, I wondered how Amber felt

about the urgency of the situation, whether it had reminded her of her mother's murder, or how Zach's life had been threatened.

"So I was thinking that since you won't be able to drive for a while, I could get my hardship license –" Amber's conclusion was interrupted sternly by her father.

"No."

"But I –"

"No one said I couldn't drive for while, just not for a few days or when I'm taking narcotics," I stated.

This statement garnered me an even sterner raised eyebrow from Zach.

"But what if –" she tried again.

Both adult voices said in unison, "No!"

Maybe her expression was a pout, but she knew better than to argue with Zach, so she huffed off.

When we heard the door to her bedroom slam, we both burst out laughing.

Until Zach stopped, suddenly serious. "She's right. You shouldn't be driving."

"I don't intend to go fetch us a pizza for supper tonight, Zach. You don't go back to work for two weeks, right? You can drive me to Portland for the orthopedic appointment, then I should be cleared to drive."

"Yes, but since you mentioned me going back to work," he said, sitting in the chair next to the sofa. "I'm thinking about resigning from the agency."

I opened my mouth to respond, but my brain provided nothing to say.

Nope, nothing.

"Really? That shocking," he commented, picking up a cracker and nibbling. "Stunned to silence is not the reaction I'd expected from you."

"You mean, just quit?" I stammered.

"Yes, or officially no. I'm tired of being shot. I'm tired of feeling like we're losing this war on drugs and that I'm only an expendable soldier for the government's ineptitude." He leaned back in the chair. "I hate what they put you through in order to catch someone stealing money. That's unforgiveable. But mostly, I just miss being with you."

"Wow," I replied, unable to think of anything more expansive. "I had no idea you felt that way about the Gordon case."

I was referring to when the FBI told one of its agents, Jamie Gordon, that his wife was dead to see if he would try to get the money she'd stolen electronically and stashed out of the country. Only they knew he'd tried to kill her. And that he'd shot Zach. His effort to get the money involved enticing me to get it because his wife and I were dead ringers. Turned out his spouse was no more dead than mine was, but I got to keep Zach. Rebecca Gordon would forever be on a ventilator, paralyzed. And Jamie would likely be in prison for the next twenty years.

How would any of that been different had Zach not pretended to be dead?

"Julie, the look on your face when you saw me standing in the kitchen that night proved to me just how bad it had been. I can't promise I'll be here tomorrow," he said, "but I don't want it to be because of one more meaningless government project."

"What about my job?"

"Work if you want to. It doesn't bother me." He nodded at my foot. "After you get this all back to normal, that is."

I winced and changed the subject slightly. "Did you see Amber's face when I passed out? I can't imagine what went through her mind. But I don't want her to worry either every time you leave for another assignment that you won't come home again."

"Then it's settled. I'll cash out my paid time off and be done with it. You can deal with getting the insurance coverage changed and stuff."

CHAPTER
5

"Have you asked Amber what she thinks about you resigning?" I asked.

"No, because I don't think her input has any relevance to our decision," he stated, getting up and walking to the bay window. "It's really up to you."

"No," I said, swinging my feet off the couch. "It's not up to me. I will support you in whatever decision you make about this. You're not asking me because you want me to say yes or no to your decision, but whether or not your decision to take such a big step is okay. It is okay, Zach."

"You really think so?"

"You're telling me you no longer want to be a part of a team that risks your life but that you can't believe in."

"That's about the size of it, yes." He turned back toward me, eyeing my feet on the floor as I scooted to stand up by myself. He smiled. "Going somewhere without your crutches?"

Using a pathetic whiny and helpless voice, I begged, "Please, sir, could you help me get to the bathroom, pretty please? Maybe you can just carry me?"

Shaking his head, he picked up the pair of crutches and handed one to me, and I used the handgrip on one side and Zach's arm on the other to get to my feet, then placed them under my arms.

"This is just unforgivably inconvenient and painful," I mumbled as I took the first few baby steps, holding my throbbing left foot off the floor.

"I seem to recall that you fell all by yourself," he said, scooting a recliner a bit to one side to make a larger path for me.

"It's not my ankle I'm complaining about," I said, finally getting to the downstairs bathroom. "It's the sore muscles and bites from the attack by a mad dog that hurt. Maybe I'll have another pain pill and a nap."

❧

Although I hated feeling dependent on Zach or Amber, I asked for help when I needed it to get up and down, especially up the stairs at bedtime. I was very grateful when Amber asked if I needed help with the wraps after I'd bathed the next morning.

My ankle was dark purple and swollen, even keeping it out of the hot water without the compression bandage. The wounds on my arm were very tender but only slightly red at the edges. When she asked, I directed her how to clean them, then she dressed and wrapped my arm again. I kept thinking how good she was at so many things medical and forensic.

During lunch, she and I discussed the duffel bag she'd found in the forest while riding with me on a search almost a year ago. The bag had been old to begin with, and what little evidence we could track had yielded nothing. Then the whole disaster that had been Zach's faked death had occurred, and I didn't follow up on the case after Amber went to New Mexico.

Now she was interested in continuing the search for the owner of the bag, and the person from whom the tattoo had been removed and the patch of skin tanned.

"I talked to a taxidermist in Albuquerque when I was there, and he thinks the tanning metals used wouldn't have caused the skin to shrink more than about ten percent, but it could have been restretched, too," she advised me, looking at the photocopy of the design I'd made for her. "Because this looks like a Buddhist love knot, and you said

Dr. Bishop said his daughter had one similar but not this exact one, I wonder if this came from someone who had it done first and then Catherine Bishop had one done to match it."

I bobbed my head, not having a definite conclusion one way or the other. Her theory was as good as any I'd concocted.

"So there has to be a body somewhere," she stated. "I know we looked around where the bag was, but thinking like a criminal, if I had that piece of skin, I wouldn't have dumped a body anywhere near it."

"A theory which leaves the other 2.9 million square miles of the U.S. to search. Think the horses are up for a ride?" I asked, trying to keep the sarcasm lighthearted.

"Well, you can subtract the square mileage for all the cities and roadways," she offered, playing along. "I'll just add that number up and get back to you next week."

Sometimes she just doesn't act like a teenager.

"Okay, so you're young. Walk through her life and see where you go," I suggested. "There are a few things we knew about her personality before she disappeared. What things about a person are not likely to change versus those that would change as she matured?"

Amber tilted her head. "I really may have to get back to you on that one," she replied. "But let's see. Things I don't think would change about me would be stuff like my intelligence and my likes for certain subjects. We assume by the library card that she liked to read, but apparently not complicated science topics."

"Good, keep going." I made notes, filling out index cards as we had been doing all along.

She shook her head. "Your turn."

"Okay," I said. "She got one tattoo, which was not a common thing for young people then. Perhaps that was either to rebel against authority or to be accepted by someone. Which would you think is more likely?"

"Why ask me? You grew up much closer to that time," she observed, getting up to refill her iced tea glass from a pitcher in the fridge.

"But you are closer to her age when she made those choices.

Both points are valid, however," I conceded. "I believe she did it to be accepted by someone or some small group. The image might be a Buddhist symbol, but there was nothing to indicate she practiced or had friends of that religion."

"Am I supposed to take the other side?" she asked.

"Not at all. We can agree, so long as your belief has a valid basis, whether or not it's the same as mine."

Zach came in through the kitchen door from the garage, and she poured him a glass of tea, too.

"What are you two working on?" he asked, sitting down opposite me.

"Amber and I are trying to determine what happened to Catherine Bishop, so we're predicting behavioral patterns we can make suppositions about," I said, taking a drink. "We can't search everywhere, so we're trying to figure out who she was and how she might have made certain decisions so we can narrow down a search."

Amber looked at me. "Is that what we're doing?"

I wasn't sure if she was stumped or being cynical.

Zach just nodded and sipped his tea.

"Dad, when's your next assignment?" Amber asked him as she folded her legs beneath her like a pretzel.

Makes my bones hurt to watch her do that.

"Well," he said, glancing first at me the back at her, "probably not for a long time now."

"Long time? Like another month?"

That's a long time?

"How about forever?" he replied.

She rolled her eyes. "No, Dad, I'm being serious!"

"So am I. Julie and I talked it over, and I'm going to resign," he told her. "Maybe I'll just work for Del Clinton once in a while to help him."

"Seriously?" Her voice ended an octave higher, looking from him to me and back, to see which of us would laugh at the joke first.

"Seriously."

"You mean you won't have a job at all?"

I understood. She was worried that having one less income might significantly impact her attempts at getting an early license and getting a car when the time came.

She has no idea that income is not a big issue for us.

"I'll probably look for something eventually," he said, taking another sip. "But I think I'll take a few months or so and just bum around the house."

I could tell by the sound of his voice that he was egging on the money issue, too.

"You can't just do *nothing*," she argued.

"Why not? You don't have a job. And I just don't feel like working any more. Think of all the time I'll have to be around here. We could rope and team pen together," he offered. "I can help you with training Waldo."

"Dad, you can't make Julie work all the time, and right now she's hurt and can't work," she stated, getting to her feet. "And I don't want to have to sell the horses."

Zach gave in before I would have, but it was his lead. "Amber, whether or not I work, we're not depending solely on Julie's income to keep this place running. I promise we won't have to sell the horses or stop eating meat. Deal?"

She glared at him. "So you *are* kidding about quitting, right?"

"No, I'm not."

With a disgusted *Hmmmph*, she turned her back and marched outside.

For the second time, we laughed at her.

"I'll explain it to her later, about her great-grandmother and my inheritance," Zach said, leaning over to kiss me as he stood. "For now, I need to run to the vet for some horse vaccines. Need anything?"

"Nope, I'm all set," I said, getting up and situating my crutches to hobble to the couch in the living room. "But because I'm hurt and I can't work, I think I'll take a nap."

We laughed again.

❋

My appointment with the orthopedic surgeon went worse than I expected. No expert at reading x-rays, I could only tell that there were no obvious fractures in the bones in my lower leg and foot. He advised me to return if I had continued pain after a couple of weeks as he would then consider putting my foot in a heavier boot or even a cast, and to stay off it for at least six weeks.

"Recovery from this depends on your compliance to my directions. Absolutely no weight-bearing at all," he said in a humorless monotone. Then he scolded me for walking on it in the first place. "In four weeks, you can start range of motion exercises but not walking. You'll see me again before then. And nothing but desk duty for at least two months."

A stranger to me, he might have been a great orthopedic doctor, but he had the personality of a rock. I mean, I don't need to discuss the family vacation and my favorite sports teams, but a little consideration to my intelligence and line of work were in order, I thought.

Maybe I'm just being crabby.

Then he sent me for a magnetic resonance imaging at a stand-alone center. Not a problem except my appointment was not until four o'clock that afternoon.

Zach and Amber and I ate lunch at a local spaghetti place, a unanimous favorite.

"Do you want to go see Geo at the hospital?" Zach asked as we finished a giant meal. "We certainly have the time."

"I'd like that."

Both he and Amber had met Georgia several times, especially when we were helping Delbert Clinton with the girls once Daphney came home from the hospital and after Zach was not dead.

So after lunch, I called Geo to see if I could bring her anything.

"No, thanks, but I really appreciate you asking," she said, her voice strained in exhaustion.

I didn't tell her we were coming to see her.

When we got to the waiting room where she sat between brief visits with her sister, she looked even more tired than she'd sounded.

"Are you getting any sleep at all?" I asked, hugging her.

"No, and heavens, girl, what are you doing on crutches?"

I explained about the fall and then the attack by the dog at Dana's house.

"Dana doesn't have a dog, so he must have taken one over there," she stated, meaning Jack Browning. "Is he still in jail?"

"For assaulting Wade and other things. Has Dana agreed to make a statement that will help us?"

She shook her head. "She still insists it was an accident."

"I found a gas container near the fire," I said. "I suspect he threw gasoline on her. That certainly makes more sense with her burns than falling."

"That's what I think, too. I just can't imagine. . ." Her voice trailed off.

"You know we'll help," I said, "But from here, it's up to her just how much we can do."

"What about the rest of us? What if he really is a threat to me or my folks?" she asked.

"As a deputy, I'd advise you to make sure you report any suspicious activity. As a friend, I'll tell you to be very cautious of him, and if necessary, to defend yourself and your family."

She nodded. "Yes, I will do that. But I can't be both places at once. My mom's been here a few times, but she hates to drive in the city. Dad's memory is getting bad, and Mom doesn't bring him with her. I think he has Alzheimer's. Mom might not be able to care for him much longer."

"Tough choices," I admitted.

What else could I say? Most people don't want to put a loved one into a long-term care facility, but with Alzheimer's or other dementia, observation and control of the environment becomes necessary twenty-four hours a day at some point. Her parents had to be in their mid-seventies or later, and her mother was a tiny little woman who couldn't possibly take care of assisting or controlling her husband physically once he needed fulltime help

"Thanks for coming," she said.

"Geo, you need to get some rest, too. Is there someone you know here in Portland you can stay with?" I asked, putting a hand on hers.

"No, I've been driving back and forth."

"Will you go to a hotel here?"

"I can't afford to do that."

Zach spoke up. "She asked if you would go, Geo. If you will go get some sleep, we'll get you a room here as long as you need it."

Tears pooled in Geo's eyes. "I couldn't ask you to do that."

"You didn't ask. We're offering," he insisted. "We'll find something close. Julie will call you with details in a little while."

Her gratitude streamed down her cheeks as she hugged each of us, even Amber.

As we walked out, Zach stopped at the information desk and asked to use a phone book, looked up a couple of places, and we went on out to the truck.

"How can we afford to pay for a hotel for her if you quit your job?" Amber demanded when we got in and belted.

She is red-hot mad.

Zach turned around in the driver's seat. "I promised I'd take care of you and Julie and the horses, and everything else. It's just money, and it's a worthwhile cause. Maybe you can do some extra chores and pitch in to help," he suggested.

Again, she made that teenage *hmmph*, crossing her arms and at least mentally dismissing the subject.

Zach winked at me as he turned back around.

Obviously he hadn't told her yet we weren't going to be destitute without his income. And, watching Amber stew about money, I didn't think his goal was a bad thing at all.

CHAPTER
6

"Six weeks!" Amber exclaimed when I told her about the orthopod's directions, as if I'd grounded her for that long instead of myself.

"No horseback riding. No cleaning house. Probably no cooking, either," I embellished as I watched her set the table that evening while Zach was outside grilling hamburgers. "Good thing Zach's quitting his job."

"Enough already. You guys think it's funny I'm worried about eating next week or buying hay for the horses, but neither of you think it's a big deal."

I couldn't stand to see her consumed by the issue anymore. "Honey, the truth is, due to circumstances way before you came to stay with us, we have enough money to live without either of us working, assuming we don't go blow it all on a race horse and a yacht."

"So we can buy me a new car?"

Yep, that's what she was worried most about.

"I doubt you get a new car when you get your license, and you'll still have to pay for gasoline and insurance for it, which means you get a job."

"But you just said we have the money —"

I stopped her with a hand in the air. "I didn't say *we* to include you. You don't get to spend it at will. You won't starve, and I doubt you'll ever go without anything you need, but that doesn't mean you get everything you want."

Her forehead and upper lip wrinkled.

"Remember when I first met you and we stopped at the travel store, I said you could get anything you wanted but that you should be reasonable about it, right?" I asked, and she eventually nodded. "Same here. Having a new car for a brand new driver is not prudent for a number of reasons. Giving you everything you want without any effort on your part means you haven't made an investment in it. When it comes time for you to drive, we'll make choices then."

Her expression didn't change much from anger toward understanding as she pondered what I'd said.

"Don't forget the pickles," I reminded her, changing the subject.

But just like that, the financial crisis she'd imagined stemming from Zach no longer working for the DEA evaporated.

Zach brought the burgers in on toasted buns, cheese melting over the meat already.

The gallon of tea Amber had set out to sun brew before we left was gone by the time the meal was finished, but so were seven hamburgers, a bowl of macaroni salad, and a basket of potato chips. Amber cleared off the table and loaded the dishwasher, then excused herself to her room.

"That was a strange meal," Zach observed. "I don't recall seeing her eat like that before."

I shrugged off his concern. "She didn't eat much for breakfast."

"Yeah, but she ate three helpings of linguini for lunch."

I pushed myself up to my crutches. "Maybe it's just another growth spurt."

I was almost to the couch when the phone rang.

Amber yelled that she would get it, of course, then called downstairs that it was for me. Zach brought me the cordless phone we'd seldom used until I was incapacitated.

"Hello," I said.

"Mrs. Samualson, this is Trent Fields from Harmon and Fields, Attorneys at Law," the man answered.

The hamburger I'd just eaten congealed into a rock in my

stomach at the mere sound of his name. I didn't ask him to continue. Didn't acknowledge his statement at all.

Perhaps it wasn't his fault he practiced the type of legal services that had put him on the opposite side of a courtroom from me after I'd helped Laura Randall when she went into premature labor six months ago. I certainly resented her for suing everyone who worked so damned hard to save her life as well as that of the unborn twin boys she'd contracted to surrogate.

He sensed my lack of conversational engagement, so he continued anyway.

"The second twin died yesterday of the many complications it had suffered since birth."

"He." I said. "Not 'it.' That twin was a boy. A person. As much as you would like to just see dollar signs, he was a living person."

I saw Zach raise his head at my comment.

The lawyer swallowed hard. "Yes, you're right. I just thought you might want to know," he said, lacking the previous egotism his voice had projected.

"Off the record, Counselor," I asked, still angry at his intrusion into my day. Into my life. "Just what exactly would you have wanted me or anyone else you dragged into court to be held responsible for this catastrophe to do differently?"

"Honestly, nothing. Mrs. Randall is lucky to even be alive, and probably wouldn't be if you hadn't helped her." He sighed. "I tried to tell her that."

Exactly. But you let her file a suit to hold me accountable for her decision to carry the surrogate pregnancy and for trying to save her and the babies.

"Thank you for calling." I pushed the button to disconnect and dropped the phone to my lap.

"What was that about?" Zach asked, sitting on the opposite end of the couch where I'd made room for him. He put my feet back in his lap and rubbed the uninjured one.

Bless him, I could feel the tension drain out with every little circle his thumb made on my sole.

"Laura's lawyer," I said. "The twin that no one wanted died."

He nodded, kept rubbing.

"It's a shame," I said, leaning my head back onto the pillow fluffed behind me, relaxing.

He rubbed maybe ten minutes before speaking. "You know, it wasn't that no one wanted him," Zach said softly. "I thought about asking you if we should take him."

Had I not already been so calm, I'd have hurt myself whipping my head up to look at him. Instead, I took a deep breath. "Really." Not a question, just an observation. "Even knowing he probably would not survive past his first birthday?"

"Sure. We're all going to die. The crime is dying without being with someone who cares."

I didn't know what to say. I sat up and scooted toward him. "Why didn't you ask?"

"I intended to talk to you about it when I got back from Seattle, but things didn't work out."

Yeah, the government made everyone believe you were dead in order to catch a criminal while you were recovering from a gunshot that cost you a kidney.

I only nodded. "I'm not sure I could have done it, given all the politics involved, then knowing he would die."

"That's understandable," he said. "But it did cross my mind."

"I'm disappointed I can't have a baby now," I said, almost surprised the words came out of my mouth.

"So am I, but I'm just glad you're still alive."

"Ditto," I replied, leaning into him. "And I'm glad you're back."

On Saturday afternoon, Zach took Amber to a penning competition, a time-limited event where three riders cut three like-marked cattle from a herd of thirty and drive them into a small fenced pen. It was something all three of us had done, but they had hoped to catch a third rider at the arena since I couldn't go.

Late that evening, I heard the truck pull in toward the barn to unload the horses.

Amber came in through the garage, looking as limp as a potted plant left baking in the sun.

"I know Dad wanted me to help him with the horses," she told me, reaching into the refrigerator for water, "but I'm just exhausted."

Instead of asking how they did, I held the back of my hand to her forehead. "You don't have a fever, do you?"

She rolled her eyes. "No, I just need a nap."

With the bottle of water and her hat, she dragged on through to the stairs and clomped up them in what sounded like slow motion.

Through the kitchen window, I saw Zach walking toward the house from the barn, talking to the dog trotting at his heels. Before I could finish loading the dishwasher, I heard him come through the garage door.

"What's up with her?" he asked. "The longer we were out, the more listless she got."

"She says she's exhausted," I repeated, wondering how an energetic teenager could be that way after just a few weeks of summer working two days a week on trail rides with Del Clinton and one day sitting with his granddaughters Courtney and Daphney.

Daphney was still in a wheelchair, which meant that getting her around to errands in town was more than either she or Del could manage yet, so Amber stayed with the girls for the afternoon while Del tended to shopping and other matters.

Zach shook his head. "I don't get it."

I shrugged. "It was tough coming back and getting caught up again the last two months of school. She's keeping up her chores and stuff, so who can complain if she says she's tired now and then?"

About to say something else, we heard a loud thud above our heads.

"Amber?" he called.

When there was no answer, he whirled around toward the stairs, taking them two at a time ahead of me, hobbling as fast as I could on crutches.

In her room, Amber's pale body lay crumpled on the floor.

"Amber?" he yelled again, patting her face.

When he looked up, I was already dialing the phone for an ambulance.

CHAPTER

7

The EMS crew would arrive within twelve minutes, I was told, but time seemed to stretch like Silly Putty by while we waited.

"Are you sure she didn't hit her head at the penning?" I asked.

"Julie, I wasn't with her every single moment," Zach answered in a defensive tone, then he inhaled once and closed his eyes for a moment. "No, I didn't see anything, and she never mentioned it."

"Sorry, I'm just trying to figure out what's wrong." I felt her pulse, which was rapid and faint. Her breathing, fast and deep. "With a head injury, her heart rate would be slower," I said, talking to myself.

By the time the ambulance was pulling into the driveway, Amber was awake and able to speak, but she was weak and confused.

"There's the EMTs. I'll go down and let them in."

"No, Amber's better off with you. I'll go down." His legs trembled as he got to his feet. He left me with his daughter, still a crumpled heap on the floor.

"Tell me what happened, Amber," I said, knowing she probably couldn't.

She looked up at me, squinting as if she couldn't focus. "Can I have a drink?"

I shook my head. "In a little while. You'll have to go to the hospital first."

That upset her to tears.

"Honey, you passed out. We need to find out what's wrong."

Footsteps thumped up the stairs, and Zach led the crew into her bedroom.

Unable to add anything to help clarify why we'd called except that she'd collapsed, I let Zach help me to my feet, and we sat on her bed out of their way.

Getting the gurney up the stairway to her room was not going to be possible, so while they were debating whether to put her on a backboard, Zach bent down and picked up Amber's weak body. "Go get the gurney out of the ambulance for us," he barked. "I'll carry her down and meet you."

Nobody wanted to argue with him, and his solution seemed to be the most efficient, so the medics grabbed their gear and hurried downstairs. Following as Zach carried Amber, I waited until they cleared the steps before I started down, lest I fall and take us all to the bottom.

By the time I got outside, Zach had already put Amber on the gurney, and it had been loaded into the ambulance. The crew was inside, working on her – oxygen, EKG, an IV start.

Amber whimpered when stuck, but she continued to pant into the mask. The medic collected blood in a syringe before connecting the IV tubing to the catheter for the fluid to run, giving his partner the blood to put into lab tubes and use a drop for the glucose meter.

The expression on her face was more than surprise as she held the meter to the medic to show him the result, then together they turned to look at me.

"Her glucose is so high it won't even read," the medic told me, and I knew it had to be over 500. "Is she a diabetic?"

"No," I said, mentally putting my hands on my hips. "I would have told you if she was." But I felt like banging my head against the door, realizing Amber's symptoms matched those of diabetic ketoacidosis – when there is no longer enough insulin in the body for the cells to use glucose as fuel, the body begins to use fat for energy, resulting in high levels of ketones, making the body acidotic. I was about to turn to Zach and explain, when Amber leaned over the side of the gurney and threw up on the paramedic's boots.

As we followed the ambulance to the hospital, I wondered if we wouldn't be going to Portland as our next stop.

After a brief exam, Dr. Sanderson – the same ER doctor who'd taken care of me just days before – took us aside. "Her blood sugar was almost 850, and she was already acidotic," he said, knowing I spoke his language but that I'd have to translate this for Zach. "We've started her on an insulin drip to get her sugar down and given her some potassium, but we'll need to watch her closely the next twenty-four hours to bring her glucose down to normal."

"Does this mean she's definitely a diabetic?" my husband asked.

"She'll need to see an endocrinologist in a few days for more complete testing, but unless there is some other very odd reason her glucose is so high, such as a serious infection," Dr. Sanderson said, "then yes, probably so."

"Like insulin shots and all that?" Zach pressed, frowning.

The doctor nodded.

To both my and the doctor's surprise, Zach spun and hurried away.

I excused us and followed him out to the parking lot before catching up. "What on earth is wrong?"

When he turned, tears spilled down his cheeks. He gathered me up into his arms and cried silently for several minutes before he managed to pull himself together.

He wiped his face with both hands. "Her grandfather was a diabetic who was never well controlled. I'm guessing Amber saw Agatha's husband go through seizures and shots and many hospitalizations as long as he was alive."

"Zach, diabetes is an easily controlled disease now," I said, think about the barbaric treatments patients had received in the previous century.

"What if –"

"No what if's tonight, Z'. We get through this emergency and we take the next step, then the next."

"How can you be so nonchalant about this?" he asked, his voice just short of demanding.

"I'm not making light of it, but diabetics can lead normal lives," I said. "And wasn't it you who wanted to take in a baby who was blind and going to die before his first birthday?"

"That was different," he argued.

"No, it's a lot better. This is not a death sentence for Amber." I reached up to dry his cheeks. "We'll get through this together."

He finally nodded, and we went back inside to wait.

Within the hour, Amber was transferred to an ICU bed, with oxygen, EKG and monitors for her vital signs, a Foley catheter, and IVs all attached, but she was sleeping.

The nurse tried to get us to go home for the night, but her suggestion fell on deaf ears attached to a very tall body that pulled a chair close to the bed and sat in defiance of hospital visiting hours.

I shrugged an apology, pointing to my crutches. "I'm not supposed to drive."

She dragged in another chair for me, and we sat all night watching Amber breathe, watching IV fluids run in and urine come out of her still body, watching every hour when the lab tech came to draw blood until her glucose level dropped below 200, then every three hours till shift change.

At the end of his shift the next morning, Dr. Sanderson came in to check on us, explaining that labs showed Amber was doing better – her glucose was down to 135 – and that our family doctor would be in to see her in an hour or so.

Zach apologized to him for being so emotional the night before.

"Honestly, if it had been my daughter," Dr. Sanderson replied, "I'd have reacted the same way."

CHAPTER
8

By Amber's second day in intensive care, my nerves were nearly frayed, listening to her and Zach commiserating. Then I realized neither of them saw the behavior as needy like I did.

When we left to have lunch, I cautioned Zach about keeping up his supportive position of her "new handicap" as she called it, because I thought he needed to encourage her to be responsible for learning how to take care of herself.

"How am I supposed to make her be responsible when she thinks of it as a handicap?" he asked, frustrated at my comments.

"She is almost old enough to drive a car, so it's not like she can't learn to do a fingerstick and inject insulin," I pointed out. "It's not rocket science."

He inhaled sharply, nostrils flaring a bit as he considered my words. "Maybe it's not so hard to do the physical tasks, but to be hit with such a life-altering diagnosis at her age, when everything revolves around image with friends and peers? That has got to be an emotionally devastating wake-up call to life as an adult."

Wow, what a huge point.

"You're right, and I agree. I am looking at this from my perspective, thinking it's not tough to face. She needs a parent who is there to hold her hand – especially when none of her friends have come up here. But diabetes is still not a handicap."

"Do any of her friends even know she's in the hospital?"

I shrugged. "She didn't ask me to call anyone. You?"

He shook his head. "Should we?"

"No, not without asking. If she has those image issues, she might not want any of them to see her. That," I said, lifting my foam cup to make a point, "I can identify with."

"Really?"

"After David cut my throat, I didn't want anyone to see me. I'd have been devastated to know you'd been there," I said. "I wouldn't even let Eric Rader visit." Sometimes, even in the years since, I mentally had to stop my hand from reaching to cover the scar on my neck.

"I brought you a gift, and you said some not-so-kind things to me," he stated, lightening the mood. "I understand now after everything else that's happened. And for the record, I'm really tired of seeing you in a hospital bed."

Time to change the subject . . .

"You should ask her if she'd like to call any of her friends, or even her grandmother," I said. "It would mean more coming from you, I think."

He nodded and bit into the banana he'd bought with his sandwich.

I thought about taking a bite, but I couldn't bring myself to do it because it made me think of Jamie Gordon.

"I know you think everything will be okay, Julie. But even if it's not scary for you, it's terrifying to me. The 'what-if's' are chewing me up inside, not knowing what's ahead."

"Think about this: You had no idea how things would work out after you met me, but you stuck it out, day by day. Sometimes minute by minute. You never knew the next what-if that could come along, but you were committed to the belief that our relationship would all work out," I said. "And it has, even though some moments you'd never have suspected have happened. But here we are. Amber is no different. You made a commitment to her safety, then to her life. You didn't know what would happen when she came here with us, but she did and we've all adapted. And it's okay, right?"

He nodded.

"So a complication to her health is no different than when I broke my arm or sprained my ankle, except diabetes doesn't go away. Still, it's one day – sometimes one moment – at a time. And we're all together."

❀

Back in Amber's ICU cubicle, she looked glum, pale against the white sheets that I knew from much personal experience were bleached, disinfected, and stiff even if they lacked actual starch.

I made a show of telling Zach I needed to go to the restroom, giving him time to ask her about her friends. Before I got back inside the unit, Zach met me at the double doors in the hall.

"I left her my cell phone so she could call somebody," he said, taking me arm and leading me away. "And she could use a little privacy."

Eager to know who she'd called, I was miffed when Zach didn't volunteer a name.

We went to a waiting area and sat. He picked up a worn magazine, flipping through pages that had lost their gloss a hundred family members ago.

"Okay, I give. Who is she talking to?" I finally blurted in my curiosity.

"She doesn't want you to know," Zach said, tossing the magazine back onto the table, "but she's been talking to Cody Randall ever since she got back from Albuquerque."

Cody's mother, Laura Randall, had been the woman who had filed a law suit naming me and a dozen others as responsible for her predicament in the emergency delivery of the twins, one with fatal complications, I learned just days ago from her attorney.

When the legal papers had been delivered by Trent Fields, Amber had immediately called Cody and ripped into him, severing their friendship and whatever else might have been on their teenage minds.

Was I angry that she was talking to him again?

"Good," I finally said. "None of what happened was his fault."

Zach reached to touch my arm. "I hoped you'd say that. Have I told you today how much I love you?"

❦

The following morning, Amber was transferred to a regular room.

She was happy to get most of the wires and tubes removed, which I suspected was part of her hesitancy to see Cody.

I was not surprised when he showed up that afternoon, holding a slender vase of daisies.

When I saw him standing outside the door, I excused myself before she even looked up from the booklet left by the dietitian. I smiled and nodded as I passed him, and as I closed the door behind me, I overheard a bashful hello.

CHAPTER
9

Being home from the hospital only led to arguments about what Amber could eat versus what she wanted, future doctor's appointments, and the sudden appearance of Cody Randall in our lives.

"He's just a friend," Amber insisted for about the sixth time the second day.

"I get that, really," I said, hobbling with my crutches to clear the breakfast table. "But still, he can't stay here all day every day to keep you company. It's time you got out and did something on your own."

"Yeah, like what? You just want me to do your housework ever since you messed up your ankle," she retorted.

I've had just about enough of this.

"I haven't asked you to do anything extra on my behalf," I said, stopping her rebuttal with a finger in the air. "But you live here, and you are expected to pitch in and do what needs to be done."

"Grandmom Vera never made me –" she began, but I interrupted her again.

"And this is not, under any circumstances, Grandmom Vera's house to keep. How she treated you and expected you to act is not relevant here."

"You don't want me to have any fun!" she yelled, whirling away from me.

"Amber," I said in a low voice, very much opposite to hers – one she had to stop to hear, but she did. "I want you to have fun. I *want* you to get outside and *do something*. And I'd be tickled if it sometimes involved Cody. But you cannot sit in your room all day, listening to music and hiding from the rest of the world."

"I'm not hiding," she replied, but half the angry ego had deflated.

"You are. You haven't talked to any of your other friends," I said. "No one else has come to see you. You haven't asked to go see them."

"I don't want to have to carry all that crap around with me," she said, hands on her hips. "It makes me feel like a moron."

"You sit here and get your insulin and diet adjusted when you're not doing anything and then go back to a completely different level of activity with different requirements, you'll risk having low blood sugar episodes," I explained. "Would you rather your friends see you like that?"

She frowned, then shook her head.

"We've agreed to eat what your diet says, but if you won't manage your own care, there is no reason why Zach should go out of his way to fix meals that meet your standards."

"I hate this!" she whined.

"I hate it for you. Zach hates it even more. But we can't change it," I said. "This is no different than being diagnosed with cancer – it's a disease that requires close attention and treatment to manage or it will kill you."

"No it won't."

"Yes, it will. Slowly and painfully. Letting your blood sugar run out of control will clog your kidneys, making them fail. The only solution to that is dialysis – hooked to a pump for hours a day, several times a week. Is that how you choose to live?"

I knew the diabetic educator who talked to her had listed other nasty consequences of unchecked glucose where the sugar crystals become like glass shards in the body, damaging eyes to cause blindness, limbs to cause pain and loss of sensation and eventually amputation. Having uncontrolled diabetes could also cause severe infections because bacteria have extra sugar to feed on. So many complications a teenager did not need to face.

The ego balloon continued to deflate. "Why me?"

I wrapped my arms around her. "There is no reason for this any more than why any of the other bad things have happened to you or Zach or me," I said, stroking her hair. "But we have each other to help muddle through them."

"You know, some days I could really hate you and your logic," she announced, pulling away from me and wiping away her tears. "But not today." She took a deep breath.

"Why don't you go see the horses? Denali's really missed you."

A flash of uncertainty was replaced by a decision. "We have any apples for them?"

She gathered a shirttail full and went to the barn, where Zach was restacking hay before our first summer cut arrived. If she asked, I was certain he would drop anything he was doing and go riding with her, and I kept peeking out the kitchen window in hopes that would be her choice.

I saw them talking, but then Amber took the apples and a few grooming tools with her to the corral where all four horses came to her.

Not riding, but grooming. Still, it was one step toward getting her back to her previous life, I thought.

My cell phone rang, and I had to crutch my way over to the table for it.

"Julie," the sheriff began. "I know you can't go out on patrol, but with Geo still in Portland, I was hoping you'd come help in dispatch while we're out searching."

"Sure, Wade," I said. "What's going on that you need me?"

"It's Mitch's wife. She's missing."

"Missing?" I echoed. Mitchell Seaver was one of the county's veteran deputies, a co-worker.

"He transported a prisoner to Vancouver yesterday," he explained. "When he got home after lunch, she wasn't there. He said he didn't think anything of it. Her car was gone, so he assumed she had gone shopping. After a few hours, she still hadn't returned, so he asked if we could do a local BOLO," he said, meaning a be-onlookout. "He said it wasn't like her to be gone like this. He called and went to all the places she might have been – her mother's, the store, her friends' houses, but he came up without any clue. We started looking about dark last night."

I waited, knowing there was something besides a bunch of deputies looking for a woman in a car.

"Blake Erwin found her vehicle off a dirt road just west of Bonneville Dam an hour ago," he said. "There was no blood, no signs of a struggle."

"Did she just leave?" I asked, astonished.

"That's the best I could hope for, Julie," he replied, sounding heartbroken. "Worst case is that someone could have dragged her body to the river and thrown her in, but there's a whole lotta nasty possibilities in between."

CHAPTER

10

The sheriff's department offices were a beehive of activity and noise.

I went to the dispatch room, sat down beside Bette Donovan, who was having a conversation on her headset, but she nodded acknowledgement I was there and slid a legal pad toward me.

On it, she'd listed all the on-duty deputies and more than a dozen volunteers who were active on this investigation, I presumed.

I heard her giving a description of Rachelle Seaver to the person on the other end of her call. Nothing that Wade Fordham hadn't shared with me.

Behind me, Wade's voice echoed through the hall, barking orders about evidence.

Bette finished her phone call, turned her head to me and mumbled, "Welcome to hell."

I smiled weakly. "Wade called me to come help you. Tell me what you need."

She shook her gray curls. "He might have asked you to help me," she said, holding up a finger to interrupt our conversation and acknowledging a deputy checking out at a scene. "But truly he needs you to coordinate the evidence being collected, which seems to be getting incrementally larger each hour."

"All right," I said, getting back up and pulling the crutches toward me. "I'll go find him and get started there. But you let me know if you need something – coffee, bathroom."

I hobbled down the hall toward Wade's office. The pain in my ankle hadn't been bad enough that I'd used any narcotic medication in two days, but I was already wishing I'd taken some ibuprofen before coming. Although I'd driven myself, Zach had offered to take me.

"Amber needs to be outside and doing something," I'd told him, shaking my head. "And you need to stick around and be here for her."

That had seemed to make sense to him, so they stayed.

I was almost to Wade's door when Mitch Seaver came rushing out, head down, almost knocking me over.

"I'm – Julie?" He seemed confused, but he did steady me. "Sorry. Damn," he mumbled, then hurried around me, breaking into a jog as he turned the corner.

Wade came out to see what had happened. "Oh," he said when he discovered the calamity he'd heard was Mitch tackling me. "I'm glad you're here."

"What's up with him, besides the obvious?" I asked as I sat in the chair across the desk from Wade. "He ran out of here like his tail was on fire."

Wade just shook his head. "It's been an ugly day so far, Julie." He palmed his eyes for a moment, giving away the headache behind them. "I sent him home, or to his mother-in-law's, or anywhere but here. He's pissed off because I won't let him participate in this investigation."

Which explains all the yelling I heard a few minutes ago.

"So how can I help you?" I asked. "Bette sent me back here."

"We're getting digital photos by the hundreds – since photography is no longer limited by the amount of film one can expose," he explained, holding up a half-dozen memory cards in a clear evidence bag. "I'm not good enough with a computer to get these organized, but I know you can. And that's just the first wave of evidence we'll be getting. Fingerprints will be next, I'm sure – all those will need to be sorted and catalogued, even though I've asked the Washington State Police to help process them. You can coordinate who gets what and keep track of where it goes, right?"

I nodded.

"Keep me posted if you see anything worthy of my attention. As it stands, I'm stuck believing Rachelle Seaver was kidnapped and likely murdered. Lacking a timeline for a possible river dump, there's no way we can have divers search the Columbia downriver far enough to find a body in the next hundred miles." He paused. "On the other hand, there's always a nagging chance she staged the whole event to escape her life here."

"Any reason she would do that?" I asked, getting to my feet.

"Not a clue, Julie. But it's still a microscopic possibility I'd dearly like to hope for."

So I set up shop in the evidence laboratory – a square windowless room at the back of the station – not because it was comfortable but because it had all the equipment I'd need. Starting with a computer, I copied all the digital photos to the hard drive before storing the cards as evidence. Then I reviewed the photos one by one, reorienting those that were vertical, moving those that were useless due to blurring or under-exposure to a separate folder, and organizing the images into groups of subject matter – the car, the scene, and so on.

When I looked up, Blake Erwin stood in the doorway.

His shoulders sagged when I waved him inside, weariness practically dripping from him after what was probably his twentieth hour on duty.

"Sheriff told me to bring this to you," he said, eyeing the stool in front of a microscope. He handed me a lunch-bag-sized brown paper sack.

I opened the carefully folded top to find a stack of fingerprint cards.

"Thanks, Blake. You need a rest. Go grab a sandwich in the break room."

He nodded, then turned to go, saying nothing else until pausing at the doorway. "Thanks for coming to help." And then he was gone.

I had no idea if he intended to come back or not, so I turned my nose back to the photographs to finish the section I was doing before tackling the fingerprints, not knowing if they might turn out something more critical than images of a scene after a crime that might or might not have been committed there.

After finishing with the photos, I dumped the cards on the table. The prints had been taken from Rachelle Seaver's car, inside and out. Obviously, like searching for a body in the Columbia River, we could dust for prints on every flat surface in the county and still not yield a single lead. Nonetheless, I found a magnifying glass and began separating the cards into piles of similar patterns before attempting to identify their owners.

An hour later, I had six piles. Two of these almost certainly could be eliminated as they belonged to children, most likely Mitch's two kids who lived with their mother in Pasco and only visited one weekend a month. He had no children with Rachelle.

One set I would have to presume belonged to Rachelle as they were the most pronounced and greatest in quantity, including those collected from the steering wheel and driver's door handles. Second were those I'd have to determine were Mitch's. Four cards had prints from the passenger side that might be Rachelle's mother's. That left one set of cards – actually just three individual prints – belonging to someone else.

Throughout the afternoon, I received other evidence, including possible blood samples from the car. Photographed, then swabbed, this minute amount of reddish stain required prep for lab and possibly DNA testing. I would need DNA and fingerprint comparisons from Rachelle's belongings. I asked the next deputy who came in to go gather items from the Seaver house, providing him with a list of potential objects for collection.

I'd been so busy I didn't hear Zach standing at the office door three hours later.

I never hear him. He's like a shadow.

Silent until I looked up, he held out a brown paper sack. "Lunch."

"You didn't have to bring me –" I started to say, but I felt my stomach rumble in disagreement.

"Just a couple of sandwiches," he said, lifting a shoulder to dismiss my scolding. "I thought maybe I could whisk you away out to the riverfront for a half-hour break. Looks like you need one."

Looking down at the tabletop in front of me, at the piles of bags and logs and notes I'd been making, my initial thought was that there was no way I could leave. Until I straightened my back, muscles tightening into knots, which changed my mind.

"Yes, I do."

I locked up the evidence and then gathered my crutches and my bag, which Zach took away from me to carry, and I made sure to lock the lab behind me.

We headed out the back, only to have the crash bar ripped out of Zach's hand when a deputy hurled the door open and plowed into us, yelling, "Where's the sheriff? Mitch's out in the parking lot, holding someone at gunpoint!"

CHAPTER
11

Richard Langley, the deputy who'd nearly bowled us over in the entrance, continued to speak at a speed and volume that almost exceeded human capacity to comprehend, moving on down the hall like a pinball, bouncing from wall to wall.

Zach, however, focused on getting outside after Langley stumbled on by us.

My husband, despite my hesitation to walk into a volatile situation, marched right out to where his Suburban was parked.

I followed him out the door on the crutches, hoping I wouldn't have to dive for cover.

Sure enough, on the far side of Zach's truck, Mitchell Seaver had Kenny Underwood by the shirt collar at arm's length, a gun pointed at his head.

"Mitch," Zach said in a casual voice as he walked toward them, "I see you have Kenny in custody."

Yeah, that's putting it mildly.

Kenny Underwood was, and will always be, a severely paranoid schizophrenic with probably unsubstantiated rumors of violent tendencies. I'd met him several months ago when his twin brother tried to frame him for murder. Although the trial for Benny was still pending, Kenny was free. During the time when Zach was pretending to be dead, he and Kenny had become friends somehow.

"He killed my wife!" Seaver's voice warbled. He pulled his gun closer to his upper chest, arm bent.

From where I stood, I could see Seaver's fingers around the grip were white. His hand was trembling.

"Then let's take him inside and book him," Zach said, demonstrating a calm I could not fathom, inching closer to the pair. "Do you have your handcuffs?"

Wade Fordham had hurried out the door, sliding to a halt when he saw Zach reaching to hold Kenny while Seaver stepped back and holstered his weapon then reached to his belt for cuffs.

With blinding speed, Zach pulled Kenny away and whipped Seaver around to his right until the deputy stood with his face against the Suburban, his gun arm twisted behind his back.

Wade and Richard Langley then hurried out to intervene, probably still unsure what they had just witnessed.

Zach stood with one hand wrapped around Seaver's wrist, his other forearm against Seaver's upper back, securing him against the vehicle.

"What are you doing?" Wade demanded of Zach, who appeared no more frazzled than he had when he offered me lunch.

The lunch and my bag sat on the hood of a cruiser two spaces to my left.

"He was holding Kenny at gunpoint," Zach said, not relinquishing his hold on Seaver. "Making accusations that Kenny killed Rachelle Seaver."

Wade stood, confused by all the possibilities.

"Kenny couldn't have been involved," my husband continued. "An hour ago, I picked him up from the hospital in White Salmon where he's been for the last two days with kidney stones." With this alibi stated, Zach let go of Seaver's arm but reached to take the firearm from his holster before stepping back to let him go.

All this to defend Kenny?

"You have no authority in this county," Seaver said with a snort.

Zach shrugged. "I've got none at all. I resigned from the DEA." He smiled and handed Seaver's gun to the sheriff. "But I just kept you from killing an innocent man, and I don't need a badge for that."

Wade took Seaver by the arm, marching him toward the building. Zach came toward me. "Maybe we should take your truck."

Astonished, I looked from him to Kenny, who was walking toward the street, and back. "What about him?"

"He was going to go to the church to work on –"

"No, Zach. Why did you confront Mitch Seaver for Kenny?"

"You couldn't have done it on crutches," he said, eyeing me. "And judging by the look in his eyes, Seaver was much too close to pulling the trigger to wait for the sheriff or anyone else." He turned to see Kenny cross the street. "Kenny wouldn't have raised a finger to defend himself, even against that sort of threat."

"He carries something that looks like a gun," I countered.

"But he only uses it to scare people away when they harass him. This was different."

"How do you know that?"

Zach opened the truck door for me after I clicked open the locks with the remote and gave him the key to drive. "Because I made it for him."

"No," I said, although I was a little surprised at the fake gun's history now. I climbed into the seat and arranged the crutches. "How is this different?"

He shut my door, then went to grab our lunch sack and my bag before returning. He got behind the wheel and started my truck, then backed out before speaking again. "Kenny is not stupid, Julie. He knows when he's really in trouble, like when his brother set him up. Seaver probably approached Kenny right after I went in the building."

I sighed. "You're sure he wasn't involved?"

"Absolutely." Zach turned the corner. "Not only was he in the hospital, I'm positive Kenny could not have harmed anyone intentionally."

"I can't imagine what Mitch must be going through," I said. "The sheriff sent him home hours ago. I understand the extreme stress of knowing a spouse won't return, but to not know for sure is a totally different monster. He must be torn between hope and fear."

"That's the only reason I didn't hurt him." Zach parked so we could see out over the Columbia River. "And I'm sorry you understand. Leaving you to believe I was dead was not my idea."

I opened my door and set my crutches so I could slide out of the seat. "I know. But that doesn't mean I don't still want to hurt someone else for it all." Even now the whole situation could raise my blood pressure.

Zach nodded, carrying the sack and two bottles of water, letting me lead the way to a bench. We sat, and he opened the sack and pulled out two sandwiches in cellophane, a bag of potato chips, and two cookies in a plastic bag.

"This was prepared by our loving daughter," he stated. "Who complained to me as she brushed down all four horses that you jumped all over her about sitting around doing nothing." He unwrapped his sandwich and took a bite, chewing and swallowing before continuing. "But she also admitted you were probably right. I took her over to Sav's before I picked up Kenny."

Savannah Fordham was the sheriff's teenage daughter, who shared Amber's predicament of being a cop's kid. Though not best friends, they were more than passing acquaintances.

Although I'd watched him disarm a potentially fatal situation, Zach showed no sign of being disturbed by the events of the last fifteen minutes. Quiet, collected. I imagined him as a hostage negotiator, calm and logical, able to strike at the perfect moment for a peaceful outcome.

"Do you miss it yet?" I asked him about his job.

Zach shook his head.

"Not even a little bit?"

He dug in the brown bag for a paper napkin to wipe his mouth. "I asked you before we got married about quitting. I have always liked the job," he said, picking out a potato chip. "But I am not good at the politics of how the decisions get made." He crunched the chip.

"Just checking," I said.

We ate without speaking, watching the river.

"Time for you to get back to work," he finally said, wadding up our trash in the sack. "I mean, one of us has to keep a job so we can feed the horses and pay the electric bill, right?" He winked.

I wrinkled my nose and stood. "I hope the sheriff didn't put Mitch in a cell to calm down."

"Where would you put him?"

Where, indeed.

❈

Sheriff Fordham had initially put his own deputy in a holding cell to cool off. By the time I got back from our brief lunch, though, Mitch Seaver had been taken home with strict orders not to show up at the station again.

"What a tremendous strain," I said, unsure if I meant that in his defense.

Wade Fordham looked a decade older just since I'd shown up a few hours ago to help. "Don't doubt it, but I can't afford to have him running rampant through this investigation and shooting anyone he concludes committed the crime."

No, he can't.

I returned to the lab. Standing my crutches in the corner, I eased down into a rolling chair, unwilling to admit to anyone how badly my ankle ached. So I got back up and went to my locker to find some ibuprofen, which I washed down with water gone warm.

Turning back to the tasks, I wasn't surprised when Wade dropped off a dozen more fingerprint cards and a toothbrush, the exemplars collected by another deputy. Now I had visual comparisons taken from items in the Seaver household – examples of individual belongings, such as Rachelle's purse and toys for the kids. I could pull Mitchell's fingerprint card from the departmental set in the files used if we needed to clear a deputy's prints at a crime scene. I compared those to the prints lifted from the vehicle. Magnifying glass in hand, I was able to match those of Rachelle, Mitch, and the kids. I still needed a set from Rachelle's mother, but that still left one partial set unidentified.

I scanned those and set one computer to running the prints

against the AFIS database, which slurped up all the PC's resources. Changing gears, I rolled my chair around to another table so I could prep samples for the lab. Each tube held a pair of cotton-tipped swabs, and I separated these – one for the state lab, one to keep.

While the sample appeared to be blood, I did test it first to be sure.

Wouldn't want to send strawberry jam to the FBI lab.

Blood it was, but based on its appearance under the microscope, I suspected it was older than forty-eight hours. It had been collected from the passenger compartment sliding door molding of the minivan, so it might have even come from one of the kids. It would take blood typing and maybe even DNA to determine.

Although I like the results the crime lab analysis offered, I found that doing the work was tedious compared to actually gathering the evidence.

Four o'clock came and went, but I continued, back to organizing the photo files.

"What was Zach thinking, grabbing Mitch like that?" Wade Fordham said from the door, surprising me. "He wasn't even armed."

"I think it was protection mode," I offered. "And I'd be surprised if he didn't have a firearm on him somewhere, but would you tangle with someone his size?"

Wade shook his head. "Foolish."

Zach or Mitch?

"Letting Seaver shoot someone would have been foolish, especially when it was the wrong someone."

"Don't suppose you've found a guilty subject yet?" he asked, nodding at the table and lightening the mood a little.

"Not yet, Sir, but I'll be here another hour," I said with a smile. "You never know."

But one hour wasn't enough to find out the truth about what happened to Rachelle Seaver. Neither was a day or a week.

CHAPTER

12

"Julie," Amber asked at lunch the next day, "is Dad really okay?"

"I think so. What makes you ask that?" I replied.

"He retired. That might not seem weird for some people, but he really liked working, didn't he?"

I waited for her to sit down across the table from me. "Maybe it is a bit odd that he decided to quit doing what he liked. But to him, the few months he wasn't here just so another government entity could catch a criminal crossed a line."

"So it's nothing to do with losing his kidney or anything. Like, he's healthy, right?"

"Why don't you talk to him about it?" I suggested. "If you show a genuine interest, I'm sure he'll tell you all his reasons."

"I don't know. Sometimes I feel like I'm still just his kid, so he doesn't have those kinds of conversations with me," she said, spreading mustard on her bread. "But you always talk to me like an adult."

"Except when you're not acting like one on some rare occasion," I said with a wink.

Zach, I knew, was outside working with one of the horses.

He's adapted to not having a job pretty fast.

"Looks like it's gonna storm," she said. "I miss the sunshine."

That was an odd switch of topics. "Very different climate here than in Albuquerque, isn't it?" I wanted to tell her that she'd get used to it, but with her allergies still bothering her every spring and early summer, I wasn't sure it was true. "But I like how my skin doesn't feel so dry. And I don't shrink when it rains."

She shot me a look of annoyance, though it was playful.

"How's the blood sugar testing and shots going?" I asked.

Her next look of annoyance wasn't so playful.

"Just asking," I said. "Making conversation."

"I hate it," she announced, the mood darkening like the sky. "Cody's afraid I'll have some sort of seizure or something. Even Savannah didn't want to leave her house with me the other day."

"You have to –" I started to say, but she cut me off.

"I don't have to do anything with them. If they can't treat me like nothing's changed, then I don't want to hang around any of them!" She slammed her napkin onto the table and kicked her chair back so hard it fell against the fireplace hearth before she marched off toward the stairs without picking it up.

Oh brother.

Maybe, I thought, Zach should handle this one. So far his approach seemed to be more appropriate to realigning Amber's attitude toward her new diagnosis. Although she might have felt more comfortable talking to me about other things, this diabetes subject was not one she intended to discuss with me.

I didn't want to have hurt feelings over what she'd said, but I did. I pondered gimping out to the barn on my crutches to talk to Zach, but before I finished my sandwich, the clouds finally loosed the rain.

As I got the table cleared off, one handful at a time, I heard Zach stomping in the garage, probably shaking the droplets from his hair the same way Laser did. Only Zach had let his hair grow out.

After loading the two plates and knives into the lower rack of the dishwasher, I straightened up to find him standing right beside me.

"You two have got to find some neutral ground on this," he said without so much as a greeting. "She called me. Even though she could see me out her window, she *called* my cell phone to complain that you were harassing her about her testing and shots."

"First of all," I said, feeling my anger rise, "I didn't harass her about either. I asked how she was doing with them, thinking perhaps she could say it was either going fine or that maybe she needed a little guidance. I *do* happen to know a little bit about diabetes, you know. And second, I can't keep her from calling you or complaining about anything."

Zach stepped back and nodded, pressing the heel of one hand against his temple. "This feels like when I was seven years old and had two best friends. No matter what was going on, two always ganged up on the third person." He leaned down and kissed my forehead. "This cannot turn out to be a perpetual confrontation."

I agreed more than I could possibly say.

He turned and went to the stairs, trudged up them in his socked feet, making noise very uncharacteristic of him.

Through the ceiling above me, I could hear the two of them talking, with Amber's voice getting louder. In less than a minute, I heard a distinct shout, then a slamming door.

Not good.

My intention was to go upstairs and console Zach, but the phone rang.

Oddly, Amber didn't get it by the second ring, so I picked it up and said hello.

"Julie?" a female voice asked, then continued without an answer. "It's Geo. I'm at Dana's house, trying to clean it up. Jack Browning showed up and told me to go home, or else."

"Or else?" I asked.

"It sounds benign, but his voice was really threatening, Julie."

"Is he still there?"

"No, he grabbed a couple shirts and a half-full bottle of booze, then he left." Her voice vibrated in fear. "But he said he'd be back."

"I can't come out there, Geo, but I'll call Wade and have him send a deputy to her house," I said. "Go sit in your car, engine running, parked where you can drive away without backing up or turning around. Do not leave without someone to escort you unless Browning comes back. There's no telling what he might do if he thought you crossed him."

And I fully believed that. He was a perfect example of how flabby muscle and enough alcohol could make a man think he was always right and invincible. From what Geo had said about the evidence of assault on Dana so far in their two-year relationship, he thought he was right a lot.

We disconnected, and I called the sheriff's department dispatcher. "It's Julie. Send a unit out to Geo's sister's house. She's there alone now, but Jack Browning's been by and made some threatening remarks. And if anyone finds him, he's probably DUI," I told Stephanie Potter, the dispatcher on duty.

"Will do," she answered, "but hang on a sec' before you go. Sheriff wanted to talk to you anyway."

A series of clicks, then ringing.

"Fordham," he said, sounding sour as a lemon.

I said my name and waited.

"Do you remember seeing photos of a footprint and tire treads around Rachelle's car?"

I thought a moment. "No. Who took them? Maybe I missed loading a memory card."

"Langston says he found two foot prints, about ten feet from the driver's door. Probably in the middle of his bunch. He also snapped a dozen of a tread mark he found."

"I don't remember getting a media card from him, Wade." I thought back.

Wade sighed. "He brought his in first, about an hour before you arrived," he said, but his cadence slowed down when his memory began processing details. "He'd put it in a bag, so I just kept adding to it. They were on my desk."

"Each memory card is coded," I suggested, "so we can correlate it to the photographer, subject, date and so on. But what's on each one separately would be a wild guess."

"Langston said he only shot one card full," he replied. "I remember him telling me what he'd found when he gave it to me."

"Who else overheard him tell you that?"

His pause was punctuated by the sounds of papers shuffling on his desk. "Hell, I don't remember. Bette could have heard. I think Mitch was still here. Maybe others."

Well, if I didn't get the memory card to start with, I couldn't have made copies to the workstation, either. And a ground print could be viable evidence.

"Any chance the prints are still there and intact?" I asked.

"I doubt it. We had half a dozen people there before the wrecker came to get the car," he answered. "I'll send Langston back out to look, just to be sure."

"Any other leads from the prints or other trace collected?"

"No, nothing so far," he said. "The one print you were searching the database for came back to a Thad White, who happens to have a criminal history of petty stuff and who now works at the grocery store where Rachelle shops. Based on the age of the prints and the location on the rear door handle, I don't think he had anything to do with her disappearance."

After a few more minutes of catching up on the case, we hung up.

I was bummed that nothing found so far had led to any sort of suspect. But now, somehow, one piece of evidence was gone.

Had Rich Langston made a casts of either?

Even in the new age of zippy digital prints, tangible evidence spoke the loudest to a jury, so I'd have done plaster casts.

I called the dispatcher back and asked to speak to Langston. The system clicked a few times, then a phone rang. When he answered, I was certain the call was cellular.

"It's Julie Samualson," I said. "Sheriff says your memory card is missing. Any chance you casted the prints?"

"Yeah," he said, hesitating. "They both turned out pretty crappy because the soil was so wet. Maybe I mixed the plaster wrong."

"Something is better than nothing. Do you still have them with you?" I asked, hoping he'd not turned them in because they weren't great samples, leaning on the photo images to be sufficient.

"Yeah. I'll drop them off next time I get by the station," he said. "I'm out east on Highway 14 now."

"Don't leave them with anyone but me," I said. "And don't tell anyone else you made them."

"Something wrong?"

"Can't say for sure, but one missing memory card out of a bag sure seems hinky."

I disconnected and was pondering the disappearance of the media card when I heard the shower upstairs. Seemed like all three of us needed some space and time to decompress. I knew I needed to get away from the aggravation of Amber's strangely extreme reaction to the diabetes and its effect on her social life.

Problem was, I had a handicap on ways to escape. My preferred way – going to the barn and taking a short ride – was out of the question. A dip in the hot tub wasn't off the list, but the thought of submerging my foot in hot water made it throb even more. That pretty much left the option of going to work, which seemed to be in order for at least two reasons.

I considered changing clothes, but decided against it since I'd have to go upstairs to get a uniform shirt. I didn't intend to do any public image tasks today anyway.

Leaving Zach a note, I hobbled out to my Suburban, with Laser at my side.

What the heck, I'll take the dog, too. He can use a ride.

Happy to be invited, Laser hopped into the back seat without me having to ask twice. As I backed out of the driveway, I lowered the window for him. He rode with his face in the wind the whole way.

The trip down Wind River Road into town was peaceful. I parked behind the station, opened the door for the dog, who jumped down with a renewed energy of having a purpose, even if it really didn't exist.

I looked around the parking lot, back to where Zach had disarmed Mitchell Seaver.

Why did that seem weird to Wade? Zach kept a deputy who was at the breaking edge of stress from shooting an innocent man.

The incident bothered me more now than it had after it happened, but I couldn't put a reason why into words.

The dog and I went inside and into the lab where I'd been

processing evidence. Trying to stay out of the way, Laser went to a far corner and made two circles before curling into his patiently-waiting-by-taking-a-nap pose.

I wouldn't even have to tell him to stay.

Looking around the room, a combination of evidence laboratory and spare office, I saw nothing out of place. I sat down in front of the computer and clicked through the copies of the photographs I'd copied, taking a closer look at those taken outside the van. Over a hundred photos on one card, none a new discovery. The next memory card I'd copied had photos taken prior to the first one I'd viewed, so I saw the photographer's approach to the car and the area around it.

Using the program's zoom feature, I increased the size of parts of each image, hoping I'd find a shot that would show the tire tracks or the footprints. At about the thirtieth image of the file, I found what I'd hoped would be here.

In the past, using film to document a scene had been limited by the frustration of reloading the camera after each short roll, delays in processing the film into photos, then selecting those requiring enlargement and the wait again for those. Few small law enforcement agencies could afford to keep a darkroom for such purposes, forcing them to use commercial resources. I'd even experienced the unfortunate incidence of film being blank or being stolen by employees in photo labs.

Digital photography offered a vast solution for those problems, but a digital photo image could be altered, which had reduced its validity in court initially. Depending on the subject recorded and the provenance of the image, more juries were seeing them these days.

The first image of the tire track was from about fifteen feet behind Rachelle's minivan. The photograph, though not directly of the track, had captured it at the bottom of the frame. No detail, but a start on where to keep looking.

Two images later, the photographer had turned his lens downward, recording a spot-on view of the track left by the tire. Tread marks were visible in the wet soil, clear enough to use to make a comparison for identification of the tire.

I felt like getting up and dancing.

No chance of that with this ankle.

I copied the photo out to a separate file, where later I could retrieve it and any others for printing and enlargement, then I kept reviewing.

Two hours and several hundred more images later, I'd reached the end of the line – no more photos of either the tire tread or the shoe print. Just the one photo we could use. One I hoped would be a step forward.

CHAPTER
13

Still sitting in the lab, I looked up when I heard a muffled noise from Laser, who'd been asleep in the corner until a figure in the doorway woke him.

"Julie, I brought those casts by. Sorry it took so long," Richard Langston said, stopping abruptly when he saw the dog. "Stolen property call."

I waved him inside. "That's Laser," I told him when he hesitated. "He was a police dog in Michigan."

Laser relaxed his head back to his paws, eyes and ears drooping.

Rich brought two brown cardboard boxes to the table where I'd been working.

We carefully pulled each plaster casting from its box then from the wrap.

"I told you they weren't very good," he said.

The tire casting was below average, yielding hardly any identifiable tread pattern. But the shoe print he'd cast was good.

So good I forgot to mention to him that I had found a photo of the tire tread instead.

"Lugged sole," I said as I examined the plaster mold.

"Not like mine," he commented, stepping back to hold his left foot up so I could see the bottom of his work boot. The logo in the heel would have distinctly stood out on an impression, but it was absent on the cast.

"Not the same brand, no. This looks like a less aggressive tread, maybe something off a cheap hiking boot."

"I only found the one," he said with deep apology.

"You looked, though, and you did find one. That's fantastic."

The pattern looked vaguely familiar, but I'd seen hundreds of prints since coming to work in Washington. Rodeos, ranches, mountain trails. I sometimes played this mental game to see how far I might track a particular print.

Richard dipped his head and turned to go, stopping at the door.

"Ma'am? Do you really like working with dead bodies and stuff?"

I smiled. "Yes, because bodies often give up as much evidence about what happened to them as all the other pieces we find."

He nodded and stepped out of view into the hall, his footsteps fading until I heard the back door open and close.

I'm not sure I convinced him that I like what I do, but someone has to do it.

Richard had only been with Skamania County for a year as a deputy, but he came from the Seattle Police Department, bringing four years of experience with him. Nice enough guy, but to someone my age, he was still a kid of twenty-six or so. Someone had called him Bear once, a nickname that hadn't followed him from Seattle and didn't really fit him.

After printing the photo image, I reached for the phone and dialed the sheriff's extension, even though his office was two doors down the hall.

He answered on the third ring.

"Wade, you need to come see this," I said without introduction.

"Julie? What are you doing here?"

"Just come down to the lab." I hung up.

I heard the squeak as he rolled back and lifted his weight from the chair, then heavy steps down the hall.

"You don't need to be here this late," he said, holding his watch so he could see it, as if he didn't already know the time.

"Needed to find what was missing." I smiled. "And although I didn't find Richard Langston's memory card with the photos, I did review the others again, and found something in those taken by Blake Erwin." I pushed the image printout across the table. "We might be able to get a match to this."

He pulled the reading glasses he kept perched on his head, balancing them on his lower nose. Slowly, he nodded. "Yes," he said, the short word taking about three seconds to say and sounding more like a snake hissing. Then his mind changed gears, and he looked up. "Best news I've heard all day, Julie. Good job!"

"Oh, it gets better, sir," I said, motioning him around to where the plaster casts lay. "I asked Rich if he had casted any of the impressions he'd also photographed. He told me the tire tread cast was so poor he didn't expect it to be of any use, so he hadn't even logged it in." I pointed to one. "Not great but certainly usable. More importantly, he'd casted a shoe print I found in no other photo."

I thought Wade Fordham was going to hug me.

"You'll get these sent to the proper people for matching, right?" He looked back at his watch. "In the morning. Go home. It's already past supper."

I glanced at the wall clock, not surprised it was almost eight o'clock, but I felt good knowing the time investment had been successful.

Packing up the two molds, I was interrupted by my cell phone. I slipped it out of my pocket, opened it up and almost said, "Madigan," before I caught the mistake. "Samualson."

"Julie? It's Nolan Forrester," the voice answered. "How are you?"

I checked the clock again and added the three hours to get Eastern Time for Michigan. "I'm great, Nolan, and you?"

"Fabulous, just spectabulous, even," he said in a lively voice belying the time.

Or else he's not in Michigan.

"And what makes you so chipper tonight?" I asked.

"I just wanted to thank you for introducing me to Olivia," he said.

Olivia Palmeri had been a med student turned lab tech trying to raise her son after her husband was killed in the military overseas. She had been living with her mother down the street from me in Traverse City, Michigan, when I met her. It had been her great memory that had helped us solve a case and save my mother several years back. When I moved to Washington, she bought my house.

"Er, you're welcome, I guess." I stammered, not knowing what else to say.

"You know we've been living together, more or less, even though I'm still working out of Grand Rapids," he explained. "I'm going to retire in two months, and we're getting married in Las Vegas in October!"

"Wow!" I was stunned.

Nolan's first wife died, scarring him deeply. His second marriage, doomed from the start, had been something his friends and coworkers urged him into. We'd discussed our pasts after I met his first wife's parents, but I would never have thought he'd get married again.

Never say never.

"Vegas, eh?" I repeated. "Have you picked a date yet?"

"Not yet, because I was hoping you and Zach could come, so we wanted to be flexible."

In the background, I heard a woman's voice. "Did you tell her about the baby?"

I heard Nolan cover the receiver and *Sshhh* her.

He returned to the call. "So check your calendars and see when a good weekend might be for you both."

I laughed. "Only need to worry about me, Nolan. Zach retired, too."

"What?" he said, almost as shocked with my news as I was with his. "He loved working drugs, and he was so good at it."

"I think this last escapade pushed him past loving his job," I said, knowing Nolan had been a part of the incident. "But I'm glad he's home."

Sometimes, at least.

"Terrific," Nolan said. "Then you let me know, and we'll have a great weekend. Bring Amber, and your mom, too, if she can make it."

After a few more rounds of catching up, we said goodbye. I just sat there, wondering what Olivia had really meant about "the baby," and why Nolan hadn't said anything about it.

Before I got back on my feet, my phone rang again.

This time, it was Zach. "Are you going to stay at work all night because you're mad at me?"

"I'm not mad at you," I said. "All of us needed a little time to cool off, and I thought I could finish this project here at the station."

"Oh, good. Would you pick up dinner for us on your way home then?"

I agreed, and once more attempted to get all the evidence secured.

But the call I'd received from Nolan still weighed on my mind.

Why wouldn't he tell me what she'd said? Does he think I'm too fragile about pregnancy to tell me if they are expecting?

After I'd slipped the plaster casts into protective bubble wrap sleeves and cardboard boxes, then stacked one on top of the other, I picked them up together and turned from the table to a cabinet shelf.

And stumbled.

In less than a second, my crutches, the evidence, and I were all in a heap on the linoleum floor. I didn't even have to open the boxes to know the castings lay beside me in shattered pieces.

I wanted to cry.

Laser was on his feet and at my side in seconds.

Maybe the sound of the fall had echoed through the building, or maybe I'd cried out as I fought for my balance, but the room was suddenly alive with men and women in uniform – those who had not yet gone home from the day shift.

Blake Erwin was the first into the lab, coming around the table only to face Laser in his best protection mode, teeth bared and a low growl coming from his throat. Enough to stop Blake in his tracks.

"Laser," I intended to shout, but my voice was tinny, tears already running down my face. "Laser, sit. Sentado!" Not exactly the correct command for *do not attack*, but close enough.

"Julie, are you all right?" Tina Romero asked, pushing aside the deputy almost twice her size to drop to her knees beside me. As a dispatcher, she didn't perceive the danger of the dog that the deputies did.

I nodded, unable to speak. Tears flooded my eyes. Embarrassed, by the fall, by the crying, by the destruction of evidence we might have used to find Rachelle Seaver.

Laser crawled to me, maybe thinking he'd done something wrong. He put his head on my left thigh, my lower leg bent under me. The slight added weight, or maybe just my focused attention, caused excruciating pain to shoot from my ankle to my hip.

I clenched my teeth and patted his head.

❧

An hour later, I was back on a gurney in the emergency department in White Salmon, Zach and Amber at my bedside.

"This time," Dr. Sanderson announced, "you did break something."

Very funny, I thought.

Zach appeared to be taking the news of my injury with complete seriousness.

On the other hand, a broken bone was nothing compared to the devastation I felt about the loss of the molded casts.

Sanderson continued after neither of us responded out loud. "You have a small fracture of your fibula, through the malleolus, and I suspect a syndesmotic injury as well."

I nodded. Zach looked confused.

"He means that the ligaments holding the two lower bones of my leg together may have been damaged, Zach." I looked back at the doctor. "So does the fracture make the joint unstable?"

"Oddly enough, I don't think so. But ankles are very complex joints, so you'll be seeing Dr. Atkins again. And we might as well schedule you for an MRI before you go, because the results will be the deciding factor on surgery."

"Surgery?" Zach and Amber said together.

That was the only word Amber had said so far, tucking herself into a corner and pouting.

"Possibly. I'll try to get in touch with him now, but I'd like to admit you tonight if he doesn't want you to go directly to Portland." With that, Dr. Sanderson left my cubicle.

"You're sure costing the county a lot of money with this ankle thing," Zach said with a weak smile. "Surgery?"

"Probably a titanium screw to pull the two bones back together while everything mends. Ankles are difficult to heal due to getting the poorest blood flow, having so much swelling, and when a patient won't stay off it," I explained. I was curious about the x-rays but not enough to get up and go look.

"Why did you have the dog with you?" Zach asked.

"Laser likes being in the car, and I wasn't going to do anything but work in the lab, so I took him. None of this was his fault," I said.

Poor guy was sitting in someone's car even as we sat here waiting in silence, the future weighing heavy on the three of us.

Twenty minutes later, a nurse came in, asking what time I'd last eaten.

I'd had lunch, but nothing since. In fact, I was starving, a thought I didn't share.

"Dr. Atkins wants to transfer you to Portland tonight, do any scans needed, then plan surgery for morning," she explained. "There's no reason you can't go by private car if you wish, but you should only have a light supper before you check in to the hospital."

"That sounds like a grand idea," I said.

We exchanged signatures and instructions, and in another twenty minutes, I was ready to go.

"Can you just take me back to the house?" Amber whined.

"No, I will not drive you back there and leave you alone," Zach answered.

"See? Everyone treats me different because of diabetes," she stated, angry as a hornet.

"This has nothing to do with diabetes," Zach said. "I wouldn't take you home and leave you a month ago, or a month from now. This isn't about you."

The sheriff peeked in around the curtain. "Bad time?"

"No, we're just getting ready for a trip to Portland," I said.

"Amber is welcome to come stay with Savannah tonight, if that would help," Wade offered. "I can take her home to get her things and drop off the dog."

"That's not necessary," I was saying, but Amber was already on her feet. "But we appreciate your hospitality."

❧

The next afternoon, I rested in a hospital bed, having had an experimental surgery where my tibia and fibula would be held together at their far ends by a fiberwire, as it was explained to me by Dr. Atkins, who talked me into the alternative to having screws. The biggest advantages seemed to be a quicker recovery to full weight-bearing and less need to worry about the screws breaking. Although my leg ached, it was no more so than it had in the last few days.

The plan was that I would be discharged the following morning.

Though he had stayed the night with me at the hospital, I talked Zach into returning home while I was in surgery, to feed the animals and to check on Amber.

She had returned with him after noon, in somewhat more positive spirits, bringing broiled salmon on a salad and baked potatoes for us all. It smelled much better than whatever had been delivered on my tray for lunch an hour earlier, which had included the requisite green beans I detested.

"Geo came up to visit me a little bit ago," I said between bites. "She looks better. Her sister is due to go home in a few days, but Geo is worried that the boyfriend will return."

"Geo should have her sister file a restraining order," Zach stated.

"A restraining order is great for keeping away anyone who wishes to abide by the law," I argued. "I don't think Jack Browning is a man who cares much about what a judge says he shouldn't do."

Zach nodded. "Yes, but we both know it's a step she has to take for anyone to take her complaint seriously. If she won't do that, then the legal system remains neutral until he actually does something you can prove breaks the law."

"What if his next attempt at breaking the law kills her this time, Zach?" I asked, knowing the answer already.

"If she's like the majority of other abused women I've encountered, she might separate herself from him while she's healing, while the pain makes her believe he might do it again. After that, chances are she will go back to him."

Amber's head lifted from her plate. "Why would she go back when it's so obvious that the guy will only hurt her again?"

"There is no answer that makes sense," I said. "Lots of lame excuses why the woman takes the blame for her partner's bad behavior and puts up with it."

"That's just stupid," she concluded.

"From the outside looking in, it sure appears that way." Zach wiped his mouth with a paper napkin. "But it's difficult to pull a woman from an abusive situation. I know," he said, gesturing to his left shoulder with his fork. "I took a shotgun blast trying to separate a couple that looked like they'd been wrecking the house and each other with baseball bats."

"You got shot?" Amber asked in amazement.

I could almost hear her thinking, "That's so cool!" but she didn't say it aloud.

Zach only nodded.

"Anyway, Dana is going to stay with Geo in town while she needs assistance with the care for the burns, which could be six to eight more weeks, maybe longer," I said.

"Where do Geo's parents live?" Zach asked.

I didn't know for sure, but somewhere relatively close. "Neither of them is able to take care of Dana, much less defend her from Browning."

"The question is, is Geo?"

A serious question, indeed.

"Does she own a firearm?" Zach persisted.

I shrugged.

"Maybe she needs a little education in self-defense," he concluded as though he'd mentally made note to do that himself, then he changed the topic for discussion. "What time will you be ready to go in the morning?"

"There's no telling. Hospital time means nothing," I said. "I'll guess around ten."

"We'll be back by then," he said. "Del's going to feed the horses in the morning. Amber and Kara and I are staying up late tonight to go see a new movie."

"I want to see *Dr. Doolittle*," Amber said. "Kara said she heard it's hilarious."

Finally she demonstrated interest in something besides moping.

I nodded. "Sounds like a good plan then. You can see the movie, I can get more pain medication tonight, and we can all have supper in the comfort of our home tomorrow."

"We can get Dad to grill," Amber offered. "Mrs. Fordham has a great recipe for Italian chicken with rice I'd like to try."

Maybe Amber should be a chef instead of a cop.

"We can pick up the ingredients on our way through town tomorrow," Zach said, finishing the last bite of his salad.

I almost laughed, because I knew despite Amber's new dietary restrictions, he was dying to have a giant greasy hamburger with melted cheese and jalapeños, and a pound of French fries.

Actually, so was I.

CHAPTER
14

Burgers were not on the hospital's supper menu, either, apparently. I ate the standard dry baked chicken, served with mashed potatoes and brown gravy, and of course the other of my absolute favorite foods to hate – gelatin. Red gelatin.

Gross.

The nurses came and went throughout the afternoon, changing an IV bag here or dispensing pills there. Someone from physical therapy came to make sure I knew how to walk with my crutches, though I was pretty adept at using them. Mostly I had the time to myself. Time I used to chastise my clumsiness and to wonder what had become of the tire tread photo when it went to the state crime lab for matching.

Nothing on television was worth watching, though I already knew that. We had a satellite at the cabin but seldom ever watched anything but the news. I wished I had brought a book.

After shift change, the hospital halls became quieter, the nurse's visits less frequent. I tried to fall asleep, but I just couldn't.

Midnight came and went, and the nurse peeked in to see if she could bring me anything.

"I can't seem to wind down to sleep," I complained.

"Are you having any pain? Do you want me to see if the doctor ordered something to help you sleep?" she asked, trying to be helpful.

I shook my head. "No, thanks. I don't want a pill. But I will take a wet washcloth, if you would be so kind."

She was, and I folded it to drape over my eyes, promising to let her know if I needed anything else.

Darkness, absolute behind closed eyes and a cool cloth to keep me from opening them, was a trick my mother had taught me when I had trouble sleeping years ago.

Mom. I hadn't given her more than a passing thought for a week or so. I'd have to call her when I got home.

And then, apparently sleep came.

Only to be shattered by noises outside my door a few hours later as the staff responded to a cardiac arrest in the next room.

I recognized some demands and statements made, though I had to struggle to hear others. They were finished in twenty-seven minutes, when a male voice stated, "Call it. Time of death 0341."

They hadn't been successful in reviving the patient. That was sad, but I had no idea what sort of life the man or woman had been living. However, I did know it was likely the efforts made would have an impact on the staff.

The nurse – her name was Cindy – opened my door and stuck her head in to see if I was sleeping.

"Sorry about the patient next door," I said quietly.

She seemed surprised I had heard, that I had correctly concluded the outcome.

Cindy stepped inside my room and closed the door behind her. In the very dim light, I saw tears on her cheeks. "Thank you." She wiped one side with the side of her hand. "After six years, it hasn't gotten any easier. Sometimes I just feel like what I do doesn't change anything."

"My mother's been a nurse all her working life. She once told me that if you don't think you're making a difference, you probably aren't," I said. "You made a difference to me tonight. You tried."

She only nodded and wiped her face with her hands. "Can I get you anything?" she finally asked.

"No, I'm okay for now, thanks."

As she stepped back toward the door, I heard her say, "No, thank you."

I suspected that she had intended to come in and just stand in the dark, composing herself alone, had I been asleep. Hopefully my being awake offered her the same temporary escape.

When I worked on the ambulance, I remembered going to a SIDS death early in the shift one morning, but then late the same night, we responded to another. In the emergency room, long after the doctor had called the code, I sat on the back steps of the truck, crying. A nurse came outside for a breath of fresh air and asked me if that was my first SIDS baby. I had to look at her and say, 'No, it's not even my first one today.'

You think that you can't work on a baby until you are called to do it, then you just do. And when it's through, you think you could never do it again, and you go hug a child and go back to work, until the next one.

That is what making a difference seems to be about, I thought, pulling the washcloth over my eyes again and drifting back to sleep for a while.

❧

Getting discharged from a hospital under the best of circumstances takes time and patience – I had plenty of one but a shortage of the other. After I'd finally signed all the medical forms, someone rolled me to the business office in a wheelchair, where I waited half an hour just to argue that while I *could* pay the out-of-pocket balance, this whole ordeal was a worker's compensation claim, so I shouldn't have to pay anything.

Zach, who had displayed all the patience of a monk throughout the morning, had written the check for just over a thousand dollars, just so a young man would finally push my wheelchair down the hallway toward my eventual release.

To change my state of mine as the doorway got closer, I asked Zach where Amber was.

"She's over at Del's, helping with the girls," he explained as we waited for someone to move through the doorway before us.

"Daphney's doing really well."

Really well, considering her older sister had accidentally run over her with a riding mower, blades turning for some reason I still hadn't figured out. There had been more than enough guilt to go around between Courtney and Delbert over the accident, so asking the question aloud would serve no real purpose.

Daphney had survived, yet she had lost a kidney and most of one leg. The accident had left her like a Chihuahua, shaking in fear of the world around her.

Which makes me grateful that a broken ankle is the least of my current worries.

"Lunch?" I asked, changing the subject.

"I thought you'd never ask," he said. "How about that little place where we like the steak and lobster?"

"Real food? I'm in!"

We laughed as we finally made it to Zach's truck.

"So have you heard anything more about Rachelle Seaver's disappearance?" I asked.

"Nothing else except that Mitch went down to Corvallis, Oregon, to his sister's place to get away." Zach opened the door to the Suburban for me and helped me in, took my crutches to put behind the seats, then went around to the driver's side to get in.

"Get away from what?" I asked, doubting the media could be a real problem in Skamania County.

"Erwin didn't say. He pulled in beside me when I was leaving Del's this morning, thinking you were with me." Zach drove through the city traffic with ease. "He said to give you his best wishes on recovery."

I had made a mental *hmmm* about Mitchell leaving town. Perhaps I'd escape from town, too, if my spouse were missing, I thought, but I hadn't left after Zach's reported death. *Hmmm.*

We rode without talking until Zach parked in front of our favorite restaurant in Vancouver, Washington. I could see the Surf-n-Turf gleam in his eyes as he handed me the crutches.

Inside, the hostess greeted us like long-lost friends, commenting how we hadn't been there in months. I couldn't imagine anyone staying employed at the same restaurant for that long, much less remembering who we were or that we hadn't been there.

She flashed a wide smile at my husband.

Ah, she doesn't remember me, but Zach does make an impression on the women.

She didn't mention my new accessory crutches or the black orthopedic boot as we walked through the restaurant, which was okay with me.

Seated in a quieter portion of the dining room, we perused the menu for no good reason except passing time – we both knew what we wanted – until a waiter arrived with glasses of water and a basket of warm cornbread muffins and honey butter.

Zach announced our selections, asked for a meal for Amber to go, and handed back the menus.

With a nod, the waiter was gone.

Zach reached across the table and took my hands. "I've missed you so very much," he said. "No regrets about having Amber in our family, but I miss having you and the cabin all to ourselves like I'd dreamed about for so long." He lowered his voice. "And I miss sneaking in and scaring you once in a while, too."

"I miss that, too." I smiled. "I'm sorry I can't seem to connect with Amber about her diabetes. Conflict is not my intention, but I don't know what sets her off."

"It's only been a week since she saw the specialist," he said. "Maybe it's like losing her mother – rollercoaster riding up and down until she's come to grips with it."

"Might be. Almost everything in her life has changed since Amy died, so perhaps grief is a good parallel."

Salads were delivered, but Zach held one hand a little longer after we were alone again.

"I just want you to know that I love you." He slid a blue velvet box across to the center of the table. "Thank you for being in my life."

"Zach, you didn't have to –"

"No, I didn't have to. I wanted to." He pushed the box closer. "Open it."

I did, discovering a brilliant pair of diamond earring studs. "They're beautiful!"

By the time I got my old plain gold hoops out and the diamonds in my ears, we'd ignored the salads so long our steaks and lobster tails had arrived.

"Who needs lettuce, anyway? We came for meat," he said, pushing the salad aside. "They look great on you."

On me, without makeup, without having had a shower in days. I felt unworthy of such dazzling jewelry.

"You shouldn't have," I said, pulling my hair back over my ears to let them show, "but I love them."

And with that, we settled down to the very large lunch, including baked potatoes and roasted veggies.

"And I miss lobster," he finally said after swallowing a bite. "Too bad this isn't on Amber's diet."

"True, but I think she's glad we don't separate her food choices from ours," I said, cutting another hunk of lobster. "At least very often."

He chewed slowly, savoring each bite.

"So are you really happy to be retiring?" I asked between bites, knowing his answer would have the same culinary delay.

He nodded at first. After swallowing, he confessed. "I'm not even technically unemployed yet, and it's already more boring than I ever imagined." He set his knife and fork down, leaning back in the booth. "I don't see how you did it for so long."

"For so long? Which time?" I took a bite of potato.

When I was recovering from which injury?

"Any of them. Is there some secret? Am I just not relaxing enough?"

I had to cover my mouth when I laughed, before I could speak. "Honey, you need something to do or else you'll end up with cabin fever. As you told me, there are lots of possibilities. You could go back to school. You could write a book." I waved my fork at him. "But you do need to relax and enjoy this for a while."

He sighed. "I'm not sure I know how."

"Practice." I smiled. "We can work on it. At least it's summer, and you can get Amber back involved with the horses and events. That would give you both something to do. Get Waldo saddle-broken, that sort of thing."

When we were finished, Zach tossed his napkin on the table and leaned back. "Don't you dare tell Amber we ate all this," he said.

"Oh, not a chance. But I'm thinking I probably have half a dozen more doctor appointments we'll need to come to Portland for," I said in a hushed conspiratorial voice. "So maybe she won't want to come with us to all of them."

"Good point. You know, it hasn't even been two weeks since we started eating what she's supposed to eat, and I'm feeling like I've been condemned to life as a vegetarian," he said. "I sure wouldn't do it if it weren't for her."

"Unfortunately, it won't be bad for us, just different."

"Oh, I'm thinking it could make being bad even better."

The waiter came by to offer a dessert menu, but we'd eaten way too much to indulge in cake, so he left the ticket and moved on.

Zach paid the tab, and we practically waddled out the front door with a much more sensible entrée for Amber in a bag.

❧

Finally at home, Zach helped me get settled on the couch again, pillows fluffed, a dose each of the antibiotic and painkiller. I closed my eyes and let the narcotic do its thing, unwilling to confess my leg had been throbbing for almost two hours. The dog bites on my arm still hurt. My hip ached where I landed on the stairs. I was grumpy about being stuck on another flat surface.

The list goes on and on, but at least I don't have diabetes.

I vaguely remember hearing Zach go out through the garage door, probably to check on the horses. No idea how long he'd been gone, I was startled awake when he came slamming through the door again, headed to the foyer closet.

"Someone shot Laser," he yelled as he opened the gun safe on the top shelf.

I was upright before I realized how lightheaded the medication had made me, but even requiring the arm of the sofa to stay upright, I needed to know if the dog was okay.

"It's serious," Zach said, slipping his gun into the small of his back.

"You're not going to shoot him!" I exclaimed.

"No, Julie, but whoever shot him might still be out there," he said with a grim face. "I'll take him to the vet. Do not get up by yourself."

I nodded that I heard his order, and yet I didn't want to sit there with no way to protect myself.

Apparently reading my mind, Zach brought me his Kimber .45 from the closet, too.

"Don't shoot me when I come back," he told me.

"Allergic to bullets?" I teased.

"Yeah, and you're a much better aim than the last person who shot me." He winked, then stomped out the door. He could have meant when Jamie Gordon had shot him in the abdomen, which I assume he was comparing to the two bullets I'd put center mass in my previous husband's chest after he'd cut my throat.

Someone shot my dog? Who would hurt him?

Thinking about it, the list was not as short as I'd hoped and included a lawyer and a few criminals from the county, including Jack Browning.

I tried to stay awake, but the Percocet was just too much to battle. I rested the firearm by my thigh, hoping I would neither need it nor wield it without being fully aware of who was at the receiving end.

As Zach had said, I'm a pretty good shot, even when I'm under the influence.

CHAPTER 15

Dozing, I thought of Amber – how would she take the news about Laser? Although he'd been mine before she came into our lives, there was no doubt about the bond the pair had now.

Considering Zach hadn't just announced that the dog was dead, I only felt more helpless it hadn't been me who found him, and I wasn't with him now.

I could hear my mother arguing Laser was "just a dog," but he was more than that to me.

Maybe I should call her, I thought. But when I looked at the phone, I realized I was probably a little too drugged and far too preoccupied by the shooting to hold a rational conversation with someone who would ask a hundred questions.

Checking the clock, I was surprised that almost two hours had passed since Zach left. I felt less groggy, but still I didn't want to get up without someone being with me, and Zach had been pretty blunt about that. Yet because I was thinking about it, the urge to go to the bathroom was even stronger than before.

Needed something different to distract my thoughts.

Zach's retirement, for example. The fact he wasn't working didn't bother me, but I had noticed during the last few days how irritable he had become about little things here at Five Aces, as we'd named the property when I'd told him he stacked the deck before he asked me to come live here with him.

To me, this cabin, this hundred acres, this region was heavenly.

Living in Michigan, living with my mother while I recovered from the life-threatening injuries in New Mexico – all of it seemed so distant now that I lived here.

I thought back to how I'd met Zach, a year after I'd almost died at the hands of the man I was married to. Though my mother and Zach's had been friends and coworkers at a hospital in Albuquerque, he and I were seven years apart and thus not playmates as children. Even after we'd met as adults, our relationship had gone through several years of uncommitted connection and several earth-shaking catastrophes before I landed here at this cabin as his wife. But we were together now, and his retirement and Amber's new diagnosis aside, all was peaceful and happy.

Whatever our plans had been for being here, we had not spent a single night together in the cabin as husband and wife without Amber, his daughter. Talk about a shock – going from being single to married to the parent of a teenager in a matter of weeks... Still, that was probably not as weird as Zach finding out he was her father in the first place.

My mind kept wandering through the past until I looked up and saw another hour had gone by. And I really had to go to the bathroom.

Defy Zach or wait?

Although I was leaning toward reluctant defiance, I sighed when I saw he'd moved my crutches out of my reach. As in across the room and out of my reach. Hopping on one foot to get them did cross my mind, but I knew better and reached for my cell phone instead. If he didn't want me to get up, he should be back by now, I thought, dialing his number.

"Yeah, I know," he said, "I'm on my way home."

"How's Laser?" I asked.

"It's not good, but the vet thinks he'll survive." I heard the truck accelerate. "I'm going to pick up Amber on my way. Shall I get something for dinner?"

I laughed, because his request that I bring home dinner several nights before had ended up with a hospitalization and surgery. "I'm not going to be hungry for the rest of the month," I said. "And I really need some help."

"You haven't gotten up?"

"No, because I was told in a very stern manner by a very large man not to do so."

"And you listened?" he asked with mock astonishment.

Making a *pththth* sound, I hung up.

Half an hour later when he and Amber showed up, she stormed up the stairs without so much as a hello.

"What is that all about?" I asked Zach as he helped me to my feet.

He rolled his eyes. "I'm not sure if I was too early or too late picking her up," he said, offering me the crutches. "And then there's the teenage reaction to news about the dog."

"I see," I said, but I really didn't. Through the bathroom door, I kept talking. "So what caliber bullet was the dog shot with?"

"Don't know, but something small and fast. Went all the way through," Zach replied.

I heard the pull-top of an aluminum can as I finished up washing my hands.

Had to be a soft drink – all the beer was in bottles. Now, however, all the cans contained diet drinks.

"Could it have been an accident?" I asked when I opened the door to come out.

With the cola can still turned up to drink, he shrugged a shoulder. He finished without taking a breath, then crushed the can with his hand and tossed it into the recycling bin. "But I don't believe in that kind of accident." He stifled a burp, then excused himself.

I think it's Jack Browning, but what if he thinks it has something to do with Pauly Brodenshot? Even dead, I fear that man will somehow remain a menace to our lives.

Pulling a cola from the fridge for myself, I balanced my weight on the crutches to pull the tab and take a drink before I spoke. "I'm glad the vet thinks he'll be okay. How long do they think Laser might be there?"

"A few days at the very least."

"Where did you find him?" I asked. "I didn't see him when we pulled up to the house."

"He was out in the shade by the barn. And yes, I looked – all the horses are okay."

"You don't have to do that, you know."

He raised an eyebrow. "Do what?"

"Read my mind."

"Okay, then I won't tell you why I don't think Pauly had anything to do with this."

Damn it! That's as frustrating as when he moves like a ghost when he wants to be noiseless.

"That's not fair!" I complained.

"Maybe not, but that's the way it is. But no, I don't think there's any connection," he said. "It's over and done, despite what you think."

Even after Pauly Brodenshot had been killed in a firefight in an El Paso warehouse, I couldn't help but despise him. He'd been one of Zach's DEA partners, a friend from his teenage years even, who had turned against the agency and the men he worked with, eventually killing two of them, as well as Amber's mother, trying to exact his revenge on Zach for catching him trafficking drugs. He might be dead, but I still hated him.

Zach turned to go up the stairs. "Of course, I could be wrong."

Out of my reach, even with the crutch I thought about smacking him with, I heard him laugh about four steps up.

"Not funny!" I yelled.

I crutched my way back over to the couch, trying hard to carry my can of cola and thinking that I shouldn't have opened it till I sat down.

Should we file a complaint about the dog? I wondered, then answered myself aloud that we should.

As I reached for the phone, I heard footsteps on the stairs.

"Julie?" Amber said in a quiet voice. "Are you okay?"

I motioned for her to sit. "I'm fine. How about you?"

"I mean, your ankle and all. Then the dog." She was talking about one thing, but I suspected this conversation was really going to be about something else completely.

"A little orthopedic hardware, no big deal. Actually this should get me back on my feet sooner than before, providing it heals on schedule," I told her, taking the opportunity to prop my leg onto a footstool. "And Zach tells me the vet thinks Laser will survive his injury."

Her eyes reddened, but she fought back the tears. "Just seems like everything around me is dying."

"You've had a tough few years," I said, "with the deaths of so many people close to you. I'm sorry. I wish I could make you feel better."

She wiped her eyes then sat up straight. "I'd really like to figure out what happened to Catherine Bishop," she declared. "That would make me feel better."

"We can work on it, but I'm still not positive we can solve it."

The case of Catherine Bishop, the adopted daughter of the county medical examiner, had gone cold since her disappearance in 1975. No one had worked on finding her in almost two decades until Amber found a bag partially buried off a forest hiking trail. Inside, we'd found a wallet containing a tanned piece of human hide decorated with a tattoo, and a library card for Catherine from a small Texas town, and a faded photograph with two or three people.

Amber nodded. "Did your friend ever make the photo image any better?"

The photo was so aged and melded to the plastic sleeve holding it that the image was barely visible. A contact I'd made at the state crime lab had promised to work on it to improve the picture.

"I haven't checked back with him in a while," I said, "but I'll call."

Honestly, with the circumstances of Zach's reported death, then with Amber leaving to go live with his mom back in Albuquerque, I'd given up on the case completely. Now that my world was right side up again, I hadn't followed up on our leads, sparse as they were.

"It might be a day or so before I'm up to going to the station," I confessed. "My foot will swell if I don't keep it elevated."

"Sure, I understand. I have a list of questions and ideas when we go." Amber got to her feet with an ease I envied. She wandered to the kitchen and opened the refrigerator, taking out the meal we'd brought home for her. "And I knew you and Dad pigged out on lobster at lunch without me."

"How could you tell?" I asked, trying to sound innocent.

"The bag, and Dad has a butter stain on his t-shirt." Looking over her shoulder, she said, "Thanks for the baked salmon, and for not eating that other stuff in front of me. But I would love a bacon cheeseburger with fries and a chocolate milkshake."

✖

Three days later, the soreness in my arm and hip had decreased, as had the throbbing ache in my ankle. I felt like going to the station to catch up on the investigation of Rachelle Seaver, even if I didn't have anything specific to do.

My visit began in dispatch, the clearinghouse of most information in our department. I agreed with Bette Donovan that the disappearance of a deputy's wife was just too close to home in such a small community.

"I tell ya," she began in her slow Carolina drawl. In person, sometimes I wanted to speed her speech up from 33 to 78 rpm, though the reference seemed to be lost on Amber when I mentioned the comparison, thanks to the digital age. "Mitch and Rachelle's family must be goin' through hell, just not knowing. I don't blame him for leavin' town – there was nothin' here for him to do but wait."

I agreed with her about the situation, but it occurred to me that I hadn't heard anyone mention Mitch going to see his kids. Maybe there was some custody issue I didn't know about, I thought, then mentally moved on.

All in all, my visit to the station was mostly a waste. Nothing definitive had been determined from the photos, and no other fingerprints had been located after Rachelle's van was brought back to the impound area. The castings I'd dropped were useless, though Rich Langston had made an attempt to glue the pieces back together.

He and I concurred that there had been nothing unusual about the shoe print pattern, although we'd agreed it was most likely a boot, nor had the size seemed to be overly large or small. The opinions were worthless without actual evidence, though. The lesson I'd learned from the catastrophe was that I needed to photograph or otherwise duplicate all evidence submitted from now on. And that it shouldn't sit on the sheriff's desk to accumulate, either.

"Didn't expect you in for another week or so," Wade Fordham said as I passed his office on my way out.

"Not working, just catching up on the news," I said, backing up to stand at his doorway. "Maybe next week I can get back for some light duty."

He nodded. "Did you get a complaint made about the shooting?"

"Yeah, I filled out everything and had Blake sign it," I said. "I'm going to pick up the dog next. Vet says he was lucky."

"Who do you suspect, off the record?" he asked.

"Jack Browning is the latest in a list of people angry at me for doing my job, but there's no proof. When is Geo coming back to work?"

"She's back tomorrow. They swapped so she won't be on nights for the next schedule."

"She's afraid of him, Wade. For her sister and herself. That's not unreasonable, but if he did shoot my dog, then this may be a completely different escalation of behavior."

"You just be careful out there, then."

My next stop was the veterinarian's clinic. The young receptionist behind the desk looked frazzled, locks of hair loose from a ponytail, a big wet spot on the leg of her jeans. She asked me to take a seat, though I wondered if her tone was really irritation or perhaps frustration one word away from tears.

In the back, dogs barked and howled, an occasional cat screeched, and a loud bird called out, "Peeper! Peeper!"

While I sat there, a woman and two young blonde children came in, explaining they were here for the bird. What I caught from the conversation was that their cockatiel had gotten out a week ago, and they'd almost given up finding it when the vet called them, saying someone had caught a bird matching their description and brought it in. Its name seemed to be Peeper.

As the receptionist brought the bird out in a small cage, it proudly hollered its new vocabulary, mimicking a crowing rooster – *er-er-er-er-ER!* Apparently the bird had been staying in the chicken coop.

I laughed, thinking how ugly those chickens must have thought that cockatiel had been.

When I looked around to a healthy-sounding *Woof!* I saw Laser on a leash, tugging at the hand of Cody Randall.

"Mrs. Samualson," he said with a tentative hush to his voice. "I've brought your dog."

"Thank you, Cody," I replied from my seat.

Laser pulled the lead from Cody and trotted to me, and I leaned over and hugged him

"I was so worried about you," I said, ruffling his thick fur. In return, I got a happy wet noseprint on my cheek.

After our brief reunion, I stood and picked up my crutches. "Let's go find out how much it's going to cost to get you outta here, shall we?" As I took a step, the dog moved back to give me room, not needing a leash.

"No need, Ma'am," Cody said. "Your husband brought by the insurance papers and a check yesterday. I've never seen medical coverage for an animal before."

"Laser is a retired police dog, and part of his original purchase agreement from the trainer included coverage for his care. I'd never have thought about using it, so I'm glad Zach brought it in." I reached down and scratched Laser's ears. "I guess we'll go, then."

"He might still need a hand getting up into your truck, Ma'am," he said, walking to the door and holding it open for the dog and me. "I'll walk you out."

I thanked him and waved to the receptionist.

When we got clear of the building, Cody looked at me. "Ma'am, I know you don't much care for me."

Not sure where this was going, I interrupted. "No, Cody, you're wrong. The things that have gone on with your parents have nothing to do with you, and it does not affect how I feel about you."

He hesitated, then nodded and continued. "Thank you. I was just going to say that I'm worried about Amber. Only thing I know about diabetes is what I heard my grandmother saying years ago, and she was always sick. Is that how Amber's gonna be?"

The worry on his face crinkled his eyebrows together.

We got to my Suburban, and I opened the door to the second row of seats. "No, Cody. I think once Amber gets her diet and activity levels established, she won't be plagued by the many ailments your grandmother or her grandfather had. Diabetes is managed so much better now than in that time. She needs encouragement to get out and do things, though. To not be afraid something bad will happen or that her friends will make fun of her."

We looked down, and although Laser knew I had opened the door for him, he sat. Cody leaned down and lifted him into the seat.

"I hope I can help with that as easy as I did the dog, Mrs. Samualson," Cody told me. "I really like your daughter, but I know she's been hiding out at home."

"You keep working at getting her to do the things she loves, Cody, and I think it will all work out."

CHAPTER
16

Zach helped Laser and me both out of the Suburban when we arrived at the cabin.

"Any news on Seaver's wife?" he asked.

There hadn't been, and although I hated to admit it, I'd lost all hope of finding her alive, and almost any for finding her at all. There were just so many places to get rid of a body where no one would ever look. Even dumping one into the Wind River reduced exponentially each day the possibility of finding a body. Rachelle Seaver had been missing eight days now, so unless she had chosen to leave, I doubted we'd ever find her.

I didn't have to elaborate any of that to Zach. He understood the ramifications of a disappearance with suspected foul play. Amber's mother had been kidnapped and later killed in similar circumstances, leaving no clue at the location where her car was found.

Following Zach to the back deck, we reclined in the afternoon shade.

Laser found a favorite spot and curled up to sleep.

"I talked with Cody today at the vet's office," I said. "Maybe he can get Amber motivated to get out and do what she likes again."

Zach only nodded slightly.

"He said he knew I didn't like him, but that's not true."

Behind his mirrored sunglasses, I couldn't tell if Zach's eyes were open or not. He very well could have gone to sleep in the moments between my two statements.

I leaned my head back and enjoyed the breeze, apparently dozing off.

When I opened my eyes, I was staring at Kenny Underwood. Standing about three feet from my nose.

Zach had apparently gone in the house or to the barn, and I was alone when Kenny approached.

"Hey, Kenny," I said, trying to hide how startled I was.

"Mrs. Zach," he said, stepping back and touching the brim of his cap. "Good day."

"Good day. What can I do for you?" I asked.

"Mr. Zach asked me to keep an eye on this place since your dog there got shot," he announced with pride at such responsibility. "I wanted to tell Mr. Zach that I saw someone parked out by the fence," he pointed to the gate on the south edge of the property, not the fence line along the highway. "Maybe it was yesterday."

"Do you remember what color the car was?" I asked, very interested.

"It was dirty white," he said. "One of those kinda like what you drive, only littler."

An SUV?

"Did you notice whether the license plates were from Washington or Oregon?"

"Nope." He did not volunteer information unless asked.

"How many people were inside?"

"I don't think but just one. But I was hiding in the trees so I couldn't see very good."

Zach came out the dining room door. "How's Kenny today?"

"Kenny is just dandy," Kenny stated, posing with his chest out.

"I hear you saw someone parked by the gate yesterday. Good job, man," Zach said, pulling out his wallet. "By the way, I still owe you for cutting down those two trees last week, too. Is fifty dollars right?"

"Oh, yes sir, Mr. Zach," he said, dipping his head as if embarrassed, but holding out his hand while my husband counted five ten-dollar bills for him. "It's mighty nice of you to pay me so fast."

"You did the work when I asked," Zach told him, "I should have paid you a few days ago, but you weren't around."

"You just couldn't see me," Kenny told him with a sly smile.

"We'll be having supper in a little bit," I said. "Would you like to stay and eat with us?"

"No, Ma'am. I don't want to be imposing on you, what with you gimping around like that," he said, pointing to my crutches.

I tried not to laugh. "It's no bother, I promise. Zach was going to grill some chicken, and Amber's making vegetables and rice."

"I best not, but I do thank you, Mrs. Zach." He backed up a step before turning to go.

"Thanks for watching out, Kenny," Zach called.

We watched him walk north into the trees until he was out of sight.

"He says it was a small dirty white SUV," I explained. "Do you think he really meant it was dirty, or that it was beige?"

Zach shook his head. "But now we know what sort of vehicle to watch out for."

"Laser's still staying in the house at night, though," I said. "Should we tell Amber?"

He shook his head again. "No sense getting her upset when I don't think this has anything to do with her."

"But it may have something to do with one of us," I argued. "Was Laser shot because it missed you or me?"

"Neither of us were here, so I don't think that's the issue. I'm out around the barn all the time, so I wasn't the likely target," he said. "Probably just some idiot out with a new gun, thinking how cool it would be to shoot an animal."

"You're just saying that to make me feel better, aren't you?"

"I don't know. Did it work?" He smiled and kissed me on top of the head. "I'm going to see if Amber's ready to start supper yet."

And like that, the whole discussion ended.

Inside, I heard Amber bounding down the stairs.

"Is he home?" she asked Zach, then tore out the dining room doors to find the dog, who'd made it to his feet with only slightly less exuberance than normal.

Much louder than necessary, Amber and the dog played their normal greeting game, with Amber down on her hands and knees, barking and howling like the dog, who finally tussled her over and laid his paws on her chest while they both panted.

That looks like how Amber would normally act.

While they recovered, I pulled myself upright, taking my crutches and going inside where Zach had taken chicken breasts from the fridge.

Looking at Amber's scribbled recipe, he asked, "Do we even have all of this stuff?"

"Honey, you are king of the kitchen," I said, making an attempt at a fake bow. "How should I know if we have," I looked down at the card, "bread crumbs or buttermilk dressing powder?"

Our eyes met, and we laughed.

He wrapped his arms around me. "I guess I'll just have to wing it."

When the phone rang, he let go of me and reached across the counter to answer. He said hello, but then he held the receiver away from his ear in surprise.

Even from several feet away, I heard the loud screeching high-pitched noise.

Zach replaced the receiver in the cradle.

"Did that sound like a fax to you?" he asked, but I shook my head. "I didn't think so, either."

I could see the gears churning in his brain, but he said nothing, instead turning back to the chicken.

I picked up the receiver, listened for a dial tone, then called the station. Geo answered, as I'd hoped. I wanted to know how things were going since Dana got home. The conversation went on, interrupted by two radio transmissions and one phone call for which I was put on hold.

"Dana's staying with me at my house for now," she said. "But she's already talking about moving back to her house."

"I wish she wouldn't do that," I said. "She doesn't need to be there alone, and she sure doesn't need him back around there."

We commiserated, then I finally said goodbye and hung up.

"You can be so sentimental," he said. Holding up the recipe card, he read, then commented, "I'm supposed to pound these flat and then grill them?" He sounded like that was a criminal offense.

I shrugged. "That's what it says. Ask Amber, it's her recipe." Instead of supervising him fixing supper, I went back to the living room and turned on the television.

Our limited reception had prompted installation of a satellite dish, but we only subscribed to a few dozen channels. I flipped to a twenty-four-hour-a-day news station.

The headline story was about a line-item veto act from two years previous being found unconstitutional by the U.S. Supreme Court.

Politics... I don't care.

On another channel, the world heard that Demi Moore and Bruce Willis would be filing for a divorce.

Gads, who cares?

In other news, the scientific stir was all about a rare southern summer causing an increase in temperatures on a Neptune moon.

Really? Is there no local or national news?

There was some short mention about the life sentence handed down to Terry Nichols for his role in the Oklahoma City bombing.

I turned off the television and fell sideways onto the pillow, appreciative of the silence, even though I'd been the one responsible for the nonsensical noise.

Next thing I knew, Laser had his head on my knee, whining.

"Julie, supper is ready," Amber said softly.

I blinked, sat up and stretched.

Then to my surprise, she offered me a hand to get up, provided the crutches, and stepped out of my way to go to the dining room.

The meal turned out to be roasted onions, peppers, mushrooms, and tomatoes on skewers, baked chicken breaded with parmesan cheese and dressing mix, and cheesy rice with peas and corn.

"This is wonderful, Amber," I said, taking another bite.

"Thanks for helping cut up the veggies," Zach told her, and I noticed she beamed at the compliments.

Halfway through the meal, the phone rang again. Amber hurried to answer it, but as soon as she lifted the receiver off the cradle, I could hear the screeching noise again.

"Hang up, Amber," I think was what Zach was trying to tell her, when an explosion rocked the house, shattering glass, knocking pictures off walls, and blasting the garage door in almost to the wall.

CHAPTER

17

Zach told me later that when he got around to the driveway from the deck, my Suburban was on its side in flames.

Of course, so was everything else in a thirty-foot radius – his Suburban, the house, the back end of his Mustang in the garage, the grass . . .

The fire chief surmised that the burning gasoline from my vehicle apparently sprayed all over, sort of like napalm. He said Zach's quick thinking with the water hose – although not the brightest thing he'd ever seen – had extinguished those flames of the other vehicles before the fire department arrived, likely saving the house by preventing the Mustang's tank from exploding. Although there was extensive damage to all the vehicles and the outside of the building, Zach had contained it from spreading.

Me? I think I had some flashback to when the cabin in Michigan blew up, ducking onto the floor, pulling down Amber to protect her from the debris. Although lots of things in the house fell, none actually fell on us. Still, my mind replayed that scene from my past a half-dozen times before I came to my senses and found Amber in tears, Zach outside spraying water, and Laser hunkered down in a corner behind the counter.

After the flames had been extinguished, we stood, looking over the destruction outside, talking with the fire chief.

"You say you got a phone call just like this one earlier?" he repeated, as if hearing it once didn't satisfy him.

Zach nodded. "When I answered the first time, nothing happened. I didn't consider it a threat, though I had this funny feeling about what it was then. We dismissed it as maybe a computer dialing the wrong number."

Chief Turner knew Zach's history in law enforcement as well as my own.

"Then Amber answered it the second time," Zach continued. "The explosion happened within a second of her picking up the receiver, but we all heard that loud tone again. I remember now how it reminded me of a training video where a bomb was set off with a cell phone call. Only this call was to the house, which doesn't make any sense."

Turner nodded. "Can't say I've got much experience with bombs, Mr. Samualson, so I'll just have to assume the two are somehow related, given the coincidence of timing."

I inserted myself into the conversation. "If we find any other pieces of the device, we'll send them on to the state crime facility," I said. "But when and how this bomb was placed is probably more relevant to identifying its maker than the device itself. I was running errands today, so my truck was parked at several different locations in town, including the station and the vet's clinic."

Cody couldn't have done it, but could his conversation about Amber have been to distract me while someone else planted the bomb?

Wade Fordham strolled up, having parked out on the dirt road beyond our gate.

"Julie, you've become quite a trouble-magnet," he said, half-grinning. "This is serious business, bombing a car. Geo was hysterical when she called me, poor gal. Now I understand why." He stuck his hand out to shake hands with Chief Turner and Zach before turning back to me. "Good thing you didn't have a take-home cruiser in all this mess."

Hadn't occurred to me, but he was right. Insurance would have covered its loss, but being down one squad car was all we could tolerate. As it was, we'd been sharing take-homes with duty shifts since one car was in the shop for a transmission repair.

I looked over and saw Cody had arrived, too. He and Amber were standing near the gate talking. She was pointing to where the explosion had occurred, describing it in vivid animation with her hands.

I nudged Zach and nodded toward them.

"Good," he said. "She's got someone her own age to share this with."

Nothing to disagree with about that.

We walked through the house, starting at the deck entry to the dining room. Zach began shooting pictures with my digital camera as we went. The French doors had eleven broken panes of glass out of thirty, with two completely missing already. The window over the sink was cracked. Three framed pictures littered the floor in the dining room, glass shattered and metal bent or wood splintered. All three glasses on the oak table had been knocked over, and I took a moment to wipe up the contents. In the kitchen, a cup had fallen off the drainer into the sink and broken. Going through the foyer, I noted two of the pantry shelves hung crooked, threatening to spill their contents to the floor. Through the doorway to the garage, where the double garage door had been blown inward, pieces of it had struck the inside wall.

"I called the insurance agent," Zach explained. "He asked me to snap photos, and to get fixed what needed to be replaced tonight, like the door glass and entry door to the garage."

That explained the camera – he wasn't just recording this for our albums, I thought. As I followed him around the lower floor of the house, I felt a growing raw burn in my guts.

I stopped our tour long enough to empty the shelves in the pantry, needing Zach to reach the stuff on the top. Less-frequently used appliances, plastic storage bowls, cans and jars of food all wound up stacked on the counter in the kitchen.

"I'm going to go upstairs, but you don't have to come if you don't want to," he told me.

Honestly, I didn't want to see anything else broken.

Ten minutes later, he returned. "Four of the glass bricks in our shower are cracked, but a number of them will need regrouting."

That was halfway through the house, which made me worry about the rest of the structure.

"I didn't see anything broken in Amber's bathroom, but it's hard to tell without moving everything. She has more stuff on the counter and in the shower than you do, if that's even possible." He sounded as though the emotions were starting to catch up to him, too, despite his attempt at humor. "Didn't find anything obviously broken in the office."

I closed my eyes, feeling the mix of anger and loss chipping away my composure.

"Nothing else except the mirror over our sink. It's cracked in half."

Great, like we need seven more years of bad luck.

Amber came inside, but Cody waited hesitantly at the door.

I waved him inside. "Zach says there's stuff broken in our bathroom," I told her. "Please be careful, but go check in your room and bathroom, too."

She responded with a wild-eyed silent nod as Zach told her to look for cracks or anything that seemed to have moved or been knocked over.

I almost let my mother's voice slip out of me and tell them to make sure to leave the door open, but honestly I didn't think Cody had any intention of crossing that line today.

Wade Fordham stepped in from the deck, the door now propped open to keep the rest of the glass from falling out. "I think the mop-up is through here, Julie. We don't have room for all of you to stay, but I'd be happy to take Amber home with me if you'd like. The motel in town where we –"

I interrupted him. "Thanks, Wade. Maybe she'll want to go spend the night with Savannah tonight, but I'm not leaving this house so someone can come rifle through our belongings because we can't lock it up," I said, realizing how irrational my statement might have sounded to someone who hadn't been a victim.

Wade and Zach exchanged looks.

"I'll go ask Amber if she wants to go," Zach said, escaping the conversation and heading to the staircase.

"You don't understand my past, Wade. In Michigan, a killer broke into my house and set bugs to record what I did. He read my journals, left a computer disk for me, and sent me drugged candy while I was in the hospital before I found out anything else he'd done," I explained. "Not knowing who is doing this or why, I'm not willing to leave my house open to another invasion like that."

"As you wish," he replied. "I don't need any lengthy explanations. Just be careful."

I heard part of the discussion from the rooms overhead. Amber was apparently not willing to leave either.

"Okay, then," Wade said, having heard her decision, too. "If she changes her mind, just call and I'll come get her."

Outside, I heard the fire trucks pull away from the house. "Thank you for the offer. We'll get this all cleaned up. I'll drop by the station tomorrow, and probably come back to office duty starting Monday. I hate that you're two deputies short."

"I'm just glad it's not permanent," he said, going out the dining room doorway. Pointing to the glass, he asked, "You have stuff to cover these?"

Zach answered from behind me, though I hadn't heard him come down the stairs. "No, but someone's coming tonight to fix the doors and glass, and the tow trucks should be here shortly, but thanks."

"I'll have someone bring up a take-home cruiser for you later tonight then, so you'll at least have wheels."

Zach nodded, and Wade disappeared around the corner. Then Cody came to say goodbye, too.

What was left of dinner, now at room temperature and ruined. I started to collect the dishes, hoping the dishwasher was worked.

"I was thinking about pizza delivery," Zach joked. We both knew there was no such thing so far out of town. "But I guess we'll have to make do with sandwiches."

Once again, we gathered in the kitchen, dusted off the cabinets and table, fixed turkey sandwiches, and ate in silence.

"Who?" Amber finally demanded, slamming her glass down hard on the table, used to having placemats. "Why would someone want to kill one of you this time?"

Good question, Amber.

"If we knew, he'd already be in jail," Zach said in a low voice. "We don't."

"It's not fair! Now Cody says his parents don't want him to come over here for fear he'll get blown up or shot," she whined.

"Nothing in life is guaranteed to be fair," Zach said. "We do with what we have how we're able. You have more than most."

"Me?" she exclaimed. "What have I got?"

"You have two people who welcomed you into a loving home. You have a room to yourself with all your electronic gizmos. You have a selection of horses to ride, and two legs to go take care of them," he began, setting down his sandwich. "And you've got your health, even if you think having diabetes has changed everything."

"That's not what I mean!"

"You don't have to worry about having enough food or clean water or getting an education," he continued. "You don't have to work to make ends meet or help feed a dozen more children in your family. And you –"

"All right already. But still, I'm the only kid in Skamania County whose house nearly got leveled by a bomb today."

"Probably in Washington," he said, looking at me in amusement. "Well, maybe not in Seattle, but the rest of the state." He yawned intentionally. "So what is your point, Amber?"

She sat back in the chair and pouted like a four-year-old. "I don't want anything to happen to any of us."

"That's a reasonable wish. Still, when bad things happen to good people, it doesn't seem fair. You've lost a lot in the last couple of years, I understand, so any threat to upset the apple cart seems like it's added to your past," he said. "But like I told Julie several years ago, you have to quit judging your life by its catastrophes and just find a rose to smell once in a while."

I felt my face flush in embarrassment, so I took another bite to hide it.

✖

By bedtime, the glass company's guy had come and gone, at least reducing the bugs entering the house. When the two tow trucks had removed both Suburbans, I watched Amber help Zach pull the twisted remains of the double-width garage door out, panel by panel, leaving it wide open. Zach pushed his Mustang out of the garage – it would need paint and bodywork, which was no surprise.

Neither motorcycle seemed to have been damaged, maybe because of the cover on each and how they were parked on one side against the wall. We hadn't ridden them nearly as much as I'd hoped, since Amber had come to live with us.

Won't be riding any time soon, either.

When we finally had the house secured as well as possible, Amber retired to her bedroom. Zach and I curled up together on the sofa, with the stereo playing low.

"Quite an afternoon," he said.

"Let's not do that again anytime soon," I suggested, snuggling into his chest.

I felt him nod, then his breathing changed, and I knew he had fallen asleep.

But he'd left his pistol on the coffee table in front of us.

CHAPTER 18

With Zach making things happen, most of the repairs to the garage and the cabinets throughout the house were completed the next day. People who had worked on building the cabin were happy to come back, which told me he had paid them well and paid them promptly. The plumber told Zach it might take a week or more to fix the glass bricks in the shower because the guy who'd done the enclosure the first time had moved.

"Nothing I can do about that," Zach said as we ate lunch. "I considered having a security system installed in the house. But so far, it's likely neither of the incidents was caused by someone on the property itself."

We hadn't figured out how or where a bomb had been attached to my vehicle, nor did we have any information back on the explosive used, but it made less sense for it to be done at the sheriff's department than at the vet's parking lot. While we also assumed that the detonation was set off by the same person who'd made the phone call, it also made no sense that the phone call to the house had actually been the trigger. And despite digging around in the small crater left under where my truck had been, we found nothing.

"I met a bomb expert at one of our crime scenes in Michigan," I said, mostly to change the subject as he retrieved a pitcher of tea to pour us each a glass. "He was missing a couple of fingers. Said it made him more careful."

Zach chuckled. "I bet it did. He probably wishes he'd been more careful just one time sooner."

"The number of explosive events in this country every year was astounding. Like idiots who make pipe bombs or mix chemicals to blow up stuff for the hell of it," I said. "I remember a woman who'd bought a used car that had some grayish powder in a gallon jar left in the trunk. When she tossed it and the spare tire out on the ground, it exploded. Potassium perchlorate, I think it was."

Didn't matter what it was, why or how it had exploded. It had sent her to the hospital.

"Amber's right about someone trying to kill us, though," I said.

"I'm not so sure," Zach said. "That bomb could have gone off when you were in the truck, any time after it was placed there. Instead, someone waited until you were safely here at the house. The phone call was to distract you, maybe. Or make sure we were all inside."

"Oh, that's just too logical," I complained. "Nevertheless, a bomb it was. And a bullet. Both are potentially fatal."

"Perhaps. Or maybe someone just wants you to stop what you're doing."

"Which is what?" I pointed to my crutches. "Stop hobbling around?"

"How many cases are open right now where someone would want you to not find something?"

How many? There was the case with Jack Browning, the case where Laura Randall delivered twins and one died, and the bag Amber found in the forest, and the disappearance of Rachelle Seaver, and a half-dozen more or so. Oh, and Pauly Brodenshot's friends.

"Several," I conceded, "but why now?"

"I don't know, Julie," he said, frustration growling in his voice. "But I do know we need to figure this out before distraction becomes disaster and someone does get killed."

He looked up to see Amber standing two risers up on the stairs.

"I'm sorry, Sweetie," he called, but she turned and headed toward the garage, slamming the door behind her. "Great. Sometimes I wonder if I'm built for this kind of parenting."

"What kind is that?" I asked with a smile. "The difficult kind?"

"I'll see if she'd like to go for a ride," he said, draining his glass of tea before getting up. "You'll be okay for a while?"

"Oh sure," I said. "I don't have anything to do, so I might go have a dip in the hot tub."

He shook his head. "I found out this morning that the explosion cracked the liner, so all the water ran out under the deck. It's almost empty."

I shook my head in disgust. "Maybe I'll just grab a book and go upstairs to that tub," I said. "If it's still usable."

He went outside to find Amber, and I sat there alone, pondering how long it would take us to discover all the broken things caused by the bomb.

❖

I didn't bother to go soak in the tub, however, as I feared getting out alone could be more work than the relaxation could balance. Instead, I leaned over the kitchen sink to wash my hair, thinking how it was at that horrible in-between length where another few inches would make it a reasonable ponytail again instead of a stubby one. Then I hobbled up the steps to go to our bathroom to dry my hair, put on a little makeup, and change into something more suitable to wear to the sheriff's department than shorts and a Harley-Davidson t-shirt.

While I was at it, I removed the boot and unwrapped the dressing around my ankle to take a better look at the surgical incision, which was about an inch vertically, a little pink right at the edges. My foot was wrinkled from the texture of the wrapping, which I replaced, then fitted the protective boot back in place.

I hadn't finished getting dressed when I heard my cell phone ringing. Downstairs.

No way can I get there in time from up here. That's why there's voice mail.

A uniform shirt, a pair of loose dark slacks that fit over my orthopedic boot, a right shoe but not the left. I was off to maneuver the stairs again, happy I'd decided not to have the surgical screws in my leg if the experimental procedure would speed up my recovery.

In the kitchen, I picked up my phone and saw the caller was from the medical examiner's office. Well, technically, he wasn't the medical examiner all the time, so the number was actually his private practice office for living patients.

I reviewed the voice mail.

"Julie, it's Boyd Bishop. Listen, I was digging through some stuff at the house, and I think I found something that would have Catherine's DNA. Esmeralda had kept Cathy's baby teeth as she lost them. I'll await your call."

Yes, I thought. There's a chance that DNA could be recovered from baby teeth, especially since I understood him to say there was more than one.

I dialed the number and hit the send button.

"Dr. Bishop's office," his wife, who also ran his office, said cheerfully.

"It's Julie Samualson," I said. "Dr. Bishop just called me a few minutes ago."

"He did? Well, and then he leaves to go to the hospital to deliver a baby," she explained. "Shall I have him call you back when he returns?"

Esmeralda might not know he's been looking for a DNA sample all this time.

"Sure. I'll have my phone with me. I'm headed to the sheriff's department now."

"And how's your foot, Julie? Boyd said you'd ended up having surgery on it."

"It started as just a bad sprain, but then I fell and actually broke the fibula, so they did a procedure called a tight-rope to pull the tibia and fibula together," I said.

"Amazing what they can do these days," she commented. "You take care now." And she hung up.

Kind of an abrupt goodbye, I thought.

I grabbed my truck keys from the hook, then almost slapped my forehead.

My truck had been rolled back over onto its tire-less wheelbase and dragged onto a tow sled last night, a burned out, deformed shell of a vehicle. No need for those keys. Ever again.

On top of losing my truck, the one Zach had picked out in Albuquerque with all its fancy options, I'd kept a medical kit and dozens of CDs inside. I'd need to make an inventory so I could put together another pack.

After a brief search, I found the keys on the kitchen counter for the take-home unit now sitting in the driveway and walked out through the garage, its double door still missing. But the smells of burnt wood, metal, rubber and gasoline lingered inside. Odors that triggered mental images of the cabin where Kim Katz and I had been held captive. Where Matt had died.

Where I'd killed him.

Crap, I had to get those memories out of my head.

I unlocked the cruiser door and got inside, finding it impossible to get my crutches in the cab with the cage and the radio console limiting space.

Struggling, I felt like crying.

"Here, let me put those in the back for you," Zach said, having appeared out of thin air. He took the crutches out of my grasp. "Are you okay?"

"No, I guess I'm not really." I wiped a tear just before it rolled down my cheek.

Zach squatted down beside the car and took my hand. "We'll make it through this, Julie, just like we've made it through everything else that came before it."

"I know," I whined. "I'm just a little overwhelmed by the bomb and at discovering each new thing damaged by it."

"You grabbed your other keys, didn't you?" he said, smiling. "What color truck do you want this time, since you really didn't have a choice before?"

Responding without hesitation, I said, "Red."

His eyebrows went up in what must have been surprise.

"I've never owned a red car before. Just seems," I thought a second, "different. I could use different."

"Red it is. We'll go shopping on Monday."

"Better get us a rental car," I teased. "I don't want to be seen in your Mustang in its current condition."

"Me, either, darlin'." He hugged me, stood and closed my door, watching as I backed up and drove out the gate.

The ride to the station, listening to the radio traffic turned low, gave me time to get my head together. In the parking lot, however, I faced the newest predicament of getting the crutches from the back by standing and hopping, I supposed. But when I opened the car door, Doug Logan came rushing over, saying that Zach had called, requesting someone come out and help me.

"He did?" I asked.

"Didn't want you jumping around on this gravel on one foot, Ma'am." He handed me the crutches. "How are you today?"

"Other than watching the cleanup of a car bomb in my driveway? I'm pretty good, I'd say," I announced. And after hearing Zach tell Amber about the things she had, I vowed to make a better attempt at being satisfied with what I had.

Like Zach, for example. Not everyone gets a dead husband back alive.

I followed Doug to the building's back door, where he pushed the buttons on the keypad to unlock it, then opened it for me.

Inside, he went on down the hall, but I detoured at the lab, the last room in the building, save the decontamination closet, as we called it because of its tiny size.

All the evidence in the Seaver case had either been processed and reviewed or sent out. Nothing for me to do in that regard. I checked the log for the gasoline can the sheriff had collected from Dana Watson's house, here for fingerprints. The only prints on it came back to Jack Browning, which was neither conclusive for an assault nor a surprise.

I wondered if Geo had talked her sister into getting a restraining order or filing criminal charges yet.

Then I mentally moved on to the Catherine Bishop disappearance and the bag Amber found in the forest. I remembered the doctor had called me, I thought, looking at my watch, well over an hour ago now.

He'd left a message saying he might have a source for Catherine's DNA. What could that mean with regard to the items in the bag? To start, we could likely determine whether the tattooed skin was hers, though by the Bishops' recollection, it was not. I still had concerns whether the tanning process could have altered the design so significantly they didn't recognize it, but now we could find out for sure.

Still, given the evidence she had been in Texas, did that mean any actual crime might have been committed there instead of here? What about the statute of limitations? As of yet, the county had not spent the money on finding or running DNA because there had been no evidence of a crime. Would determining the tattoo was Catherine's be sufficient to suggest a death? Could we obtain DNA samples from any other of the evidence, such as the sweat soaked into the leather of the wallet itself?

And if the skin was not hers, did we still have a responsibility to find her? Could we even presume there was a crime? And did we have to tell her adoptive parents we were looking, or if we found her?

As if by telepathy, Dr. Bishop peeked in the door.

"I hoped to find you here," he said. "And thank you for not giving me away with Ez'. She's not ready to hear anything about Cathy." He looked down at his feet. "I fear she won't be anytime soon."

Some people never are, I thought. To them, not knowing is better than knowing something bad for certain.

He handed me a small plastic bag, crinkly and yellowed with age. In it were nine baby teeth, mostly incisors.

"I hope you these will be helpful to you. My wife wouldn't be happy I found them – she probably stashed them away when I made her get rid of Cathy's things," he said. "I hate to ask, but if you don't need them all, I'd like to have back what you don't use."

"Of course," I told him. "I hope we can get the necessary pulp from just one."

"Do what you need to do," he said, taking a step back. "I hope it helps you find answers, even if we don't like them."

Just the opposite of his wife. Either way, one of them would not be happy.

CHAPTER 19

We – meaning the sheriff's department – had done nothing extensive or expensive with the contents of the bag Amber had found. Before I did more, I decided to check with Wade Fordham to see if he had any thoughts on where to start or connections to get anything done.

I grabbed the evidence list and looked it over. The bag, a carved wooden fetish of either a wolf or something similar, two craftsy-looking conglomerations of twigs and feathers and twine and beads that resembled small dream catchers, and a very worn men's single-fold leather wallet. Inside the wallet, we'd found a faded photo of two or maybe more people stuck inside the plastic sleeve, a library card for Catherine Bishop from a small central Texas town, ticket stubs to a circus – one adult, one child – and the two-inch by three-inch piece of tanned skin with a tattoo Amber had identified as a Buddhist love knot.

A strange thought crossed my mind – what if the tattoo wasn't a Buddhist design but something else? Did that matter?

Research. That I could do best from the library, I thought. And I needed more information about DNA.

I bagged the baby teeth as new evidence, logged it, and stored it with the other items from the duffel. Then I found the photographed image of the tattoo we'd created when asking the Bishops to identify it, made a photocopy of it, and replaced the original. I wouldn't need the photo, just a basic outline of the shape.

Using the phone next to the door, I called dispatch. "Bette, I'm going down to the library to do a little research."

"Sure thing. Did Dr. Bishop find you okay? I knew you were back there somewhere, but I was busy," she said, pausing our conversation to answer the radio. "Sorry, it's that kinda day."

I waited until she'd had a brief exchange with a deputy before telling her that he had. "He dropped off some evidence, so that's why I'm going to the library, to find a few answers," I said.

On my way back through the hallway, Wade's voice echoed. "Julie? Don't leave yet."

I stopped in my tracks.

He huffed into the hall, hurrying to where I stood. "Is it true that Boyd brought something we can get a DNA sample from?"

Nodding, I intended to explain, but he kept talking.

"If we can get a clean sample from those teeth to use, I'll authorize testing for the –" He grimaced, not wanting to call the tattooed piece of skin leather, no doubt. "For the specimen, or anything else in that bag you think might be a match."

I nodded again. "I'm off to see if I can find the best way to sample items, and then we can decide which lab might be the most qualified to handle them, because we certainly cannot do the testing here."

"Very good," he said, clapping me on the back hard enough I had to hide the wince. "Feels like we're moving forward on it again." He turned to go, then stopped. "Oh, and they found enough of the detonation device on your truck to determine for sure it was intentional."

Seeing my truck on its side in my driveway was pretty much all the determination of intention I'd needed previously.

"What comes next?" I asked.

"State Police are working on it, whatever that means," he replied, not fully happy with the answer someone had given him.

For years, I've understood that cops from different agencies, especially from different levels, don't always put aside their egos and play nice together for the good of solving a crime. Rural agencies hate big city departments, and city cops hate state cops, and apparently everyone with a badge has a reason to hate the FBI.

That might be an itsy-bitsy exaggeration.

Maybe, but I especially detested the agency, though my reasons were quite different from that of most cops – mine were personal. I could almost feel obsessive with my hatred of the FBI and other federal agencies, though part of me tried to understand that not every agent was bad.

Some days, I couldn't come close to believing even that.

We parted, and I crutched on down the hallway to the back door and outside into bright, almost hot sunshine. I found that by opening the back door of the cruiser, I could toss my crutches inside, leaving only two small hops to get in the driver's seat. However, I was pretty sure that retrieving them would take more effort.

I hadn't driven a block when my cell phone rang. I pulled over, rather than try to negotiate traffic while juggling it.

"Samualson," I said, probably just before the call jumped to my voice mailbox.

"Julie? It's Geo." She sounded serious, not at all her usual cheerful self. "Can you come over to my house and look at Dana? I think one of her burns is getting infected, and she doesn't want to go back to the hospital."

"Sure, I can do that," I said. "I'll be over in about ten minutes. And by the way, did she ever decide about a restraining order. You can just say yes or no if she's listening."

"No, I don't need anything else, but thanks."

Damn. We really needed to get her to file a complaint against Browning.

"Okay, I'll be right over."

We disconnected.

On a whim, before I started back out of my odd parking spot, I called Bette in dispatch.

"I didn't want to use the radio," I told her, "but Geo wants me to go over to her house and check out her sister. Would you have a unit just cruise by in about thirty minutes?"

She said she would be happy to do so, and we hung up.

Doubtful that it took all of the ten minutes to reach Geo's house, a small crackerbox house painted a sunny yellow with white trim. She had roses and azaleas – I think that's what she called them – growing around the front porch, other colorful flowers throughout her yard.

I parked in the driveway behind Geo's compact car.

She met me at the door, gave me a big hug, then led me inside and introduced me to Dana, who was the spitting image of Geo, only skinny as a rail and wrapped in white dressings as if she was going to Halloween as a mummy.

We shook hands carefully, and Geo waved that we should sit in the tiny living room while she got us each a glass of lemonade.

I wanted to pass, but I was working on my diplomacy skills, and somehow I knew that a drink was part of Geo's bigger plan.

Dana had gauze and net around her hands, one arm, both thighs, part of her neck, and one patch of dressing held to the side of her face. Surrounding most of the white dressings, she had partial-thickness burns, red and blotchy.

"I'm sure Geo told you I fell in the fire pit," Dana said, almost challenging me to defy the story.

I detected a slight slurring of her voice, but I couldn't tell if it was caused by the burns to her face and throat or whether it was the pain medications.

"Yes, she did. In fact, I came to the hospital to check on you and Geo a couple of times before you were released. I'm glad you're home. Personally, I hate hospitals," I pointed at my foot. "Had to have a little surgery myself."

"Oh goodness!" Geo exclaimed as she came from the kitchen with a tray of glasses. "I didn't know that or I wouldn't have asked you to come over here."

"I was at the station, Geo. It's quite all right."

Well, I had been at the station, so it was close enough.

We chatted over lemonade as if nothing bad had ever happened to any of us, just three – well Dana didn't contribute much to the conversation – gabby women passing the afternoon.

Finally, Geo did get around to her reason for calling.

"The burn on Dana's right thigh," she said, "is red and oozing more than it has been. I was hoping you might take a peek. If it's something we can get treated here, neither of us wants to go back to Portland."

I nodded and got up to go wash my hands before we started.

We went to a back bedroom to unwrap her leg, as Geo announced that she'd had it steam cleaned before Dana got home. "I wanted her to have as sterile a room as possible, so I gave the cat to a neighbor's girl and replaced the linens and curtains."

"That was quite a forethought," I told her. "And I'm sure that the daughter really loves Spanx."

I could tell Geo missed the cat, but she was making every effort to do the right things for her sister.

"Let's take a look at your leg, shall we?" I asked, pulling gloves out of a box on the nightstand.

Dana stood, and I unrolled the gauze bandage that held in place a large dressing. The wound was raw-looking, almost through the skin in an area about the size of both my palms, with lesser burns surrounding it.

Geo had accurately described the drainage that concerned her.

I put the dressing back in place and rewrapped Dana's leg.

"What antibiotics has she taken?" I asked. "Did they give her a prescription for one to take now?"

Geo retrieved a list for me and pointed. "This is what they gave her."

I didn't know a lot about burns, since my problems have leaned toward lacerations and orthopedic injuries, but Geo was correct in guessing the current antibiotic was not doing enough to treat the infection. As open as the skin was, almost any passing germ could colonize the wounds.

"You might call and see if your family doctor can culture that," I suggested, "but I suspect he's going to send you back to the burn unit to a specialist. Burn treatment can be so unpredictable, and choosing the wrong antibiotic could make things worse."

Geo nodded, but Dana only looked away.

Out the window, I heard a ruckus. When I peeked, I saw Browning had driven up into Geo's well-groomed yard and was standing beside his truck, yelling for Dana to come outside.

Dana stood up and took one step toward the doorway.

"No," I said. "You will not go out there. I'm guessing he's drunk."

She looked from me to the window and back before sitting down.

I reached for my portable radio, only to find I wasn't wearing it. In fact, I hadn't put on my duty belt, so I had no nightstick, no handcuffs, and no gun.

And I was on crutches.

"Call 911," I told Geo as the yelling outside became more obscene. Maybe that cruiser I'd asked Bette to send wouldn't be too far away now.

Hopefully, the uniform would make a difference in Browning's attitude until backup arrived, because that was all I had.

CHAPTER

20

I walked out the front door just in time to duck the beer bottle whirling through the air in my direction, smashing against the house next to my head.

Although I'd been willing to let him walk until that moment, all my good will had shattered with the glass.

"That's enough, Jack," I warned. "You can leave now or go to jail. What's it gonna be?"

"Dana better get her ass outside right now so I can take her home," he hollered.

"So you can hit her again?" I asked.

"I didn't hit her," he said, spitting on the grass. "You can ask her."

"Oh, you mean so she can fall down and get hurt again, right?"

"Yeah," he said, then realized I was making fun of him. "No! So I can take care of her."

I crossed my arms and nodded, holding my ground. There was no way I could get to my cruiser to the shotgun with the crutches.

"You can't stop me from taking her, neither," he yelled.

A squad car screeched to a halt in front of the house.

"No, but I'm betting he can," I offered nonchalantly, pointing over Jack's shoulder.

Two more cars arrived within the next fifteen seconds, heading off what could have escalated from argument to brawl rapidly due to his drunken belligerence.

"Add assault on a peace officer and DUI to the drunk and disorderly," I told Richard Langston after Browning was in the backseat of his cruiser. "He drove here, and he threw a bottle at me."

Langston tilted his head then shook it in disbelief.

"Well, maybe not at me exactly, but he almost hit me, nonetheless."

Nodding, Langston crawled in his car, requested a tow truck respond to the scene, and then backed out of the tangle of patrol vehicles to take Browning to jail.

Wade showed up, having missed the drama but hearing enough of the story from Blake Erwin before coming to where I stood on the porch. "You confronted Browning without a weapon? On crutches?"

As if I had much of a choice.

Geo stuck her head out the front door. "No, sir, I had her back, if it came to that," she said, brandishing a pump shotgun. "But if she hadn't been here, this might have gone a lot differently when he came to my front door."

I held out both hands and shrugged in a "See?" expression.

"Can I add a charge for damage to my property?" she asked. "That bottle broke my porch light, and he ran over my hydrangea bushes over there."

Wade just nodded and walked away.

"You take her back to Portland," I told Geo. "No sense in messing around with a possible infection that could start small but end up killing her."

"You really think it's that serious?" she asked.

"Yes, it's that serious."

❁

I gave up on the idea of going to the library. The quiet was just more than I could take at the moment, so I drove home.

Zach was scrubbing the cabin logs that had been scorched in the explosion when I pulled into the driveway.

"How'd your day go?" I asked, getting out of the car and hopping on one foot to open the back door.

"Nothing exciting after you left, except the yelling," he said, putting down the stiff brush to come help me. "I've been accused of keeping her from seeing her friends, forcing her to eat that crappy healthy food, and making her come up to this God-forsaken place away from everyone she knew in New Mexico."

"I see," I said, leaning on the hood of the car. "How do you plead to these charges?"

Zach rolled his eyes. "I think it's a good thing we missed her terrible two's." He handed me his glass of tea for a sip. "What wild extremes of mood she can display."

I tried not to laugh.

He had missed the many arguments I'd had with Amber while the government was having him play dead, leaving us to the pieces of story we'd been given. Then when she went to Albuquerque, partly because I didn't know what else to do with her, she found out he was alive. Apparently that blessing had worn thin already.

"How was your day?" he asked, taking back his glass.

"Oh, the usual. New evidence in the Bishop case that may provide a DNA sample. Nothing new about the bombing except they've determined it really was a bomb, if you had any doubts," I said. "And I had a little face to face time with Jack Browning before he went back to jail."

"Huh?"

That got his attention.

I told him the whole story, and then I asked him not to let me leave the house again without my gun.

"I might not ever let you leave the house at all if you keep that up," he said, then drained the glass. "Criminy, Julie. Have *you* ever thought about retiring before someone kills you?"

With a wink, I looked up and smiled. "I figure I'm good until the sheriff tells me to pretend I'm dead. I want to see what's under what you wear to my funeral before I retire."

"I can show you what's under what I'm wearing now, if you'd like," he offered, waggling his eyebrows. "Amber's gone to the Clinton's for a few hours while Del's shopping."

Although Saturday was the Fourth of July, Amber had been planning on riding in a nearby playday – more or less a smaller scale rodeo with speed competitions like barrel racing and pole bending, but not judged events like bull or bronc riding. However, not having a truck to pull the horse trailer ended that discussion right away.

Didn't keep Amber from arguing that we could borrow a pickup from Del Clinton.

"No, Amber," Zach said, ending the debate at least in his mind.

"Kara and her mom are going, so why can't I go with them?" she persisted.

"You can go," he said, not bothering to look up from the ham he was chopping for breakfast burritos. "But you cannot take a horse."

Amber, of course, made some very audible sound of disgust and frustration before storming up the stairs.

When I looked over, Zach was shaking his head.

"I believe it was you who told me she'd grow out of this," I teased. "Welcome to being home."

"No comment."

"This too shall pass?" I offered.

"So will a kidney stone, I'm told."

"At least they can give you drugs for that," I said. "Getting out would be good for her, but she hasn't been practicing, so I'm not sure what the hubbub is about."

"That has no relation to the fact she wants to go hang around all day," Zach told me. "Like that last playday we went to, she sat on Denali and gossiped with Kara and Cody most of the day. When she did compete, it was like she didn't care about winning."

A voice called from up the staircase. "It's not about winning, Dad!"

He just nodded in a *see-I'm-wrong-again* manner and went back to his culinary tasks.

Twenty minutes later, breakfast was served without Amber's

return to the table.

"She'll sulk all day, I guess," Zach said, serving himself her portion of the scrambled egg concoction he'd made.

"She does need to eat something," I told him. "But perhaps she ought to learn that the hard way."

"What exactly does that mean?"

I lowered my voice more. "It means that it's not anyone's responsibility but hers to manage her blood glucose and her meals," I said. "So when her blood sugar drops and she doesn't like the consequences, then maybe she will begin to understand that it's up to her to eat and take her insulin correctly."

Zach gave that a pondering nod.

"And she needs to understand that the world does not revolve around her, so missing a playday does not mean the sun won't rise tomorrow," I continued. "Nor does it mean that this family having a comfortable financial cushion equates to her getting everything she wants."

"Tough love."

I wasn't sure whether he was being sarcastic or just summarizing my speech.

"You told her the other day that life isn't fair," I said, stepping off my soapbox.

He looked out the dining room doors. "You know, I got most of what I wanted when I was her age, but I didn't want the things she wants. And I worked for what I got."

"Me, too."

"She can't get a regular job without a car, can't drive without a license, and can't make her own money without imposing on one of us," he continued. "Things are different."

"Maybe so, but if she expects everything to be a free ride and doesn't make the effort here at home, then we've no reason to give in to getting her a license or a car, either."

He didn't respond, so I assumed the discussion about Amber was done and switched topics.

"Dr. Bishop brought me Catherine's baby teeth, which I think his wife had hidden away," I said. "And because of that, I got the go-ahead to spend the money on DNA profiling for the skin and the wallet."

"That might get you somewhere. How long will testing take?"

"Being a cold case, it could be months, but I'm hoping to pull a string or two."

We cleaned up the kitchen, and I took a brief nap on the sofa before leaving at noon to do a little research at the library and determine the right strings to pluck to further my agenda.

The library was a quiet, cool place with that universal library smell. I wondered if a company could make that into an air freshener, like new-car smell stuff.

Picking a table close to the section I intended to browse, I dropped off my shoulder bag holding a notebook and pens, then went looking. Half an hour later, I was sitting in a well-worn chair with four texts, one the size of the dictionary laid open near the front desk and which I could barely manage on crutches, browsing for information.

First, I looked through a book on symbols, finding several images that were close to the photocopy I'd made of the tattoo on the skin and to that on Catherine's shoulder. I concluded the image might not be Buddhist but perhaps Celtic in origin, but an unending "knot" nonetheless. However, there were a dozen variations on the design.

I flipped to the larger text on DNA, still a relatively new science for solving crime, thinking the department needed books more up to date, but this way we didn't have to pay scads of money to buy them. I flipped open my notepad and began.

Can DNA be sampled from leather? Yes. And DNA sources could include human skin that had been tanned. However, in the case of the wallet, determining which was the DNA from cow versus any absorbed sweat into the leather from a human source would be very time consuming.

Can DNA be sampled from baby teeth? Yes, but for the best results, I'd need to find an expert in dental forensics.

I scribbled more notes as I read.

DNA is contained throughout the human body in blood and any cellular material from tissue or organs such as skin, muscle, brain, bone or teeth. It's also found in bodily fluids such as urine, semen, saliva, perspiration, and so on. While DNA from identical twins is an exact duplicate, other result comparisons have about a one in one billion possibility for exact matching.

Testing DNA can be done through several methods, which seemed like an overwhelming bit of information to write, so I bookmarked the pages to be photocopied. However, after reading more about these methods, I decided that we could have two separate labs doing different tests. The simpler and faster results of blood typing and mitochondrial testing would give us the first indication whether or not the tattooed skin really belonged to Katherine, with the overall assumption from this whether she was dead or possibly still alive. We could then await results on PCR – polymerase chain reaction – testing, which was more specific, to compare the teeth to the leather if needed. Although I understood the basics of the science, some of the chemistry details were over my head. Fortunately, I just had to know what was available to test, and then find out who could provide us results.

I was standing behind a woman at the front desk, waiting for the key to use the copier, when my cell phone rang.

The librarian gave me a stern frown as I stepped away to answer it.

Yes, I saw the sign about turning it off. Geez... Do you see my badge and gun?

"It's Amber," Zach began as soon as I'd pushed the button, so I heard his first few words because only he was shouting. "She's groggy and not making sense. I'd take her to the emergency room, but the Mustang won't start. Should I call an ambulance?"

"No, first you need to calm down," I said. "Get a glass of orange juice and mix in two spoonfuls of sugar, and make her drink it. She'll probably be whiney about it, but sugar is what she needs."

"I don't need to take her –" he asked, and I heard the refrigerator door open, a rack rattle as he removed a bottle of juice.

"No, it's not necessary if you can get her to drink. I'll be right there." I disconnected and stepped toward the desk. Holding up my phone, I said to the frowning librarian, "Sorry, there's an emergency. Can you copy those pages I marked, for the sheriff's department, and I'll swing by and get them when I can?"

The librarian, her name was Phyllis I read on her nametag, nodded with no change of expression. I tried to smile my appreciation, but it went without response.

The bag I carried bounced between my crutches and my hip as I hurried out the door toward my cruiser.

On the hood of the car perched one of Jack Browning's friends, I presumed, though I didn't know his name. Cleaning his fingernails with a pocketknife.

The knife would never remove all the grime.

"Get off my car," I demanded, not slowing down. "Because if you're still there when I back up, I'm not stopping to see if you're hurt when you hit the asphalt."

He slid off and folded his knife against his thigh, then stepped between me and the driver's door.

"And if you don't get out of my way, I'll shoot you and let someone else worry whether or not to scrape you up," I said. "I'm in a hurry, and I don't intend to mess with you."

By then we were six feet apart, but I was still moving like a freight train.

"I was just going to enlighten you," he said, taking a frayed toothpick from his mouth pointing it at me before tossing it on the ground and taking a step away from the car, "that we didn't appreciate Jack going to jail yesterday."

"And I didn't appreciate him throwing a beer bottle at me, either. Now move!"

I reached down to my hip, comforted my duty belt and gun were right where I expected them to be this time. With one flip of a finger, I unsnapped the holster.

He stepped on out of my way, tipped his filthy cap, and said as he turned, "We'll be seeing ya again then."

"Do you want to go to jail, too? Because I can make that happen with a push of a button."

"Nope, just saying a friendly adios." He kept walking, giving a half-assed wave over his shoulder.

I dropped the bag to toss the crutches in the back seat, then jerked the bag off the pavement and slung it across the console as I got in, debating whether or not to have him picked up for the threat.

Not worth my time, I thought. Not right now.

I started the car and headed for home.

CHAPTER

21

Amber was finally asleep, though it was mid-afternoon.

She'd drunk the orange juice Zach provided, then she'd eaten a healthy meal to make up for snubbing us at breakfast and lunch.

I'd had a long talk with her, although she sat with her arms crossed, pouting, about how she had to be responsible for her own health.

"In case you didn't know, had you been home alone, or been driving, or been out on horseback at the playday, your blood sugar would still have bottomed out because you didn't eat," I'd told her, trying to be calm and educational. "And if you fail to recognize those symptoms, you could very well fall unconscious, getting hurt, or just plain dying."

"So I'm not supposed to go anywhere or do anything alone ever again," she retorted.

"No, *you* need to be the one to manage your diet and medication properly, and then to recognize the symptoms before you have a serious problem. I don't know how you're feeling when your blood sugar fluctuates. Zach doesn't know. Cody or Kara or Savannah – none of them will know before you do. And if you don't teach your friends to look out for you, too, they can't help you."

"It's stupid!"

"No argument about that, but it's permanent, Amber. And you

have to deal with it or suffer the consequences. For example, if you let this get out of control and have a seizure, you won't get a driver's license for at least a year. Or they'll take it away after you get it."

"What?"

That hit straight in her motivation.

"It's the law, not some dumb rule I made," I said. "So you choose. You can keep ignoring this diabetes problem until it starts taking away everything you want, or you can begin to manage it like an adult. End of lecture."

I'd gotten up and walked away, leaving her to consider what I'd said.

When I came downstairs, Zach was sitting outside on the deck, enjoying a cool breeze and watching the colors in the eastern sky as the sun dropped toward the horizon behind the house. Instead of discussing the crises of the day, we talked about things that did not evoke anger or frustration. Things like the feel of a spring rain and the smell of newly mown hay. Things we missed, like the raging storms visible on the distant horizon in New Mexico, bringing fierce lightning and thunder. And the wind against your face when you were on a motorcycle.

We relaxed, held hands, and sipped wine he'd opened while Amber and I talked.

"I miss this," I said, squeezing his fingers. "I miss a lot of the moments we had when you visited me in Michigan."

"Like when I would sneak into your house?" he asked.

"Yeah," I confessed. "That, too. But like the night we went for a ride on my bike, or went walking on the beach."

"We could still do those things," he offered. "But there is less spontaneity."

I nodded. "When Amber gets more settled with her diabetes, I'd like to ride out to the Oregon coast. Maybe Newport, Cannon Beach."

"We will do that, then."

"At least we have one less job to work around," I said. "I'd like

Amber to see it, too. And our trip in October to Las Vegas for Nolan's and Olivia's wedding," I reminded him.

It seemed settled, a future trip. When Amber had better control of her diabetes, when my ankle was healed enough to ride, when I could arrange a little time away.

When.

❁

Sunday, I intended to sleep in, to revel in being between the crisp sheets long after the sun had risen. Maybe Zach would bring me breakfast in bed, just because he wanted to do it. Later I might spend time with a good book, stretched out in a hammock on the deck.

Alas, sleeping in was not in the stars.

I could tell because they were still shining when my cell phone rang at 4 a.m.

The caller was Geo.

"She's gone!" the panicked voice told me. "I got up to go to the bathroom, and I peeked in to check on her, to see if she needed any pain medication, but she wasn't in her bedroom!"

I tried hard to silence the sigh mixed with a hard yawn.

"Geo, take a breath!" I finally had to interject in the middle of her next sentence. "Did you call the dispatcher?"

"No, I just thought that," she took a ragged breath, "that you could help me find her. I think she trusts you, at least a little."

Zach rolled over to see what the call was about.

"I'll be right over," I told her, "but you need to call the sheriff's office."

"I will, right away."

She hung up.

I let my arm drop. "Does it never end?"

"What?"

"Geo's sister is gone. But I doubt it was Browning who coerced her to go, since he's likely still in jail."

"The beer bottle toss?" he asked.

"And the public intox, though I assume the DUI charges didn't hurt." I tossed the covers off and sat up on the side of the bed. "Gee, I wish this all could have happened when I wasn't handicapped."

"Or at least when you weren't trying to sleep," he added. "Want me to go?"

"No, I don't know what I can do except offer her moral support," I said, yawning again as I hopped toward the crutches, then toward my closet for a uniform. "The rest will be up to the deputies on duty."

As I pulled on a shirt, I was swearing under my breath that Browning was an idiot and the next one of his friends to show up and threaten me would end up in jail or the morgue.

"Who was it?"

I turned to see Zach standing in the bathroom doorway, naked, with his head tilted in curiosity.

"Who was who?"

"You said that the next one of –"

I held up my hand. "I know what I said. One of Jack's buddies was sitting on my cruiser yesterday when you called me at the library. I suppose you could say he threatened me, but I had more important things on my mind, so I let him walk away." I sat down on a stool to pull my pants over the boot.

"Who *was* it?" Zach repeated, slower, as if I hadn't understood his question the first time.

"I didn't ask his name," I replied, exasperated. "No one I recognized."

"What kind of threat?"

Great, he's scented this like a bloodhound.

"He just said, 'We'll be seeing you later.' It would have been a stretch to arrest him for threatening me, but I knew that was his intention," I explained, tucking my shirt into my pants. Then I went to the sink to wash my face, brush my teeth, and to do something with my hair.

Zach was sitting up in bed against the headboard, bedside light on, when I came out of the bathroom. "Please be careful," he said.

I pulled my duty belt on and snapped the keepers that attached it to the belt in my pants.

"Promise," I said.

He leaned over to kiss me goodbye. "Call when you're on your way home, and I'll fix you breakfast."

"Thanks," I said. "A girl could get used to this."

Turns out, eating together wasn't on that day's agenda either.

I arrived at Geo's house at half past four, parking in front of the house next door because two cruisers already took up all the parking space available.

When I got out of the car, I had an eerie sense of being watched. Looking at the nearby windows, I realized faces peered out at the activity from at least three houses. Odd, as gregarious as Geo was, I doubted any of her neighbors were friends enough to come to her house and ask if they could help.

Getting the crutches out of the back seat had become a less arduous task, but as I walked with them, I realized just how sore my left hip and thigh were getting from keeping my foot off the ground. I would be so ready for toe-touching, I thought, as I ascended the two steps of Geo's porch.

Doug Logan answered the door and let me in.

I was proud of the young man for growing from a volunteer EMT to dispatcher to now being a deputy. He was young and still had a lot to learn, but his willingness to work was evident in everything he did.

Inky Grissom stood in the kitchen, asking Geo questions.

Another deputy imported from the Seattle area, Inky had happily taken the nickname after a pen bled all over the front of his uniform, because his mother had named him Orville after a great grandfather. Poor guy wasn't even thirty yet, but the name conjured images of a white-headed, crotchety man of seventy. Still, he was a more seasoned officer and sometimes found more efficient ways to accomplish a task than Doug did.

I hung back and quizzed Doug. "Any sign that someone came

here and picked her up?"

"None that we've found," he replied. "But it does seem the most obvious possibility. Geo doesn't think Dana could walk very far, given the wounds on her leg."

Thinking back to when I unbandaged her thigh, I had to mentally agree that the swelling and pain would certainly slow her down.

Geo stepped around Inky and greeted me with the usual cheer then crumbled into tears when I hugged her.

I guided her to the couch and let her cry.

"I've done everything I can to make sure she's getting adequate medical care and to keep her safe," she said, finally composed enough to dab her eyes and sit up straight. "But she's been resistant, just going along with the things I've done."

The dispatcher advised Inky by radio that the subject was not located at her residence.

"So where could she be?" Geo asked, swiping her hand over her head, leaving a trail of mussed hair.

"Geo, are her pain medications still here?" I asked, thinking that taking them would give us an indication whether she planned to leave or not.

She went to look and came back with the prescription bottle.

I counted out the number of doses she was supposed to have taken since the script was filled, subtracted that from the total number of tablets provided, then dumped the remaining pills on the coffee table to see if Dana had been taking extra.

"She takes them regularly?" I asked.

Geo nodded.

"Does she ever take more than is prescribed? She can have up to six a day."

"Only twice, I think. She told me a few nights ago that her leg was really hurting, so I gave her an extra pill before she went to bed."

That meant ten tablets or so were missing.

"And you don't lock these up?"

"Why would I?"

I looked up at Inky. "Who would buy hydrocodone tablets here in town, you know, to resell?"

He shrugged. "I'll find out."

I thought about calling Zach to see what the street price would be, but it didn't matter, really. Although it wasn't yet a big problem in our little town yet, narcotics could sell on the street for five to ten times what each would cost in a pharmacy. But even at twenty bucks a tablet, there weren't enough missing to cover Jack's bail, though it might have been enough to make up for a shortfall.

"Browning's still in jail, right?" I asked Grissom. "Make sure we know if someone goes to bail him out."

He left, but Doug stayed behind for a short time until he was sure we were safe and that I would be at the house throughout the morning.

"You need anything, you just call," he reiterated on his way out the front door.

And then we were alone.

"Tell me more about Dana," I prompted when Geo and I settled into the living room. "What kind of person was she before she met Jack? Knowing that could help us find her."

Geo described her sister, four years younger, as a smart kid in school until she fell in with a manipulative older man she eventually married. "He wasn't physically abusive," she explained, "but he was just all hot air, bigger than life. A real know-it-all. The night before her small wedding, Mom and I debated just kidnapping her away for a week or so." Geo gave a feeble smile. "They were together about six years. Somehow, Dana never got pregnant. He just up and left for work one day and never came home. Divorce papers arrived via some stranger months later, and she signed. Then she started dating men in a progressive spiral down. I always thought the one before this was at the bottom of the barrel, until I heard about Jack."

"You told me about the time her arm was broken," I said. "What others?"

"She quit coming around so much after he shoved her off the porch. I knew, and she knew I did, so she didn't want to lie about any other bruises or stuff. Dressing her burns these last few days, I've noticed several other scars she didn't get as a kid."

"What kind of scars?"

"Like a cigarette burn on the back of her upper arm," she said. "And what looks like a dirty scrape to one knee, as if it healed without being cleaned."

I shook my head. How could anyone put up with that?

Fear. You know about liking fear so much you'll tolerate anything.

I blinked.

I wasn't so afraid of my husband that I'd have gone back to him after he cut my throat, though.

"Do you know where Jack lives when he's not staying with Dana?" I asked.

She shook her head.

I didn't need to know particularly so long as one of the deputies had checked there.

As with all searches – for children, for elderly, for someone who is loved – time creeps by at the speed of growing ivy for those who wait.

I encouraged Geo to get some sleep. "It could be a long day."

"I woke you, Julie, it's only fair that I stay up, too."

"No, you called a friend, and I came to be with you," I said. "I happen to be in uniform, just in case."

After the last run-in with Browning, authority image and hardware seemed appropriate.

She hugged me and then went to her bedroom.

I sat in her reclining rocker, which had a view through the sheer curtains to the front yard. If any of Browning's friends showed up, I'd be waiting. I thumbed through a stack of magazines next to the chair to pass the time.

Almost six hours later, I heard Geo go to the bathroom. When she came out, she asked if I'd like coffee or maybe tea.

"Whatever you're having." From experience, I knew she'd put on water for tea.

I'll drink it, but it's not my favorite.

"Any news?" she asked after the teapot was on the stove, but she didn't turn around to face me, perhaps afraid of bad news.

"No, nothing yet," I replied. "Have you called your parents?"

She shook her head. "Not the sort of news one sister wants to tell her folks about the other. My mother will be a basket case, and I don't want to upset my dad."

I could relate to a mother's distress at receiving news about her daughter, no matter who it came from. Every time my mother heard about me being in a hospital or when I showed up on her doorstep looking like I'd been run over by a truck, she had a conniption fit. No way could I imagine what had happened when Zach had told his mother that his twin sister had been murdered, but I doubted he'd just picked up the phone to call her.

Telephones have become such a common tool, I thought, that we often use them now without regard to how bad news may affect the recipient. A century ago, such communication might have come by mail or telegraph. Today, even when distant death notifications are delivered by police officers, often it's only a perception that the news is personal. Not that having someone stand in front of you to tell you your husband is dead is all that much better, but at least I remember I had someone to physically hate.

I remembered how panicked Zach had sounded yesterday when he called me about Amber's low blood sugar episode. Hearing the voice means you also hear the emotions.

"I probably do need to call them, though," Geo continued, and I agreed it was time.

I need to call my mother, too.

Getting up, I excused myself to the bathroom, hopefully so she would dial the phone while I was out of the room.

Sure enough, I was returning to the kitchen when I heard her.

Everyone on the block heard her.

"What? You mean she's *there?*"

I entered the living room, listening to one side of a conversation about Dana's whereabouts for the last few hours, chastising her father about all the effort that had gone into finding her sister, ending with the obvious, "She could have just left me a note, and you shouldn't be driving!"

Taking a seat, I listened to Geo's continued emotional lecture, now directed at Dana. I pulled out my cell phone and called the dispatcher to end the search.

"Oh, that's such a huge relief," Stephanie said. "Now we can concentrate everyone on finding the missing kid." Between radio and telephone calls, she told me the parents of a five-year-old woke about eight o'clock this morning to find him gone from their RV at the Home Valley Park campground. "Deputies have been splitting their efforts walking an expanding grid away from where the parents parked the night before last."

I understood all that she hadn't actually said, too. Search for a child trumps everything else a department faces, but the deputies were working hard to search for a family member of one of their own, too.

"We're about to get a formal search team going – Doreen Holland will be set up there within the hour. I'd ask, but I know you can't ride," she said.

"No, but Zach and Amber might be able to go," I said. "I'll find out and call you back."

I hung up about the same time Geo did, and I returned to the kitchen

Anger and embarrassment colored her face like a rose. "What a mess," she concluded, pulling her chair to sit at the table, then turning to the stove when the kettle began to whistle. She continued to talk while she poured steaming water over tea bags in two cups. "But she's fine. Says she woke up and couldn't get back to sleep, so she called my dad to come get her. She said she just dumped a few pain pills in her purse so she'd have them."

"I'm glad she's okay," I said, holding up my phone. "I need to find out if Zach can take Amber and go help in the other search."

"There's a real search, too?" She put both mugs on the table and hung her head. "I'm so sorry I panicked and called everyone. This is all my fault."

I stood. "No, it isn't. You did what you should have done, Geo.

And Dana may not show you how much what you're doing means to her, but it means a lot. Taking care of burns, even in a hospital, takes a special kind of heart."

"I just do it," she said. Although there seemed to be no love in the tone of her voice, there was a strong sound of conviction.

"Not everyone could."

She looked at me, face serious, eyebrows drawn together. "I'll tell you something no one else here knows," she said in a harsh whisper. "And I swear I'll deny it if you tell anybody. I spent six years in Viet Nam as an EVAC nurse, where we didn't have time for feelings. Not about patients. Not about the horrible injuries we saw. And then we came home."

I felt my eyes widen.

"My parents thought I'd run off to Europe or somewhere with a friend to bum around, but after a short time, I went to a nursing school and then basic training at Fort Sam Houston in Texas before I was shipped overseas. After all the things I saw over there, when I came back, I just let my parents believe what they wanted."

Wow. Nothing came close to expressing how that news popped my aggravation like a balloon.

"I only worked again as a nurse back in the States a few weeks," she said. "I didn't want to remember any of it. So I waited tables for ten years before I wanted something more responsible than filling a glass."

"But you're doing it for Dana," I said, still not understanding the connection.

"Yeah, but I wouldn't do it for anybody else." Her brown eyes held mine. "Not even you."

CHAPTER

22

When I called home, I explained what I knew about the search for the little boy to Zach.

"So do you think you and Amber would be up for a ride?" I asked.

The silence on the other end told me he was thinking about it. No doubt, Amber's diabetes was foremost in his mind, and I knew better than to interrupt him.

"Does Amber know what all we need for the search?" he finally replied.

After our excursion into the forest for the plane crash last summer, I figured she'd have a good idea what to gather. Knowing there was only one child in a lower altitude region reduced the necessary equipment.

"I think so. Be sure she takes her insulin and plenty of snack bars with her, plus a tube of icing from the kitchen cabinet," I replied.

"Icing?" He asked in the exact confused voice I expected to hear.

"It's a better tasting source of sugar than the tablets if her blood glucose level tanks again."

"Good to know. Maybe she'll share," he said, probably only half-joking.

"Get stuff packed up," I said. "I'll be home in a half hour to get you going."

"Could you bring me a burger?"

"No, but I'll have them ready to grill when you get home."

"Fair enough. See you shortly."

Saying goodbye and actually getting out of Geo's house took longer than I anticipated, but I was on the road to the cabin by noon.

Home Valley, where they'd be searching, was east of both Stevenson and Carson on Highway 14, and it sported a county park and campground overlooking the north bank of the Columbia River.

I considered the location as well as the behavior of a five-year-old. The missing child was a boy, which made him a slightly bigger risk-taker than a girl, except those with older brothers. Important questions to ask the parents included whether they had connections to someone local whom the child might wander away to visit, or if they were strangers to the area, which could lead to the child getting lost.

The Home Valley Park camping area only had two dozen sites, none with utility hookups. A larger recreational vehicle might require a generator for power, so perhaps the family had something smaller like a tent or pop-up trailer with no toilet.

My first guess was that the child woke up, went outside to walk to the chemical toilets, and got lost.

The problem with a child getting lost in that park was the same as its greatest attraction – the close proximity to the Columbia River.

When I pulled into our driveway, reality smacked me in the face again – Zach might have been willing to take the horses on a search, but we had no truck to pull a trailer.

Delbert's new pickup, not the old one Courtney had crashed into my mailbox when she came to tell me her sister was injured, sat hooked to our white four-horse trailer.

Geez, how stupid was I to forget that?

I parked and got out, was hopping to get my crutches when Zach came out the garage door.

"Thought I heard you pull in," he said, leaning over for a quick kiss. "Amber's pretty jazzed about this. They haven't found him yet, have they?"

I shook my head, though I suppose it was possible I just hadn't heard the news on the county radio in the last few minutes while I'd been busy slapping my forehead.

"Zach, I am so sorry," I said, pointing to Del's truck. "I was so caught up in Geo's emergency, then this, and I absolutely forgot that we didn't have a vehicle to pull a trailer."

"No big deal. Del came right over when I called him," Zach said as we walked toward the trailer. "Offered me his smaller trailer, too, but so much of our gear always stays in this one, it just seemed like a lot of extra work."

I nodded, thankful for a neighbor with a good heart, which Del Clinton had been since Zach met him when the cabin was being built, long before I ever set foot on the property.

"Julie," Del said, coming over to shake my hand. "I see you're gettin' around pretty good on those crutches."

Another reminder just how sore I was, using muscles to walk that had previously been ignored.

"Not too bad. I hope to be back on both feet again soon," I replied. "How are the girls?"

"Daphney still has rough days, but I think she's gainin' ground in physical therapy," he said of his younger granddaughter and her recovery from the horrible injuries she'd sustained. "And Court's doing good, too."

Zach had left us chatting and gone to lead the horses out of the paddock, saddles in place. Bridles hung on the horns until he stopped to move each one to a hook at the back of the trailer before loading one horse then the other.

I was surprised when Amber came bolting out of the house, both arms full of stuff.

"I got food and water, sleeping bags, and your rescue kit from the garage – I hope that's okay," Amber fired off as she went hustling by me.

"Of course, and did you get waterproof jackets?" I asked.

"Yes, and your GPS, too."

She acts as if she's done this a dozen times.

I told Del I'd run him back up to his place as soon as I found out where Zach needed to start, and then I placed a call back to dispatch for those details.

No, the boy hadn't been found yet, Stephanie told me. No, he couldn't swim. No, the family was from near Yakima but one set of grandparents lived in Vancouver, where they had visited two days prior to going to the campsite for a day or so before going home.

Doreen Holland was already at the park, coordinating the search, so I wrote down her contact information for Zach. When he came around to where Del and I stood, he asked if I could take a quick look to see if they got everything.

The only thing I suggested they add was another handful of protein bars – the ones that Amber had wrinkled her nose at last time. "They might not taste great, but it's easy energy. Stick a couple in your vest pockets. I like them better when they're not so hard."

Zach wrinkled his nose, too, but went to the house to grab some.

"You do this often?" Del asked me, nodding over his shoulder to the truck and trailer.

"Not a lot of call for a whole team searching, but several times a year we get something big like this," I said. "Having horses makes it much easier to cover ground, and with a child, there are two questions that are never in your favor – is he hiding because he's afraid of getting in trouble, or has he kept on moving even after he figures out he's lost? I'm guessing this kid is a mover."

"Guessin', huh."

"When you're searching for someone, it's a lot of guessing. You have to evaluate variables and guess which direction he has gone – up or down a hill or toward the water, for example. Whether he walks or stays put, and whether he might think he's in trouble and hide from searchers. Whether he went looking for something and got lost or just wants to not be found."

"That's mighty complicated," he said. "Best left to you experts."

"No one's an expert at searching," I replied. "We just try to do our best."

"Julie, if there's one thing I've learned about you these last few years, it's that you trying means you're doing the very best anyone can do."

My face got warm as I blushed.

"There isn't one single person I prayed more to look up and see when Daph' got hurt." Tears pooled in his eyes. "Then you stood up to that helicopter nurse to let me and Courtney say goodbye before they took off with her in the ambulance. Ain't nothing ever meant more to me than what you did for the both of those girls that day."

Tears threatened to spill down my cheeks, too. "It was the right thing to do, Del."

"People don't always do the right thing, Julie, they do the easy thing."

With that, Zach returned, gave me a kiss goodbye, then he and Amber crawled in the pickup to go to Home Valley.

I took Del home in my patrol car, staying to visit an hour with Courtney and Daphney, graciously declining the invitation for supper, then going home where I collapsed onto the couch to take a much needed and well-deserved nap.

Lunch could wait. I needed sleep more than I needed food.

❧

Apparently I needed hours of sleep because when I woke to the sound of my phone, it was past five o'clock already.

The call was from Zach, but when I answered, I could barely make out any words at all due to the static and choppy sound.

". . . find the boy . . . west of . . . lost . . . sunset . . ." was what I heard. Or something like that.

"Zach? I can't understand anything you said," I yelled into the phone, as if that would make the signal better. "Can you call me –" I was asking when the connection changed to the irritating beep indicating the call had failed.

I tried calling back, but his phone went straight to voicemail.

I waited ten minutes, then tried again.

Then I called the search coordinator. "Doreen, it's Julie," I said, then exchanging brief pleasantries. "I got a call from Zach, but it was too garbled to understand. Has the boy been located?"

Searchers had found him near the camp an hour ago, she told me, and most of the teams had returned to check out, but she hadn't heard from my husband yet.

"Just ask him to call me when they get there," I said and disconnected.

As the sun dipped lower, my concern mutated to worry. Then Doreen called.

"Has Zach contacted you?" she asked, trying to sound casual.

Okay, now I'm really worried.

"No, I haven't heard from him." I tried to outwait her silence but failed. "I take it they haven't come back. I can't imagine that Amber wouldn't remember to check back with you. Didn't Zach leave the truck and trailer where you are?"

"No. After they checked in, I sent them to the western side of the park. I asked Doug Logan to go check. He says their rig is still there, locked up tight."

Acid flooded into my stomach, I could feel the burning just under my ribs all the way up to scar on my neck.

"What about the radio?" I asked.

"I haven't heard from them since Amber checked in at four o'clock."

"You'll be there a while longer?" I tried to disguise the panic rising in my throat.

"I'll be here as long as it takes, sweetie."

Why didn't that sound encouraging?

I disconnected and sat there on the sofa, sweat beading on my upper lip and forehead, my heart thumping wildly in my chest, knowing that Zach should have returned to the trailer as soon as they heard the boy had been found.

What if they didn't hear? How long would Zach keep looking? Wouldn't Amber remember to check in every hour?

Nothing for me to do but go to Home Valley. This time when I went out to the cruiser, I took Laser, still healing from his gunshot a week ago, but he was happy to go along for the ride.

I debated stopping at the sheriff's department before going on to

Home Valley, but I couldn't think of a single reason I should.

Any information about Zach and Amber would surely be passed on to me either directly by Doreen from the campground, or through the dispatcher after I called on the radio to advise I was going to the search coordinator's location.

In fact, I heard almost no radio conversation at all about the search for the little boy, concluded except for the wrap-up, or about the two searchers as yet not accounted for. No one had used the word "missing" in regard to the pair. No one was talking about them at all.

Good news or bad?

I crossed my fingers for it to be good news that no one had thought to inform me the two had turned up. Or that no one had cell service where Zach had parked.

Or.

The list of "or" got longer as I drove, until I simply had to think about something else because eventually I got toward the bottom to the worst-case scenarios.

The sun dropped toward the horizon behind me as I turned onto Highway 14 eastbound, and I hoped the blood-red smear in the western sky was not an ominous sign.

At least twice I wondered what the hell I was doing, going down there. Not a thing I could do to find them while on crutches. Even if I could figure out why they hadn't come back or where they might be, I still had no ability to get them back safely.

Didn't matter. I didn't even slow down.

CHAPTER 23

I pulled into the Home Valley Park just as the last few rays of daylight began to fade. Behind me, Wind Mountain rose from the park's almost sea-level location. Across the Columbia River was the more scarred Shellrock Mountain.

When I parked the cruiser next to one identical to it, Doug Logan came over from a gathering of three other men, presumably searchers.

"Julie, we were waiting for you to speak with these guys about Zach's experience, to see if you might be able to provide some clue where to look," he said, opening the back door to reach for my crutches.

I told Laser to stay in the car.

The trio met us halfway to the car and introduced themselves. I caught only one name, the apparent leader of the group, Warren Crawford. Inky Grissom joined the huddle from somewhere, but I hadn't seen which direction he came from.

"I'm told you know the drill about answers helping determine where to look," Warren started. "We'll presume they have continued moving in the search grid they were given until some event changed both their ability to respond to calls and to return to their base. Fortunately, the area is actually pretty limited. Without any input from you, we'd likely just work the grid backward."

I nodded, thinking I'd probably have made the same choice.

"What would one of them do if the other got hurt?" he asked.

I hate guessing the answers to these questions about my own family.

"If Amber got hurt and couldn't ride, Zach would stay with her. She was recently diagnosed with diabetes, so he wouldn't leave her alone." I thought a moment. "But if Zach got hurt, I think Amber might attempt to ride back for help. They would have had Zach's cell phone, the portable radio, and a GPS unit that she was at least basically familiar with using."

I tried to think back to the search ride we'd gone on the previous summer.

"Based on their riding skills, what are the chances they both could have gotten hurt and ended up without the horses?" he asked.

"Zach grew up around horses, so for him to end up afoot would be rare. Amber's not so experienced but has been on numerous trails around the area, and she's competent on horseback. I can't think of a situation where they'd both be hurt, but I suppose if one was hurt and then both horses bolted, they could be stranded."

"One more question," he said. "The girl has diabetes. Does Zach have any health issues we need to know about?"

I shook my head. "He's a strapping, healthy guy."

Minus one kidney.

With a nod, the three men pulled their caps down snug, turned on flashlights and headed to the tree line behind Zach's trailer. One stopped at a vehicle and opened the door to clip a leash on and let out a hound of some sort who wandered in circles around him, nose to the ground, oblivious to the men.

The handler took the dog to the horse trailer to get a scent to follow, then they both took off, dog straining at his lead, with the other two men following.

Grissom excused himself to return to his patrol car, parked somewhere behind us, leaving Doug and I alone in the light of a lone sodium vapor streetlight.

"I'm supposed to take you back to Doreen's now," he said, but hesitated.

"What is it, Doug?"

"Nothing to do with finding Zach," he said, looking at his shoes. "It'll wait."

"No, it won't. Spill it."

He took a deep breath, then tilted his head up to the sky. "I saw Mitch last night."

"And?" I prompted, not sure how that could be news except I didn't know he'd returned to the area since he'd gone to see his sister in Oregon.

"I saw him at a nightclub in Portland. Drinking, dancing, seeming to have a great time," he said. "He was hanging all over this woman in a short neon blue dress, heels, and – " He held his hands out in front of his chest, then thought better of the next descriptor. "Didn't seem like he was concerned about his wife being missing at all."

My eyebrows kept creeping higher the more he'd talked.

"Maybe it was nothing," he said, trying to reverse his story as if I didn't believe him, but I held up a hand to stop him.

"Doug," I said slowly. "Two questions. First, did he see you?"

He shook his head.

"Second, have you told anyone else what you saw?"

He shook his head again.

"Good. Let's deal with this search tonight, then we can figure out what's up with Mitchell Seaver tomorrow."

I followed Doug back to the campground check-in lot where Doreen had set up her base – a travel trailer behind a behemoth four-door one-ton pickup.

She greeted me with a hearty hug, pulled a treat from her jacket pocket for the dog, and invited us inside her trailer.

"I just put on a fresh pot of coffee," she told me as I squeezed into the booth at a table cluttered with maps, radios, a laptop computer and printer, and so on.

Laser found an out-of-the-way corner.

I could almost inhale the caffeine in the rich earthy aroma as it brewed.

I wish coffee actually tasted like it smells when you first open the can.

After her husband had died a decade ago, Doreen had volunteered to be both the search coordinator for the county and to provide her own transportation. The trailer was always hitched, fully stocked, ready to roll on a moment's notice, and self-contained for about three days just about anywhere.

I appreciated the always-hot coffee and a place to get out of the elements when we searched, but knowing that someone had the resources to coordinate teams, knew the terrain where she sent them and kept track of everyone, and could access up-to-the-minute weather was comforting.

I was not surprised she hadn't found a definite location for the pair, but she'd provided the three men on foot with a map and the exact trail, starting time, and estimated location she would expect Zach and Amber to be at every passing hour.

Tracking in the dark wasn't easy, but if the dog was following his nose, he probably didn't care whether the sun was shining or not. The handler and trackers would.

Doreen set a mug of coffee in front of me, pushing stuff aside to make a little more table space. "Warren'll find them," she said, putting a hand on mine when I reached for the cup.

We talked. Doreen answered her cell phone and the radio a few times, pulled out her most recent printout of the current water vapor satellite image over the Pacific Northwest, indicating a line of clouds just off the coast, arching downward. "I give that about sixteen hours before we get any change in weather," she announced. "Won't be much, maybe a little drizzle."

She'd done this for so long, I took her weather predictions far more seriously than anyone else's at the news stations. If she said sixteen hours, she wouldn't be wrong by more than thirty minutes.

I closed my eyes, and when I realized they hadn't opened until my head bobbled, I half-smiled in embarrassment.

"You go right back there and get a little sleep, young lady," she told me, thumbing toward the bed over her shoulder. "I'll be right here, and I promise to wake you with any news."

Part of me wanted to argue with her, but I knew I'd be useless sitting at the table falling asleep, and even less helpful if something needed my full attention later. Laser got to his feet and followed me when I maneuvered to the back of the trailer. I slipped off my shoe before reclining. Laser took his post near the entrance.

We both fell asleep promptly.

✻

When I opened my eyes, the sun brightened the sky, but I couldn't tell if it had actually risen or not through the window because it faced west.

I sat up and swung my feet to the floor, startling Laser, who let out a whimpy *woof!*

"Sucks getting old, doesn't it?" I asked him, hopping into the tiny bathroom, barely large enough for a sink, shower and chemical toilet, with posted instructions on correct usage for those who hadn't been in Doreen's trailer before.

After following the specific instructions for the toilet, I stood and washed my hands and face at a sink only slightly larger than the coffee mug she'd given me last night, intentionally not looking in the mirror, but I hoped to look a bit more awake than I felt.

Hopping back to the bed, I gathered the crutches and squeezed out into the kitchen and dining area, finding that other than Laser, I was alone.

But I heard voices outside, so I went to the kitchen window and peeked out the blinds.

Doreen stood next to Warren, listening.

"We found the horses grazing about a mile from the parking lot," he told her, pointing to a map he held between them. "But there were no foot prints anywhere along the easiest paths from there all the way to here." He pointed again. "The dog and handler continued west, following the scent. We brought the horses back and staked them over by the trees near the truck, gave each a long drink of water, took off the saddles and put them in his trailer."

"So the horses did get away from them," Doreen concluded,

nodding. "We'll have a helo in here with infrared within an hour."

Apparently when I opened the door, it creaked. Both of them turned toward me, startled. They exchanged a quick glance, then Doreen headed for me.

"Go on back in, and I'll whip up a bite for you to eat," she began, shooing me with both hands. "I'll bring you up to speed on the details from the team."

"I heard," I said, stepping back inside. "Now we need a helicopter to find them?"

"Warren said the horses –" she said as she pulled the door closed behind her.

"I *heard* what he said," I repeated.

She nodded. "I'm sure they're fine."

Her words sounded empty.

As she promised, she served a plateful of hard-boiled eggs, Canadian bacon slices, cheese cubes, and more coffee.

Easy food to pack and store for instances like this, I thought. Then I looked at Laser, and remembered a sealed tub of dog food over in the horse trailer – I'd have to feed him in a bit.

Did I tell Zach to pack enough food? Was it all in the saddlebags?

Doreen and I sat and nibbled for a while, neither talking, until a car pulled up next to her trailer.

She got up to see who it was, finding Doug already walking to the door.

He greeted her, removed his cap and came inside.

"Julie, remember that thing I told you last night?" he asked.

I nodded.

"The sheriff got a call first thing this morning from Clark County, wanting to know when we would be transferring that prisoner, because he had some assault and battery charge there," he said, not using Jack Browning's name. "He was in our jail in late June for that fight with the sheriff, and awaiting transfer for their charges. Our records show he was taken to Vancouver." He paused. "That was the transfer Mitch was making June 25 when his wife disappeared."

I blinked, frowned, tried to put the facts into a line that would make sense. Seaver was transferring Browning the day Rachelle Seaver disappeared, but Browning never arrived at the Clark County facility.

The connection between those two events and Doug seeing Mitch Seaver at a nightclub suddenly made very ugly sense.

"I didn't want to talk to you about this until Zach and Amber were –" He struggled for a word besides "safe," I think. "– located. I probably need to tell the sheriff, but I don't want to make a big deal out of something if it's not."

"Doug, I suspect it's a very big deal. And yes, you do need to tell Sheriff Fordham."

Doreen had watched our conversation like a mid-court spectator following a tennis ball during a match, not asking but trying to decipher the words not spoken.

"They're bringing in a helicopter to continue the search for Zach and Amber," I said. "You go talk to the sheriff. He knows how to find me."

There were a dozen questions in Doug's mind, but he wouldn't ask them in front of Doreen, which I thought was the right thing not to do. She didn't need to get involved in whatever might be discovered as the case went forward another day without finding the body of Rachelle Seaver.

He politely excused himself and returned to his car, accelerating a little harder than necessary when he pulled out onto the roadway.

"You're not going to tell me what that was all about, are you," Doreen said, not really asking a question. She folded her paper napkin diagonally into a triangle, then again, sharpening the creases with her thumbnail before she spoke. "Let me put one little bug in your ear, though. I have it on good authority that Mitchell Seaver just bought himself a brand new thirty-five-foot Bayliner in Portland. A boat that costs about seventy-five grand."

"He bought a boat," I repeated, letting the statement ferment in my brain.

Ugly sense had just become a monstrosity.

If Mitch wouldn't tell us where Rachelle was, maybe Jack Browning could, one way or another.

Perhaps no one else remembered this, but Jack had been wearing an ankle bracelet for the last six months after being arrested late last fall for leaving the state while on parole.

It might take getting a warrant for the GPS records of the last thirty days' locations, but his whereabouts on the morning of June 25 could just turn out to be his and Seaver's undoing.

I was lost in thought about this when Doreen answered a radio call relayed from the search helo, giving coordinates for two adults west of the day use section in the park, in a moderately wooded area.

She copied down the information, acknowledged and thanked the search helo team via the base station for their quick response and success.

"Let me send out the guys to fetch your family back here," she said, setting about doing just that.

❧

Two hours later, Amber and Zach rode up together on a four-wheeler, one of five that had gone to get them.

As I made my way down the steps of the travel trailer, I heard Zach telling Warren how much he appreciated the ride. When he saw me, he pointed to the herd of off-road vehicles and explained, "No one wanted me to ride behind them, so someone volunteered his vehicle and stayed behind."

"Stayed?" I hugged him, then Amber.

"Yeah, at the crime scene," she said in a cheery voice.

"Crime scene?" I repeated, only my voice had gone up an octave.

"Long story. We're okay," Zach continued. "Warren says the horses are okay. And someone else gets to figure out who the dead man is who untied the horses and then spooked 'em when he shot at us."

"What??"

A county patrol car came racing into the campground, stopping in a cloud of dust and sliding gravel. Blake Erwin stepped out.

"Good to see you back on asphalt," he told Zach. "Warren called, so let's start at the beginning."

Doreen took Amber inside for breakfast.

I was torn, wanting to hear Zach's story, wanting to make sure Amber ate something nutritious, and wanting more information about Mitch Seaver. I went to the trailer.

Amber was already mouthful deep into the cheese cubes with a hard-boiled egg in one hand and a bottle of water in the other when I got inside.

"Your dad's telling his story, so let's hear yours," I said. "What happened?"

Amber she gobbled the food, spewing a few words at a time between bites, but the gist of it was that she and Zach had ridden all the way to the western point of the park, had made a short jog south, then headed back in a parallel track as directed. She checked in on the hour as they headed east, almost back to where the truck and trailer were, then again zigged south for the next leg of their search westbound. At the west end on their third trip, when she called on the radio, no one responded to her. Zach tried the number I'd given him for Doreen, but the call failed, so he called me – and I'd only caught a few words before the connection dropped. They dismounted to take a break, tied the horses up and took a short walk down to the river. Amber hadn't grabbed her saddlebag, and Zach had only taken the water from his.

"We were down by the river when we heard a loud pop. Dad told me to step into a place behind a rock, and he cut back around where the horses were, and then I heard one more popping sound, then three loud gunshots from Dad's gun." Her eyes had changed from excitement to glassy fear as she spoke. "I didn't know what to do, so I just stayed where he told me, but I was afraid he'd been hurt. It seemed like forever before I heard him call my name. When I came out, he said someone had been tailing us, tried to shoot him, but we were safe." She blinked, then tears streamed down her cheeks.

Stunned speechless, I wrapped my arms around her while she

cried, knowing she'd been too shocked last night to react emotionally.

"They found the little boy, right?" she finally asked, wiping her face with a paper napkin.

Doreen spoke up. "Yes, they did. He was in perfect shape, just lost and a little thirsty."

She sniffled. "I'm sorry you had to come look for us. When the horses took off, I realized my insulin, all our food, the compass and your GPS were still in my saddle bag," she said. "And so were the sleeping bags and our coats. Zach had those yucky protein bars. He made me eat them all."

"Sounds like you had to rough it for the night," I said. "Did Zach not want to walk back?"

"He said it made more sense to stay put until daylight because he wasn't sure if I'd have enough to eat, and we had no compass. Then he heard the helicopter this morning, so he knew someone would be coming for us."

I heard the four-wheelers start up and take off.

"You two make a great team," I said, beaming. "We'll let Blake get to the bottom of this shooting, then go home."

Amber went back to eating.

Doreen poured me another cup of coffee, then began to gather her maps and other forms, filing them into an expanding folder.

Thoughts and possibilities thundered through my head as I waited for Zach to return and tell me his version of what the hell had happened last night.

When Amber had finished eating, we drove over to the day use area to feed Laser, then to water the horses and get them loaded

"Julie, I've been kind of a pain in the butt the last few days," she said as she led Denali to the trailer. "I'm sorry. This whole diabetes thing has really freaked me out because it grosses out my friends. Only Savannah wants anything to do with me. Even Cody treats me differently."

"Put yourself in their place – if you didn't understand diabetes, you wouldn't be comfortable hanging out with someone who might over-exert and have a low blood sugar spell, and who can't eat all the junk food everyone else does, would you?" I asked. "They just don't know how you're different and how to assimilate that into their worlds."

She shrugged and put the horse in his slot, then came back outside.

"Cody really wants to be your friend," I said. "He probably understands more than you realize because his grandmother was diabetic. He thinks you're pushing him away."

"I have to stick my finger, like a dozen times a day," she said with sarcastic exaggeration, "then I have to carry the insulin and syringes and everything else everywhere I go. How can I pretend to be an average kid now?"

I reached for her as she walked by to get Rainier. With a hug, I said, "Honey, you've never been average, so why try so hard to just be that now when you've always been so much more."

She smiled as she pulled away.

She went to lead Rainier to the trailer, but I noticed he was limping on his right front leg, so I motioned for her to stop.

I moved around to his right side and tracked my hand down the outside and front of his leg, then reached inside just above his knee – I think it's a knee, I'm always so confused by the comparisons to human anatomy – and stroked down to get him to lift his hoof. Just below the joint, my fingers ran into a warm trickle of blood.

"He's hurt!" Amber gasped. "Is it bad?"

If it had been her leg, I'd have been able to make some conclusion about severity and a treatment plan, but with a horse, I truly had no idea. I gently placed Rainier's hoof back on the ground and straightened up.

He didn't put weight on the leg, which indicated to me that it at least hurt.

"I don't know, Amber. Leave him out here on the grass until Zach gets back."

She tied his lead back to where he'd been and stood there with her arms crossed, looking at him, obviously frustrated that I couldn't fix the wound.

I wiped my hand on a dirty towel, then dumped some water from Zach's spare canteen on another to wash up.

The wound wasn't bleeding profusely, and I didn't want to put a wrap on it and either have to remove it again for Zach or do more harm. I pulled my cell phone from a pocket and dialed Doreen.

"Have you heard from Zach or Blake yet?"

"No, but I'm already on the road. Is something wrong?" she asked.

"One of the horses has a leg wound, so before we loaded, I wanted Zach to take a look at it."

"They ought to be back soon," she replied. "Dr. Bishop's on his way."

"Okay, just checking. Thanks for all your help, Doreen. I appreciated the bed and the breakfast and mostly the good company."

We disconnected.

I dialed Zach's cell, but it went directly to voice mail again.

"It went dead late last night," Amber said after I left a message. *Thanks. Now what?*

She found more protein bars in her saddle pack, now hanging in the trailer, offered me one and opened the other for herself.

I took a bite and chewed, making a face. "You know, these really are pretty gross."

We laughed.

I asked her to dump Laser a half-bowl of food and water, and he ate without appearing too much to be starved.

Finally in the distance, I could hear the engines of the four-wheelers getting closer. Ten minutes later, Zach and Warren pulled up.

Amber went running to her father, the story about Rainier going at a full gallop like she was.

"Whoa!" he said when she just about plowed him over in a hug. "Who's bleeding?"

He looked at me, and I pointed to Rainier.

"Let's go take a look," he told her, peeling her away from him. "It's okay, honey. He's still on his feet. That's a good sign. He probably cut it on his way back to the trailer last night."

The pair walked, with such a similar posture of grave concern I almost laughed. At Rainier's side, Zach made pretty much the same motions I had, feeling the outside then the inside of the leg. Then he moved to the horse's left side so he could kneel and see the wound. When he reached to touch where the bleeding came from, Rainier reared partway, then danced away from Zach, who'd been so surprised, he ended up on his butt.

Amber rushed to get Rainier under control, though Zach was already on his feet, trying to calm them both.

That's another reason I didn't want to try my hand at doctoring a horse.

Fifteen minutes later, Zach had a dressing and wrap placed, Amber had both horses in the trailer, all the equipment stowed where it was supposed to go, and I was following Zach and Amber back to the cabin in my patrol car.

Not two miles from home, the dispatcher called me on the radio, asking me to phone the station.

I acknowledged, but I waited until I'd parked in the driveway out of Zach's way as he circled Del's pickup to unload before I called.

"It's Julie," I said, only to be told to hang on a second, then the clicks of a transfer.

"What took you so long?" the sheriff asked, as if his coffee this morning had been pointless. When I took a breath to answer, he continued. "Never mind. What's this about Seaver telling someone at Clark County we weren't transferring Browning yet, then logging that he did it anyway?"

"I don't know, sir. I wasn't in the station at all that day."

His tone was gruff, but I recognized it as pure frustration. The department was about to be thrown to the lions, and he knew it.

"And then Doug says he saw Mitchell in Portland? Have you seen him?"

"No, sir, I haven't. But I also heard a rumor today that Mitch bought a new boat." I paused. "A big, expensive boat."

Not that I know any more about boats than I do about horses.

He mumbled a string of expletives that would have made a

roughneck blush, then was quiet a moment. "I hate to ask, but can you come in?" he asked, rustling paper. "Or, no, wait. Damn it, I don't know what I need anyone to do."

"We've processed all the evidence we had from where her car was found. Unless we find a body, I don't know what else I can do, either."

"*Can* we find it? Cadaver dogs, that ground radar thing, anything?"

"We could start at the river and work our way north in this county with both and still never find her body," I told him, knowing that wasn't the answer he wanted to hear. "We've got to narrow down the area to search."

"How in the hell am I supposed to let Seaver just come back to work next week when half the department suspects he's involved in this?" he asked, not expecting an answer from me about that, either.

"Put him on administrative leave, Wade," I said, confirming what he already knew. "He absolutely cannot work as long as this case is active, so that keeps him off duty and out of the building."

"I guess that's my only option. I'll change the locks on the evidence lab, change the code to the back door," he said, his mind drifting to other tasks he'd need to complete. "Drop by tomorrow if you get a chance."

And then he hung up on me without even saying goodbye.

I opened the car door only to find Zach standing there, waiting on me.

"Everything okay?" he asked.

"I doubt it," I said, taking his offered hand to help me get out, then leaning up for a kiss. "Details at ten. Let's deal with the horses first, then I want to know how you ended up shooting someone last night."

"I'll handle the horses. The vet will be here in ten minutes," he said, fetching my crutches. "You go start the grill and make the burgers you promised me last night. I'm famished."

CHAPTER
24

Conversation over hamburgers – Zach ate three – was mostly carried by Amber, who explained to me about Zach's more thorough examination of Rainier's wound once he got the horse into a stall and the leg cleaned up enough to see well.

"It's from a bullet, probably from the man Dad shot and killed last night," she announced.

"I said it *might* be, Amber," Zach said before taking another bite. "There was something, but we don't even know if it was part of a bullet."

"Yeah, and so the vet had to take it out, and he'll give it to the deputy for a ballistic comparison if it is," she said, as if she had first-hand experience in the process. She talked with the energy of a toddler on a sugar buzz

Wondering if that analogy might be all too close to the truth, I asked, "Have you tested your blood sugar since you got home?"

"Before dinner," she said, smearing a baked potato wedge through a puddle of ketchup. "And I'll do it again before I go to bed, since we're pigging out." She popped the bite into her mouth and chewed, almost as if she were as hungry as Zach.

Other than the one statement, he hadn't interrupted his dinner for mere chat.

"Dad thinks the man he shot looked like a biker," she continued with way too much enthusiasm. "He probably got off one shot at the horses then one at us, then Dad killed him."

That did it.

Zach put down his third hamburger, wiped his mouth, took a deep breath, and somehow kept from exploding. "Killing a man is not dreamy or romantic, Amber. You might think it's a simple thing to do, just point a gun and pull the trigger." He took another breath. "But a man is dead because of me. Do you understand that? It's not something you brag about to all your friends. It's a bad thing, but I did it to protect you."

Amber opened her mouth to reply, but Zach held up a single finger. "And because it's an open investigation, you will not speak of it with anyone outside law enforcement or this family again. Do I make myself clear?"

She nodded, looked down. "I'm sorry. But I am proud of you for doing something like that to save me."

Zach's shoulders sagged as his anger evaporated. "Honey, there are two women in this world I would do absolutely anything to protect from harm, and I'm having dinner with them both."

We finished our meal, discussing more mundane topics, then Amber cleared away our dishes and went upstairs.

"You will tell me what happened, won't you?" I asked when Zach stood.

"Of course. But not now. I need to go check on the horses."

Without so much as a kiss, he left me sitting at the table, although I knew he had fed and watered them all when he put Rainier and Denali back in the paddock. His escape meant something was on his mind, something he needed to ponder, to work out before he could talk, even to me.

I gathered up the rest of the stuff from the table to go into the fridge or the cabinets, making four trips, taking my time.

The crutches were frustrating, though, limiting how much I could carry. On a whim, I sat the ketchup and mustard down on the cabinet, turned to lean against it, and put my left foot on the floor. Even in the boot, my calf and Achilles' tendon stretched as my foot relaxed with only the weight of my leg. I felt a pull in the ankle. Not pain, but uncomfortable. Then I tried to raise my toes, causing a cramp in the bottom of my foot that drew the second and third toes downward, pain stabbing through my sole.

Because of the boot, I could not rub the arch of my foot, nor did I really want to try standing on one leg to do it, so I let the muscles go limp until the spasm stopped.

Won't be doing that again anytime soon.

After I finished in the kitchen, I went to the recliner in the living room to prop up my foot, suddenly realizing just how tired I was when a yawn wound through my body.

The sun was still up, I thought, and I'd slept both at Geo's and in Doreen's travel trailer, so how could I possibly be tired?

Plus, I had Zach's story to hear.

And then I must have blinked but forgotten to open my eyes. I don't remember him coming inside or tucking my throw around me while I slept in the chair.

But when I woke, almost midnight according to the stereo clock, Zach was stretched out on the sofa, reading a book.

"Why didn't you wake me so we could go to bed?" I asked.

"I wasn't ready to sleep yet, so I thought we could just hang out here together."

I laughed. "I don't think you could call it hanging out if I was asleep."

He flapped a hand in dismissal. "It was working for me."

"Ready to talk?"

"How about I fix us a drink first?" he asked, folding the book jacket into the pages to mark his place. "Wine?"

"Whatever you'd like is fine for me," I said, lowering the foot of the recliner. "Are you still hungry?"

He shook his head. "I had a couple of bowls of cereal about an hour ago."

"Certainly filling, I guess." I followed him into the kitchen where he picked a bottle of wine, held it out for my approval, and then opened it. "By the way, what you told Amber about your two favorite women? I liked that."

"I don't recall calling you my favorite women," he said with mock consternation. "But I think the implication for you is fair enough." He turned to me, wrapped both arms around my shoulders. "You're my favorite a lot of things."

Acting hurt, I said, "You mean I'm not your favorite *everything*?"

"You can't be my favorite color or song or ice cream flavor," he said, smoothing my hair. "But you're my favorite wife."

I play-smacked him in the arm. "That also makes me your least-favorite wife."

"Sometimes," he told me, rubbing his arm as if I'd hurt him. "As the saying goes, 'I don't want to be your first love as much as I want to be your last.'"

"Ah, that's sweet."

"It's not quite true, though," he said. "I really did want to be your first, too. But you weren't interested in an eleven-year-old boy."

"Ah yes, the dreaded age difference. Good thing I like younger men, huh? Did you grow to this size to make up for the lost time?" At six and a half feet tall, even I had to look way up at him.

"No, but it's had its advantages over the years."

I thought back to the first time I recalled seeing him as an adult – though I hadn't known who he was – and found his size to be intimidating. I blinked back to the present, hoping I hadn't smiled at the memory.

He poured us each a glass of white merlot, then motioned me back to the living room, carrying both glasses. We cuddled up on the sofa.

"So about last night," he began. "The search began as I'd have expected, though I've never gone on one like this before. I let Amber take the lead, and she checked our position on the map, called in, did the things she said she was supposed to do." He paused to take a sip of wine. "You taught her well."

"No, she learned well," I corrected him.

"She probably told you how we had made it to the western edge of the park the third time, but she couldn't get a response on the radio. We had gotten off the horses for a break and walked over to the shore when I heard something behind us. Thinking it might have been the child, I turned just as the first shot ricocheted. I pushed Amber behind a rock, and I went to find who had fired. After a second shot, when I made it up behind him, he whirled with the gun in his hand, clearly intending to pull the trigger again, so I shot him."

Three times, according to what Amber had told me.

"You do make that sound so simple," I said.

"Training," he said. "And self-preservation."

"Amber was scared out of her skin, first that she was alone, then after the gunshots that you wouldn't come back."

"I know. When I saw that he'd untied them, I tried to catch at least one of the horses, but they were long gone. Had I caught one, Amber could have ridden, even if I'd had to walk. Without, she would have had to walk back, but we didn't have any food or that icing stuff with us. All we had were those damned protein bars I stuck in my pockets. So we stayed put."

The decision was probably a sound one, not knowing for sure yet how her blood sugar levels would fluctuate, especially after a horribly stressful event like that.

"And so what did Blake do?" I asked.

"I just took him back out there, told him the same story a second time, walking him through the place where it happened, and that was that."

"Did he tell you who it was?"

"He said a name, but I didn't commit it to memory." He drank more. "Did look like a sleazy biker, though."

"Wonder if it was a friend of Browning's?" I wondered out loud.

"You mean maybe the one who threatened you outside the library?"

I nodded. "That guy had a dirty brown ponytail, brown eyes, a dark gray t-shirt with some eagle and mountain design on the front." I closed my eyes to bring back to image.

"Tacoma," Zach said. "The lettering on the back is a dealership, Destination Harley-Davidson."

"Yeah," I said, feeling a little dismal. "That's it. So why would he be shooting at you and not me?"

"Maybe he wasn't aiming at me," he offered, though I didn't like that alternative any better. "How badly could he interfere with your life by shooting Amber? At least enough to get you out of the picture regarding Geo and her sister."

I took a large swallow of my wine. "That's a huge risk to take, wouldn't you think?"

"If he only wounded Amber and scared off the horses, it would be logical that I wouldn't leave her to chase him, right?"

"Guess he didn't know about your silent-but-deadly mode," I replied, thinking about the lack of noise with which Zach moved, even when he wasn't trying to be quiet. "Wow, maybe we shouldn't explain that to her."

"I already did," he said. "The part about not leaving her, anyway. When we were unloading the horses."

"And she didn't go berserk?"

"I didn't tell her she might have been the target, Julie, just that I wouldn't have left her if she'd been hurt." He frowned. "Yeah, maybe we shouldn't tell her that part. On the other hand, the first shot might have been toward the horses to spook them, which was probably the ricochet we heard. I'm guessing that the wound on Rainier's leg had just a piece of rock in it, nothing more. She's really more upset about the horse than about the dead guy."

"That does it," I said, rolling my head back. "Just give her a badge now."

Zach ignored my sarcasm. "I asked her what she would have done if I'd been injured, and she said she'd go for help if the horses had been there, but she wouldn't have tried to walk out."

Wobbling my head, neither shaking nor nodding, I explained, "When she went with me, I told her she had to keep track of our position so she could call for help or ride out and bring help back if I got hurt. She may remember what she was taught in one situation, but she needs more experience to extrapolate a plan for a brand new set of circumstances, even if that was the right answer."

We relaxed, sipping more wine.

"I knew that someone would be looking for us," he said, "but the helicopter was a bit of a surprise."

"Not my doing," I said, then an idea I couldn't quite catch wiggled in my head. "They were using infrared, I think."

"Really? I know the DEA sometimes searches for marijuana fields using infrared because the plants show up different from things around them – though I haven't any idea how. They found the fields, then we did our thing on the ground."

"Apparently humans look different than their surroundings, too," I said, but I still couldn't quite make sense of why this topic squirmed without revealing itself. Like a snake in a burlap bag, I could see it writhing but couldn't see its markings.

Humans, drugs, searching. I hate it when I can't focus on an idea. Maybe it's the wine.

"I'm sorry you had to shoot him," I said, resting my head on Zach's shoulder. "But I'm glad you were prepared."

He gave a half shrug, his not-quite-aw-shucks look.

"Really," I said.

We both know what it feels like to kill a man.

CHAPTER 25

Sleeping on the sofa hadn't been as good an idea as the last time we tried it, so we finally went upstairs around two, then Zach's alarm clock beeped at six. He left me to snooze while he went to feed the horses. It was a chore he liked, though sometimes I felt like we tended to their meals more often than our own.

Zach had once explained to me that a horse has a relatively small stomach for its size, so small servings several times a day and grazing were healthier than one large meal.

I had the grazing philosophy for eating, too.

Not as sleepy as I'd feared, I got up and undertook the lengthy process of unwrapping the bandages on my foot. Ten days after surgery, everything looked good. There was still some discoloration around the ankle joint from the original injury, but the surgical incision was healing.

I tried to remember, the discharge instructions said I could shower but not to soak my ankle in hot water for more than ten minutes for two weeks. Shower it was, regardless whether a bath might have been an option. I needed to rinse away the last two days' worry, if not actual grime.

Reaching into the shower in the master bathroom, I turned on the water to heat up, a typically short wait as the pipes warmed, then I dropped my clothes into the hamper before stepping into the glass-bricked enclosure. I made sure the water was not too hot before easing under the cascade with the crutches, and then, like a yawn I couldn't suppress, the tension gathered and melted away in my shoulders and back.

I reached for the bottle of shampoo – smiling a bit because Zach always complained that I always have too much stuff in the shower – from the built-in shelf. I poured a dab in my hand, but when I reached to put the container back where I got it, the shelf – also made of tempered glass – shattered.

In disbelief, I put my hand out where three bottles, a tube of conditioner and a can of shaving cream had once sat, though they now littered the floor of the shower.

Fortunately none of them landed on my feet.

I must have jumped back, which now left me standing with my back against the far wall away from the entrance, my left crutch on the floor which was also covered in shards of blue-tinted glass. I didn't dare take a step, or a hop, actually.

Rinsing off the blob of shampoo I'd just poured into my hand, I risked leaning far enough to turn off the water.

Then I debated whether to yell for Amber to come help me, or just to wait for Zach. Or maybe, I realized as I stood there, getting colder and dripping water, that a combination of the two would be in order.

Why would the shelf break like that? It was a half-inch-thick piece of tempered glass.

And then I remembered the damage to the house Zach had found so far.

The bomb in my truck.

Well, under my truck.

It doesn't matter where the bomb was.

I stood there, cool air beginning to circulate into the shower. I couldn't reach a towel or my crutches.

"Amber?" I called, suspecting I'd have to escalate to yelling after two or three tries. "Amber!"

"What?" a sleepy voice called back. "I'm in the bathroom!"

"So am I. You need to go get Zach for me – he's in the barn."

I heard her as she stepped into the hall and then into the master bedroom, where I could see her shape through the glass bricks of the shower.

"A shelf broke and there's glass all over the floor. I need Zach to lift me out of this so I don't get cut or fall."

She tilted her head. "Um, yeah, okay. Just a second while I put on some shoes."

Waiting for her to return with Zach seemed to be an hour. I kept my left foot in the air, but my step backward must have taken some of my weight, because I felt a burning sensation all the way through my leg.

I hope I didn't tear loose everything done in surgery.

Downstairs, I heard the commotion of Zach stomping the dust off his boots before he took the stairs at least two at a time. "What in the world –" he said, stopping abruptly at the entry to the shower, looking down at the tile flooring. Taking one single step in, he leaned forward and pulled me over his shoulder, then backed out again where I slid down to the carpet. "What happened?"

"The shelf broke," I said, grabbing a towel to wrap around me. A lump grew in my throat, and I fought back tears of anger about the bomb. "You said some of the tiles had broken, but I wasn't thinking about that when I got in."

I looked down at his white t-shirt, with a streak of blood on it, then down at the dark blue towel, which I opened.

Zach knelt down and touched a nick in my thigh.

It hadn't stung until that moment. But then, I hadn't known it was there. What is it they say, *Don't look and it won't hurt.*

"I don't feel any glass in it," he said, standing up and getting a bottle of antiseptic from the medicine cabinet. "Shouldn't need any stitches – it's pretty tiny, actually." I let him dab it with the liquid on a cotton ball, pat it dry, then place a Band-Aid strip on it only because it kept oozing. "Good as new."

"Are you okay?" Amber called from just outside the door.

"Everything is fine," Zach and I replied together, then we laughed. "You should shower in the downstairs bathroom," he told me. "I'll bring down your stuff."

I pulled the towel around me tightly, grabbed the crutches and headed out to the hall.

Behind me, I heard him mutter to himself, "If I can carry it all."

"Don't forget my razor and the lotion!" I called cheerfully as I turned to go down the stairs.

❧

Our Tuesday consisted of dropping off Zach's Mustang for repairs and getting the only rental the body shop had available – a three-year-old minivan. It rode okay, but I could tell being in it offended Zach's sensibilities for horsepower and style.

Shopping for a vehicle in Oregon might have offered more selection, but with the transfer back to Washington and sales tax and all, we decided that starting at the dealerships in Vancouver would make more sense.

I'd never shopped for a car with Zach before, but he was unyielding with salespeople, almost aloof. We left one dealership after only a quick look at their limited inventory.

At the next, the first salesman to greet us made the mistake of looking at what we drove up in, then telling Zach, "You probably don't want to look at those," pointing to the high-end Suburbans like we'd been driving. Zach, in his ever larger-than-life coolness, said "Thanks, that's all I need to hear from you. Now you can find me someone who wants to sell me what I came to buy, or I'll find another dealership, right after I explain to your manager why you are the idiot who let someone who will pay in cash walk off the lot, because I really want to see that."

After a quick change of sales personnel, things went a lot

smoother.

I selected a vehicle – a Tahoe instead of a Suburban. We discussed options which now included heated seats and second-generation airbags with an automatic four-wheel-drive system and a full towing package. It was red, which had less to do with it being the color I wanted than the fact all the options I wanted just came on the red one.

Zach negotiated a price with the guy, told him to call the bank to verify that we would bring back a cashier's check in two hours and pick up the truck, with the expectation it would be washed, fueled, and the paperwork ready to sign. "Minus all the dealership stuff that goes along with your sale," Zach reminded him. "Tax, title, license, warranties, and an owner's manual."

I could see that there were more forms the dealer really wanted, but after Zach had already threatened to walk off the lot once, and because the Suburban Zach had looked at was even more expensive than the Tahoe, apparently fluff forms were unnecessary for cash sales.

"And I want you to get me a Suburban with everything, four-wheel drive, towing package, everything this one has, in black. I don't see one here, and I couldn't take it home today anyway. Do a search and call me with the cost. I'll pay for it when we come back to pick this one up, but I want it here in less than a week."

"Everything?" the sales manager said, probably seeing dollar signs flashing in his head at the commission on these two vehicles.

Zach pulled open the brochure, scratched out the lesser of a couple of "either" options like the stereo choices or the seat coverings, and the garage door opener. "There. That should help."

As we walked out the showroom, Amber turned to Zach. "Does this mean I get the Mustang?"

"No." End of that discussion. "I'll find you something suitable to drive when you show you're responsible enough to have a car."

We went to lunch at an Oriental place where you go through a buffet to get raw meat and veggies, then it's cooked for you on a super-heated eight-foot flat grill. Being all-you-can-eat, Zach and I took full advantage of trying several different concoctions, while Amber had one bowl and a salad.

She confessed to me in the restroom that her blood sugar had been a little high both before breakfast and before lunch, so she ate less and skipped dessert. I commended her on making a good decision.

After lunch, Zach drove us to the mall, and likely hating every second, followed us through to a shoe store. I tried on several pairs of sneakers I hopefully could fit my foot and brace into, knowing it would be several more weeks before I got to that point, but that I'd be stuck with them for months after I quit using the crutches.

Amber wanted to look at something in the bookstore, but I was already tired of hobbling around, so she went inside while Zach and I sat in the thoroughfare together. "You're happy with the Tahoe?" I asked.

"It's yours, Julie. I didn't care what you got so long as it had four-wheel-drive and could pull that trailer."

"I didn't need seating for nine," I said. "I think this will be more suitable for the traveling I do. And I like the red."

"Just try to take care of this one," he said, raising an eyebrow. "You know, keep it away from bombers. Which reminds me, I need to call a plumber again about the shower."

No need to respond to that, so I peeked around his shoulders to look behind him.

First I saw Cody Randall, and a girl who could only be his twin sister Cady, followed by their mother Laura and a handful of younger children.

"Oh, terrific," I grumbled. "I wonder if this was planned by your dear daughter."

Zach glanced, then looked back at me. "We've got nothing to be ashamed of, sitting here. Let's see if anyone even notices."

Notice? How could anyone not notice a very tall man and a woman with crutches, sitting in the middle of a mall?

Cody broke off from the group and came around the bench in front of us, holding out his hand to Zach. "Mr. Samualson?" He nodded at me. "Ma'am?"

"How are you today, Cody?" Zach asked.

"Fine, sir. We're just checking out some back-to-school bargains Cady saw advertised. She's working here at one of the department stores during the summer."

"That's great," I said. "Amber's in the bookstore. Why don't you go say hi?"

"Yes, Ma'am, I'd like that." He made a sort of wave at us and then hurried inside.

His mother and siblings walked behind us, passing without a word.

I personally figured I'd saved Laura Randall's life, regardless of the outcome with the twins she'd carried. If she was too deep in litigation to speak to me, then screw her.

"That's not a nice thing to think," Zach said, grinning. "Besides, I was there, too."

I shook my head, laughing at his ability to know what I thought.

Namakaeha is his middle name, which means "all-seeing eyes" in his grandmother's native Hawaiian. That he was named for something as a baby that he could do so well as an adult had never been a surprise to me.

I still can't pronounce it without making several tries.

I caught a glimpse of Amber and presumably Cody toward the back of the store, having an animated conversation. Just when I was about to look away, Cody leaned forward and kissed her. She jerked back, looking around in a panic to see if anyone had witnessed it. We locked eyes for a moment before her face turned the color of strawberry jam and she whirled away.

Honestly, I wasn't sure which of us was more stunned, Amber or me.

Zach must have felt my physical reaction, which was probably similar to getting a static electricity shock sometimes when he walked on the carpet then kissed me.

"What?" he asked.

"Um, I, well," I stammered. "It was nothing. Just a spasm in my leg."

"You don't lie very well," he advised me, looking up to see Amber coming toward us. "You can tell me later."

Her face was still flushed, and she announced that she didn't find what she was looking for, so she was ready to go.

Zach looked at her, then at me, and back, nodded and helped me to my feet, and told Amber we'd follow her out.

After we left the mall, Zach stopped at the bank, and the loan officer told Zach that the dealership had just called with a total for a Suburban, too. Zach had her make the check out for it but to make the total a thousand dollars less.

Back at the dealership, my new wheels were ready to go, as Zach had indicated. The salesperson showed Zach a photocopy of the window sticker of the Suburban, currently sitting on a dealer lot in Seattle. Zach shook his head and offered a price a thousand bucks lower "for my inconvenience of having to wait," which was apparently an offer no one had to authorize to accept. He signed all the papers for the Tahoe, took the key fobs and folder of papers, then got up to leave. Then hesitating at the manager's door, he asked, "What about the other vehicle?"

"What about it?" the sales manager said.

Zach didn't say a thing.

Silence is a great tool in interrogation and negotiation.

"We can have it here tomorrow, ready to pick up after noon," he swallowed. "If that's acceptable."

For the life of me, I don't know why, but Zach looked at his watch. "I'll be here after two o'clock."

With that, we filed out of the dealership to where my new Tahoe sat, sparkling in the sunshine.

"I'll ride with Julie," Amber announced.

Zach and I exchanged glances and kissed goodbye.

"I'll stop and pick up steaks," I said, "if you'll start the grill when you get home."

That deal was made without debate or negotiation.

"Could you get me chicken instead?" Amber asked as I worked to settle into my new truck, adjusting mirrors, the seat, the temperature controls.

I had finally gotten everything adjusted in my last truck.

"Breasts?"

"What?" she asked in shock, then caught herself. "Oh, you mean the chicken. Yeah."

I nodded, trying very hard not to laugh as I backed out of the space. That kiss had really put her in a tailspin, I thought. And it didn't look like it had been a fully consensual act, given her surprise and the continued reaction.

Silence had worked for Zach, so I thought I'd give it a go with Amber.

Sure enough, we had gotten through Camas, Washington, when she turned to me and asked, "Do you think I'm too young to date?"

"Well, sort of. I think age is less an issue than maturity," I replied. "And emotionally, you've had a rough year or so. I think it's okay if you go out with a group of friends, but you're probably not ready for a commitment to one boy yet. What do you think?"

"Cody wants to be my boyfriend," she said, her face puckering into a frown. "I know you saw him kiss me back at the mall, but I wasn't trying to –"

"Amber, I did see, and what I saw was that he really surprised you. I know you like him, but if you're not ready to be his girlfriend, that's all right. This needs to be something you want, too."

She let out an audible sigh. "I do like him, but I don't want him to think I'm a freak."

"Then let's make a deal. You tell me when you want to go to events and invite him, like the roping and stuff, and if you don't want him around, you can blame me or Zach," I said. "I think he's been a very polite young man, but he's still a hormonal soup ready for your father to dump into the manure pile if he gets out of line."

Amber smiled. "You mean it's okay if I don't want him to come over for dinner?"

I nodded.

"Oh good. Can I just have steak, too, then?"

CHAPTER 26

I called Wade Fordham when we got home that afternoon.

Nothing had really changed except he had put Mitchell Seaver on administrative leave.

"He didn't seem too upset with it," Wade told me. "Almost relieved, in fact."

While Mitch didn't really have a choice, I'd expected a little pushback from him about the leave.

"Not a peep about being out on a new boat, though," Wade added.

"Did you really expect him to brag to you about it?"

"I mentioned that he should use this time to go fishing. No joy."

"Well at least you don't have to worry about him fishing for evidence now," I said. "Any luck getting Browning to talk about the day he didn't get transferred?"

"He just said that Seaver took him out of the jail, put him in a patrol car, and drove him up to Dana's place. He claims he didn't know he was supposed to have gone to Vancouver," Wade said. "Just thought that Skamania County had decided to do something nice for him."

"What a load of –" I looked up to see Amber standing in the kitchen. "Crap."

I promised her I'd try harder to watch my language, holding myself to the same standard I held her.

Wade chuckled. "Whatever you call it, it still stinks."

"It occurred to me that he's had an ankle monitor on for the last few months after his last visit to a state judge. What do we have to do to get the readouts?" I asked.

"Good question. I'll see what I can find out," he said. "How's the leg? Do we get you back any time soon?"

"No, but I'll drop the patrol car off tomorrow morning. Picked up my new truck this afternoon," I said, tossing the key fob in my hand. "It's red."

"Good enough," he replied. "I've got an appointment to meet with the county attorney in the morning, so I probably won't see you."

We hung up as Zach was bringing in three juicy slabs of beef and baked potatoes from the grill. Amber set bowls of salad on the table, then a bowl of beans.

"Anything new?" he asked as we sat down to eat.

"Not really. As hot-headed as Mitch was about Kenny, would you think he'd take it well when Wade put him on administrative leave?" I asked, slicing into a baked potato the size of a toy football.

"No," Zach answered. "But maybe he has other things on his mind besides working right now."

"Sure, the whole missing wife thing has got to be stressful."

"What if he's not stressed that she's missing," Zach offered, dumping his potato full of butter, sour cream and shredded cheese. "Maybe he's stressed that someone will find out where she is."

"If a cop killed his wife and hid the body, there's no telling where it might be," I said, taking the butter dish from him. "The van was left by the river, so I don't think he could have met her somewhere else."

Amber kicked in a one-liner. "Unless he had help."

"Apparently Mitch doesn't know yet that Clark County called, looking for Browning, making the whole alibi questionable. We may be able to track where Browning was by his ankle bracelet," I said, thinking hard. "But if he was taken directly to Dana's, then who else could have helped Mitch?"

"Dead guy in the forest," she replied. "The one Dad shot."

Zach nodded. "She has a point. Browning's trip would be Mitch's alibi, but what's-his-name could be Browning's."

"And he did try to kill us," she added. "Eddy Anderson. That was his name."

Two faces turned toward her.

"What? I overhead Deputy Erwin say it on the radio."

"Anderson," I repeated. No bells.

"So where would you hide a body?" Zach asked me. "You need to pick it up at the van, hide it for transport, then put it where no one will find it."

I watched him pull a knife blade through a rare steak, leaving a blood pool on the plate.

There hadn't been enough blood at the scene where we found the van for a murder, right?

"I don't think he killed her there, so maybe she was alive until he got her to wherever she's buried now."

"What if she's not dead?" Amber asked.

"Then I don't think he would be spending money he'll eventually get from her life insurance policy on a boat he couldn't afford when she was alive."

"Where are his kids?" Zach asked.

"They're with his ex-wife in Pasco." I took a bite and nodded my approval and appreciation of a great meal. Finally I swallowed, continuing my train of thought. "So, Mitch thinks he's in the clear. Someone else has the kids, which leaves him worry-free. Who would be the biggest threat to his new freedom?"

Two faces looked up from their steaks at me now.

"You are," they said in unison.

I didn't like it, but they were right.

Which made shooting at Amber, or Zach, or even Laser for that matter, make more sense to interrupt what I was doing.

"So the question is still where would you hide a body, given the time and geographical limitations Mitch would have had that morning?" Zach asked. "Would you stay in the county?"

"If I were driving a cruiser, yes. People tend to remember seeing sheriff's department cars in out of the way places."

"Could she have been killed at the location where the van was left?" Amber joined the brainstorming.

"There's no evidence of that, but she might have just been incapacitated."

"Any chance an accomplice could have driven her van without leaving evidence you'd have found? Or that someone drove his patrol car while Mitch drove the van?"

"Maybe," I replied. "No, I think she walked away from the van willingly where we found it, probably to get in another car with someone she knew."

"But if Mitch hadn't picked her up there, the van and the patrol car would both have to go somewhere with easy access, right?" Zach continued. "Wouldn't one of the vehicles have picked up obvious trace from the location like leaves or mud underneath?"

Had anyone looked for that?

I turned to check the clock on the microwave, but it was after 5:30, and I knew Wade would have already left the station. Pulling the cell phone from my pocket, I dialed Wade's.

"Julie?" he said when he answered. "Is something wrong?"

"Do we still have Rachelle's van in impound?"

"No, Mitch took it this morning when he dropped off the county car."

"Did the tech look underneath either of them?" I asked. "Like for evidence of where they had been?"

"The cruiser? No reason we would have," he said. "I don't know about the van. Why?"

"If there was evidence, it's long gone now," I said, feeling deflated. "If he used his county car, the first thing Mitch would have done is run it through a carwash a dozen times."

"Do you think we missed something?"

"Too late now. I'll check the logs in the morning," I told him, and we hung up.

"Damn it," I muttered, then saw Amber's face. "Sorry."

"No, I think you get that as a freebie."

❈

I didn't sleep much that night, partly because my mind wouldn't stop digging through the details that seemed to tie Jack Browning to Dana's assault and to Rachelle's disappearance. The biggest common denominator was Deputy Mitchell Seaver, whose behavior since his wife went missing was questionable at best, and circumstantially much more damning.

And partly because Zach was kind enough to stay awake with me, providing a little mental and physical diversion.

"You have a much better time when we're not having to be quiet," he said, cuddling me up to his chest afterward.

Trust me, I had a great time, just without the sound effects.

"Is there anything I can do to help?" he asked.

I shook my head, lists and images already beginning to float back into parts of my brain working again.

"Besides the obvious," he said, teasing his fingers through my hair.

Oops! He hadn't meant helping with the case.

He tilted my face up to his for another soul-shattering kiss that erased thoughts of anything beyond our bed, and I surrendered to the warmth and tenderness of a man who'd left me breathless every time we'd made love.

"Remember our first night?" he asked.

I smiled. "You mean the night you kidnapped me from a bar and had your friends drive us a hundred miles out in the country before you held me down and made me scream?"

He lifted his head to look at me, then he rolled his eyes. "Yeah, that night."

"Oh yes," I said as the rest of my memory was swept away in a flash flood of desire.

�֍

Much later, curled up again together, he whispered, "As far as I know, you've only told one person about what happened that night, and if his reaction was any indication, the next time you tell it, I'll end up in jail."

I laughed. "But it's one of the most memorable nights we've spent together," I said. "What you did changed my life."

"It changed mine, too." He kissed my forehead. "That was the night I decided you'd be my wife."

"Perhaps it was best you didn't tell me that then."

"Or maybe I should have. Who knows what might have been different?"

"Maybe."

Looking back, it was hard to believe I'd been so depressed and angry, so unwilling to feel anything good after surviving David Wesley's attack. Against all odds, Zach had stuck by his conviction to love me, even when I tried so hard not to love him back.

"It doesn't matter, though, I wouldn't change a single moment of our time together."

I'll always I wonder if that means he'd change anything when we were apart . . .

CHAPTER 27

Our repeat trip to Vancouver to pick up Zach's new truck was only delayed a short while, but in the two hours I spent at the sheriff's department before noon, a lot of things came into focus, starting with an odd comment from Doug Logan.

I'd gone to the station after picking up my copies from the library about DNA. My intention was to prep the baby teeth for testing. However, I got a little distracted.

In the evidence lab, I'd pulled the file for the Bishop case, which now included the additional photo of Catherine with her tattoo visible, and the file I'd begun for the unknown circumstances regarding the tattooed human skin spread out on a table. I was comparing the design shapes of the photocopy to those I'd gotten from the library when Doug entered, waiting patiently for me to look up.

"Whatcha got?" I asked, thinking he'd arrived with some new evidence I needed to process.

Evidence management had become a new facet of my job, not because I really wanted to do it, or even because I liked it so much, but because I was good at it and able to research new methods to help catch criminals. And because I was office-bound for now.

Doug took a step forward, staring at the papers. "I saw that one," he said, his voice sounding parched. He pointed to the photocopy of the image taken from the bag.

He had my full attention, but the color had left his face a dull plastic gray.

"Doug?" I said, trying to get him to look up. "Doug?"

Finally, like a spell had broken, he raised his head and focused on me. "I saw a tattoo just like that one the other night, at the club." He swallowed, but it sounded hollow. "Mitch has it on his left shoulder." Reaching back, he indicated where it was.

"Mitch has one?" I repeated.

I flipped open the Bishop file, looking for the photo the doctor had provided, showing the location of Catherine's tattoo. I spun it around on the table for Doug. "Like this?"

He nodded, swallowed, then said, "So did the woman he was with."

Alarm bells clanged in my head.

Why would a cop have the same sort of tattoo as a woman who disappeared from here twenty years ago? The same cop who apparently let loose a prisoner he documented taking to Clark County. The same cop whose wife disappeared.

"Do we know where Seaver is today?" I asked. "I think it's time we got some answers about all this."

"No, but he's not answering the phone at their house," Wade said from the doorway. "Blake is on his way there now to check, but I would presume Mitch left town yesterday morning as soon as I put him on leave."

"With the van," I stated, knowing that any trace evidence we might have found under it was long gone as well. I'd already checked, but no one had examined the patrol car when he brought it in, and I was certain Mitch would have washed the cruiser, too. "We need to talk to Mitch's ex-wife and Rachelle's mother then."

"Why?" Doug asked.

"To find out if all his women have a tattoo that matches this one."

Blake Erwin made arrangements to go talk to Rachelle's mother that afternoon, to ask whether her daughter had a similar tattoo. He would go to Pasco the next day to visit Mitch's previous wife, Teresa – Lopez was her last name now that she'd remarried. She had custody of their two children and had a toddler by her second husband. Obviously I couldn't go, being on crutches, a liability to the county by working anything besides desk duty, but I certainly wanted to talk to them both.

Wade thought Mitch's marriage to Teresa had been his first, making Rachelle his second wife. I'd suggested the department put together as much of a history on Mitchell Seaver as possible before Blake drove to Pasco, because I suspected that Teresa might not have been a first wife but maybe a second or even a third.

"Why's that?" Doug asked me.

"Mitchell doesn't seem like the type who wants to live alone," I replied. "The time between his divorce from Teresa until his marriage of Rachelle was less than six months. I have to wonder whether Rachelle might not have been the reason Teresa divorced him."

The Blue Rule, as one of Zach's partners had once called it, is that cops have a hard time staying faithful and staying married.

I made a set of copies of the tattoo images for Blake to take, to have Teresa verify which one matched Mitch's, and to ask if she had one. I also made a list of questions about his past that she might be able to answer, such as where he'd lived previously and where his parents lived. I also wanted to find out about his sister down in Oregon, and whether by a strange coincidence she owned a dirty white SUV.

We spent about an hour putting together a strategy for finding answers to link or break any association to the crimes against me and my family, knowing already that Mitch was guilty of letting Jack Browning go free instead of taking him to Vancouver the day he reported Rachelle missing.

You connect a dozen links and suddenly you get a chain of evidence.

I patted Wade on the back when I got up to leave, knowing it broke his heart to think that someone in his law enforcement family was the focus of such a horrible implication. He was digging through Mitchell Seaver's personnel records, looking for any additional information that might be useful.

Once I got back to the cabin, Zach and Amber were not in the house, so I changed clothes and waited in a chair on the deck, feeling the summer sun on my skin. I could hear them talking out past the barn, probably tending to Rainier, though I couldn't make out the conversation.

That a man I worked with could have committed any of the sordid crimes we were investigating, much less that they appeared to be strung together, nauseated me.

I tried to put it out of my head, but still something I couldn't figure out nagged at me.

A half hour later, Zach and Amber came walking together from the barn, laughing at something, their postures, their walk was so similar, it was almost as if they had practiced doing it on purpose.

"Sorry we took so long," Zach called, still twenty feet away. "I need to go wash my hands and change jeans, then I'll be ready."

"I'm going over to the Clintons to stay with the girls for the afternoon while Del goes to town," Amber announced.

"I'll just be sitting here until everyone's ready," I said, feeling relaxed and unrushed.

Laser came up and put his head on my knee, so I scratched his ears. "You doing better, Boy?" I asked. "How awful that someone shot you."

"I'm much better, but I couldn't agree more," the male voice of my husband responded, though I wondered if he was replying for himself or being a surrogate voice for the dog.

"Come 'ere and I'll scratch your ears, too," I told him, which was answered with a canted smile. "Ready?"

Dressed in clean blue jeans, a white baseball-cut t-shirt with yellow sleeves, and a pair of dark gray elephant-hide boots, he was more drop-dead sexy than if he'd put on a suit and tie. Much more.

"Are you carrying?" he asked me, meaning did I have a pistol on me.

"Yes, I am." I flashed him a look at the holster on my belt hidden beneath a long-sleeve denim shirt I had on for that very reason.

Nodding his approval, he offered me a hand up. "Let's go spend some more money!"

"Sure, but I thought you'd paid for both trucks yesterday," I said as we headed to my new spiffy red Tahoe. I tossed him the key. "You drive."

"Really?"

"Why not? My foot hurts."

He opened my door for me. "When's your next appointment?"

"I go back Friday to have the sutures removed, although I could take them out myself," I said, waiting to finish until he got in the driver's side. "Or you could."

"Nope, not doing that again," he declared. "Ever. I had to take out enough the previous time you had surgery to last any non-medical person a lifetime. What, eighty stitches or something in your back and," he stopped to repeat for emphasis, "*and* your shoulder. Nope. Never again."

"Okay, I get it."

Amber came running out to join us, her oversized shoulder bag bulging.

"I got all my diabetic stuff," she announced, "and I have stuffed animals I bought for the girls last time we went to Portland."

I hadn't noticed when she bought them, so maybe it was when I was in the hospital.

We dropped off Amber at the Clintons' and drove to Vancouver with about a half hour to spare before Zach's deadline. He didn't want to rush them, he told me, so we stopped by a drive-in where he ordered us a chocolate malt to share.

"You've been quiet all afternoon," he said, taking the cup back from my first drink.

"Thinking about Mitch. I don't want to believe he's involved in any of this," I replied in genuine frustration, "but that's the direction things are going. Rachelle's missing, and we presume now she's dead. There's no question he forged the transfer papers and then let Browning go on the day she was reported missing. I'm ninety-nine percent certain that Browning threw gasoline on Dana and burned her, then assaulted the sheriff the next morning, which is why he was in jail to begin with. Then, after seeing him the other night in Portland, Doug is certain that Mitch has a tattoo like the one on the leather, and like Catherine Bishop's."

My statement was met by a choking sound from Zach, who made a face and handed me back the malt. "I don't want to drink after you if I might catch your ability to talk like that."

Phthththt.

"Really, Zach. What we've found seems to link all three cases to him."

"Then go arrest him."

"We can't. There's no proof."

"Yet," he said, putting out his hand. "Give me back the malt. Good thing smart isn't contagious."

CHAPTER 28

Picking up Zach's Suburban was a less than perfect encounter, starting with the fact that the vehicle wasn't black, it was more like a very dark sparkly gray.

"The vehicle has everything you wanted," the sales manager explained. "It had been prepped for purchase in Seattle, including a repaint, for a client who died suddenly."

"It's not black," Zach repeated.

"I know, but it was still listed as black on the invoice when we arranged to get it, so we didn't know until our flatbed truck got there. In fact, in the dark, the driver didn't notice it, either."

With a look that would have made the gray paint just melt off the metal, Zach pinned the manager to his chair and said one more time, "It's. Not. Black."

"We'll knock two thousand off the price and do free oil changes for two years," the poor guy offered.

"How about two grand off and oil changes and basic maintenance on *both* vehicles for as long as we own them," Zach countered, not making it sound like a question.

"Yes! I – we – yes, that's good."

So it was done, and after Zach signed the papers, we walked out to the vehicles, now parked side by side.

"That's actually a very nice color," Zach commented with a smile, clicking the locks with the remote.

"It's not black," I said.

"I know, but it was worth being stubborn about, don't you think?"
Must be hell trying to negotiate with a big guy like him.

We got in our new vehicles and drove to a restaurant that was supposed to serve really good Mexican food.

Honestly, I was quite a skeptic – I'd found that no one this far north made really good Mexican food, or really good barbeque, either. Each geographic area has its specialty, and one should not expect good seafood in South Dakota, grits in New York, or Mexican food in Washington. Pizza, although different throughout the country, has universal possibilities to be good.

But Zach wanted to try the place anyway.

Nibbling on a basket of hot chips, straight from a deep fryer, with thick and chunky salsa, Zach asked me about the search for him and Amber. "Whose idea was it to use a helicopter with infrared?"

"I thought it was Doreen's," I said, "although I guess it could have been Warren's. Why?"

"Just wondering." Zach took another large scoop of the salsa on a chip, eating it like it was bland, which it was not.

"Finding two warm bodies against a cooler background –" I stopped, the nagging sensation now a bonfire in my brain. "Maybe we could use it to find where Rachelle is buried!"

Zach tilted his head. "But where would you look?"

"We discussed this, remember? If Mitch really did it, then he probably would not have left the county, nor would he have gone anywhere in his patrol car where he might get stuck. That helps narrow down the area, right?"

Our conversation was interrupted by the server, and we ordered, then returned to our discussion.

"If she's buried, how would infrared help?" Zach asked.

"A decomposing body under the surface is still warmer than the surrounding soil," I said.

"Okay, but it can't be cheap to pay a chopper search time, and even limiting areas could be costly with no guarantees."

"Yes, but you said the DEA uses infrared and thermal imaging to find marijuana fields, right? What if we can get them to do double duty in this county to look for both?" I asked. "Surely you have a contact who can help us."

"I can always ask Layne Sebastian," he said. "I think he owes you one."

The Mexican food was pretty good after all.

✶

Before we left Vancouver, Zach called Layne's cell phone. "He might not answer, you know. He could be –" he began telling me as he pushed the send button, but apparently the call was answered right away. "Layne? It's Zach Samualson. Yeah, how're you doing?" Pause. "Really. I know, but after that fiasco in Seattle, I just felt like I needed to be home with my family."

Layne must have asked Zach about his retirement. They continued the conversation while I window-shopped along the storefronts.

I had met Layne a summer ago when he and two members of his task force from the Portland Police Bureau came to our little rural sheriff's department, following a lead on a John Doe we'd found. It turned out to be their missing detective, who had been working undercover in an operation involving the shipping and sales of counterfeit goods and the return of money back to terrorists. The investigation into his murder fell into that gray area between knowing who did it and being able to prove it.

Then when Layne's wife was killed, a witness implicated a woman whose alibi was being in bed with Layne, which made for a disaster. That investigation ended with the supposed witness being the murderer, but still Layne had to bury a wife, lost a lover, and ended up resigning from the police department while he tried to put his life back together. At some point, Zach had recruited him to the DEA, although I didn't know that until after Zach had been "dead" for months.

I wanted to hate Layne for being a part of the agency that had put me through hell, but I couldn't. According to Zach, it had been Layne who had saved his life when he got shot, letting Jamie Gordon get away.

Behind me, I heard Zach saying goodbye.

"He thinks they can manage to do that," he told me. "Wants you to provide a map of the county with areas where marijuana might be found, as well as where you want them to look for a body."

"Terrific!"

The plan was for Layne to contact me through the department in a day or so to make arrangements, making the flight official.

Now I just had to decide where the best places to hide a body might be.

I had the whole drive home to consider those possibilities, and the best one I could think of was Dana Watson's place. Browning would have access to it. If Seaver had Browning in his patrol car, stopping to meet Rachelle by the river might have seemed innocuous to her until she ended up in the trunk of his patrol car. Driving from there to Dana's house would be both simple and provide Browning with the story that the county dropped him off there. Plus, the house sat on several acres, so there would be both ample land to bury a body, and Browning could threaten Dana if she had any knowledge at all of it.

Was that why she was so afraid of him and refused to press charges?

I was home before I ran out of mental discussion about any of this, but I valued the time alone to talk aloud to myself. No doubt other drivers thought I was nuts, or maybe they thought I was just singing – something no one would want to hear. Not even me.

It had been Zach's idea not to stop at the sheriff's department and tell Wade Fordham about the new connection with the DEA. "Make it look more spontaneous when Layne calls," he'd suggested, and I had no reason not to think it was good advice. But getting a helicopter to search was sounding more like a better idea every time I thought about it.

Zach went over to pick up Amber from Del Clinton's.

I gimped into the house, having to stop at the garage door to enter the code to open the door because I remembered that my remote was a blob of melted plastic in my old truck.

Arrgh! Another stinking consequence of the bomb!

Inside, I set down my bag and made my way on out to the deck, Laser following me, where we sat in the shade so I could close my eyes for a moment and savor the quiet.

Laser let out a small growl, and I came awake to see Kenny standing a few feet from the deck, hands clasped in front of him as if he were just waiting for me to wake up.

"Hello, Kenny," I said, startled as usual by his appearance. Not just his there-he-is-and-how-did-he-get-so-close appearance, but his unwashed clothes – some of which looked suspiciously like what Zach had once owned, size and all – and the wild look in his eyes, which never held on to any one object very long.

"Mrs. Zach," he replied with enormous courtesy. "I was hoping to see Mr. Zach."

"I'm not sure if he's home yet, Kenny. Is there something I can help you with?"

"Oh, no Ma'am, I don't want to intrude. I'll come back later."

With that, he turned to go, and nothing I said even slowed his retreat.

I wondered what it was that Kenny would show up here to see Zach about. Not telling me wasn't so much a surprise, because the only time Kenny had spent any time talking to me, it had been at Zach's direction.

Had he seen something?

I got to my feet and went inside. Thinking I should set out something for supper, I wasn't hungry yet. Zach would be, I thought, because he's always hungry. And Amber would probably need to eat, too. I pulled out chicken to marinade, though being on crutches was maddening as I tried to move around the kitchen.

A vehicle pulled into the driveway. I thought it was Zach until the front doorbell rang – while I was handling the raw meat, of course.

I yelled, "Just a minute!" and washed my hands, only to hear another vehicle pull up.

By the time I had grabbed a paper towel to dry, I could hear voices around in the garage. I opened the door to see Zach and Amber talking to Layne Sebastian, who saw me and held up a six-pack of beer.

"Nice to see you," I said, going out to greet them.

"I didn't have time to grab beer before we all showed up here last time," he said, meaning the night they arrested Jamie Gordon here in my kitchen. He hugged me. "I thought I'd better make up for it."

Coming inside, the men began gossiping about the goings-on at the DEA, but I finished up the marinade and returned the meat to the refrigerator before joining them.

"What I gathered from talking to Zach today was that you have a problem," Layne stated when I came to the dining room table to sit.

I took a breath and let loose the same sort of version I'd summarized for Zach about one of the deputies being connected to a variety of crimes at least through the similar tattoos.

"But you suspect him, right?"

"I would suspect him if he weren't a county employee," I said. "But it is difficult to imagine someone I work with killing his wife."

Layne nodded. "The catch now is finding a body, I gather?" he asked.

"In a nutshell, yes. A deputy is going to talk with Seaver's ex-wife tomorrow, and I'm curious whether she'd been coerced into getting the same tattoo, which might help determine a pattern. I haven't heard whether Mitch's current wife's mother could tell us if Rachelle had one."

"That's kinda crazy," he said, leaning back in his chair. "And I know all about crazy."

"Speaking of which," I said, changing the subject and turning to Zach. "Kenny came by and wanted to see you. He wouldn't tell me anything."

Zach nodded, frowning. "You met Kenny," he said to Layne.

"Yeah, though I don't think he liked me nearly as much as he does you."

"I got to spend a lot of time with him. Most people can't get past the fear he has of everyone, but for so many years, there was no one he could trust," Zach said. "Even his twin brother had taken advantage of his mental illness."

Our conversation turned again to catching up – Zach's decision to retire, how I broke my ankle, Amber's new diagnosis of diabetes, and Layne's recovery after losing his wife.

He agreed to stay for supper, and when Amber came in from the barn, I began setting out stuff so Zach could grill.

While Zach was outside and Amber upstairs washing up, Layne stood on the other side of the counter and said, "I just want to thank you again for what you did for me. For Sarah. And for not giving Chris Bell my resignation without a condition, even though I just couldn't go back to the bureau."

"No one you've ever met understands what it's like to be that broken more than I do," I said. "You deserved to be able to step away and start to recover for a while."

"Someday you can tell me your story," he said.

"Maybe. The best part is that it ended with Zach." I tilted my head. "He seems to be able to find the very best in people."

CHAPTER 29

"Julie," Blake Erwin said, the cellular connection scratchy as he began talking. "I went to see Mrs. Lopez today, and you were right about the tattoo. But there's sort of a catch."

"What's that?" I asked, sitting up on the sofa where I'd been napping.

"Mitch insisted she get the tattoo to match his when they got married," he said. "Then with the birth of each of her children, he made her add their names just beneath it."

"Rachelle has no children," I concluded. "No names."

"And Rachelle's mother thinks her daughter also had a tattoo, though she only saw a tiny bit of it under a shirt once." He paused. "The design is a possibility, eliminating other common images like roses or hearts."

My mind raced as I tried to fit the puzzle pieces together, no two fitting exactly, none giving me an idea of the entire picture.

Mitchell Seaver has one. Teresa Lopez has a tattoo with names for two kids. Rachelle had one but no children, so presumably no names. Catherine had one, and the photo in the wallet suggested a child. But the tattooed skin we found had no name, so was it hers?

The bigger key was that all the tattoos we had identified had the same basic design of an intertwined endless knot.

"Julie? Are you still there?" Blake asked, interrupting my thoughts.

"Yeah, sorry."

"There is one other thing," he said. "Teresa Lopez suspected Mitchell was married before they met, but she could never get him to actually say so. He was in the military and stationed in Texas before he came back here where she met him."

"We need to find out whether the marriage thing is true," I said. "Because he may have had something to do with Catherine Bishop when she lived in Texas."

"Wow, that's a bizarre connection," he observed. "I'll let you know when I get back to town."

We disconnected, and I stretched back out.

I had shown Mitchell what we found in that bag the day Amber brought found it.

He was the one who told me about the Catherine Bishop case. Could he really have something to do with her disappearance after she made it to Texas? If so, why would he have told us about her when I showed him the tattoo? We'd never have made such a connection if he hadn't pointed it out.

Or would we?

I dialed Wade Fordham's direct extension. After telling him what Blake had told me, I asked, "Did Mitchell grow up here?"

"Local boy who went off to serve his country, then came home to serve his county," Wade said. "That's what I gleaned from his background check."

"Do me a favor," I said. "Conference Dr. Bishop in to this call."

I heard a series of clicks and then I could tell the call was live again.

"I'm here, Wade," Dr. Bishop said.

"Me, too. Julie?" Wade replied.

"I'm here. So Dr. Bishop, you have been here all your life, right?"

"More or less. I went to college and medical school back east, of course, and a residency in Chicago."

"But after you married Esmeralda, you've lived here ever since."

"Yes."

"Do you remember Mitchell Seaver as a kid?"

"I should. I delivered him, doctored him for years. Removed his appendix when he was twelve, I recall."

His voice said he didn't understand where any of this was going.

"Did Mitch ever date Catherine?"

Silence.

"Dr. Bishop?" Wade prompted.

"Yes, I think it was her junior year in high school," the doctor finally said.

I think he made the connection, but he didn't like it.

"Did he leave to go in the military before she disappeared?" I asked.

"Yes, he was a year older than Cathy."

"That's the direction to start looking then," I said. "Thanks for your time. We'll keep you posted."

"Thanks," he said, but it didn't sound like that's really what he meant.

One click, then Wade came back on the line.

"Damn it, Julie, you could have at least warned me." The words sounded serious, but his voice did not.

"Sorry. Didn't mean to blindside you."

"I'll get Blake working on Mitch's military background. And for the record, we still can't find him. Apparently he didn't go back to his sister's in Corvallis. Do you want a BOLO?"

"No, we have nothing to arrest him for, as much as I'd like to know where he is." I changed the subject slightly. "Did Doug ever find out what sort of vehicles Mitch's sister has?"

"Yeah, I think so. He stuck a piece of paper here on my desk," he said, shuffling papers I knew to be four inches high or more. "Here we go. The note says 'A Honda Accord and a Ford Explorer. No colors available from DMV.' Whatever that means."

"It means I'm betting that Explorer is an off-white."

When Amber came in at lunchtime, we shared a sandwich, and I caught her up on the investigation.

"You mean that deputy who came into the evidence lab the day we found it might have killed Catherine Bishop?"

"I'm not saying that definitely," I waffled. *Wasn't I?* "But there seems to be a connection between him and several women with similar tattoos."

"So is he the one who shot Laser, who had that guy shoot at us on the search?" she asked, getting madder with each connection she made.

"It's possible, yes."

"Possible?" Her voice eeked up a notch in pitch and volume.

"Amber, yes, it's possible. However, legally speaking, there is no proof that he did any of those things."

A voice sounded from just outside the door. "Yet."

Zach joined us for lunch, making himself a thick sandwich and pouring a glass of tea.

"So you can't arrest him for any of this?" she asked.

"No, not even if we could find him. But we're still digging for answers from his past – his military service and so on."

"Will finding Rachelle's body be the cornerstone of a legal case?" Zach asked.

"I don't know," I said, feeling so far away from the investigation. "It would depend whether we can tie him to her death. We also need to wait and see if that tattooed skin belonged to Catherine Bishop. I haven't found a lab that will take the case."

I haven't been to work in almost two weeks, either.

"Layne said they would try to get a helicopter up over the weekend," Zach said. "Do you have a map for him yet?"

"No, I need to do that," I said, slumping even lower. "After lunch."

"Can I help?" Amber asked.

"Sure. I can use all the help I can get."

When we finished eating, she cleared away the table and brought a road atlas and a county map she'd picked up at some local business. "You said that driving was part of the limits he would have, so the roads would be important, right?"

Zach produced a satellite map of the area. "This was why Layne came out here last night," he said, "in case you thought he just came for dinner and beer." He winked.

In an hour, we had sketched out four zones with deeply wooded but very accessible areas that would be both potential marijuana growth targets and places it would make sense to bury a body.

Sense to us, I mean. Who knows what makes sense to someone who really wants to bury a body?

"We can drop this off when you go for your appointment tomorrow," he said, folding up the map we'd marked in two colors.

"Time for the sutures to come out," I explained to Amber, then turned to Zach, "and since you didn't want to do it, I guess we drive to Portland and back."

"We can take your truck."

"No, I was thinking we should take yours," I argued. "Otherwise, you'll just want to drive mine."

"That was the idea," he said, kissing me on top of the head before he gathered his cap and gloves to go back outside.

"Red's not your color," I said when he got to the door.

"Damn, that's the new color I picked for the Mustang," he said, and closed the door behind him.

"It was already red!" I yelled.

"Why do you two argue like that?" Amber asked.

"We're not really arguing," I explained. "We just like to fuss about things that don't mean anything."

"Kinda like flirting?" she asked.

"I guess it's what married people do when they flirt, yeah." I smiled.

Amber went upstairs, and I wiped off the countertops, thinking about how Zach and I picked at each other in fun. I'd never thought someone might mistake what we did as a real argument, but I was impressed that Amber had the guts to ask.

Even though I hadn't ventured to the barn on my crutches previously, I wanted to get out in the sunshine, so I found my floppy hat, then decided to put a garbage bag over the immobilization boot. I was just finishing when Amber came bouncing back down the stairs.

"What is that for?" she asked, wrinkling her nose.

"To keep it clean while I go to the barn," I said. "Want to walk out there with me?"

She shrugged. "I'd like to go over to Savannah's house later," she said. "I don't want to spend the night, though."

"Sure," I said. "But why not?"

She twisted her mouth and bit her lip. "I'm not ready to do that yet."

"Okay," I said, happy enough she wanted to go visit a friend.

In no hurry, we walked out through the garage toward the barn.

With its large doors open, I could see Zach rearranging the hay inside. During the last winter, most of it alone, I had removed bales the easy way, so it had become a stair-step maze. He was more organized about how he moved them front to back as we used them, and apparently he found nothing wrong with carrying each bale to a location that suited him.

"He's moved it all twice," Amber said in a low voice. "I don't get it."

"Sometimes, you don't have to get it. It just is."

She looked at me like I was two dimes short of a dollar.

"He feels like doing something," I said, keeping her hushed tones. "But I don't think he knows what to do, nor does he want to leave either of us alone."

"Ahh," she said, as if the world suddenly made sense.

"You two can stop whispering about me," he said. "I can hear you."

We exchanged looks, astonished.

He stopped what he was doing and stood with one hand on his hip. "And no, I don't want to leave either of you by yourselves until this whole case," he said, waving his other hand to indicate everything out there, "is solved."

"All righty, then," I said. "I just came out to enjoy the sunshine and the company."

"I wanted to work with Waldo for a while," she said, "if that's okay."

He nodded at us both, then returned to tossing bales from one stack to another as if they were a ten-pound bag of flour, not a seventy-pound bundle of dried grass.

When Amber had collected the tack she wanted and gone outside, I said, "She thinks we're really arguing when we fuss about things like which truck to drive. I told her it wasn't real, it was just, you know, fussing."

"Fussing." He made a little nod with his head. "Is that what you call it?"

"What would you call it?"

"Foreplay." He picked up another bale to move.

I laughed. "Yes, I guess that will work. But it's well in advance of any other intimate activities."

He dropped the hay bale halfway between stacks, pulled off his gloves, and strode over to where I stood leaning against the barn door. As easily as he'd plucked me barefoot from the shower, he leaned and lifted me so I was face to face with him. I dropped my crutches and wrapped my legs around his waist when he backed me against the frame. "Doesn't have to be," he said, peeking around the door to see where Amber was.

"As romantic as this might seem," I said, "I can just imagine you having to pick slivers of wood out of my back."

Instead of putting me down, he turned so his back was against the wooden door.

"Better?" he said, leaning forward to kiss me.

And yes, the world was back in its proper orbit for almost ten minutes, and nothing else seemed to exist until a polite cough interrupted us.

"Oh, hey, Kenny," Zach said. "I was wondering when you'd

come back around."

He nodded a greeting to me, only after Zach had put me back down and handed me the crutches.

Seeing that there would be no conversation with me around, I excused myself and hobbled toward the round pen where Amber had Waldo on a long lead.

"I don't think he likes me very much," Amber complained about the colt. "Dad can get him to work a lot harder."

"Given his size and experience with horses, he can probably make them all stand up and dance with one practice try," I said. "Waldo thinks you're a pushover, that you can't make him work as hard as Zach does."

"But I try," she said. She cued Waldquinte to reverse directions, but instead he trotted to where I stood and stopped for me to rub his nose.

"No!" she barked, popping the little whip, forcing him back into a trot. "See?"

"I can't tell you how to accomplish anything with the horses. Z' is the expert," I said. "But I'll leave so Waldo won't be distracted."

Having been dismissed from the situations of both members of my family, I made my way back to the house, Laser happily walking along with me. I chatted to him about how good the sun felt on my skin, and that I was glad I didn't have long furry hair like he did, but then he didn't have to worry about a suntan.

He seemed to agree, but he wasn't much into making conversation.

I was almost at the deck when I heard Amber scream.

Don't even try to run.

By the time I had turned to see what was happening, Zach was almost to the round pen. I could see Waldo inside, bucking like he'd been standing in an ant bed, and Amber doing the human equivalent.

Inside the fence, Zach sent her out the gate, then went to collect Waldo.

Or so I thought until I saw Zach reach behind his back and then heard a gunshot.

Not Waldo!

I hurried back toward the pen as fast as I could, and Laser ran ahead of me to where Amber stood, arms crossed, stomping her feet until she saw me coming.

"Snake," she said, explaining almost everything.

She'd probably never seen one, nor had Waldo. Together, they had skyrocketed each other's fright.

Shaking his head, Zach came out of the pen, holding a snake limp by the middle, carrying it around to the side of the barn.

"It wasn't poisonous," he said, "even though it nearly caused them both to kill themselves in panic." He looked back over his shoulder at the horse inside the pen, then at Amber. "Are you all right?"

"I'm fine," she said, still pouting. "Damned snake." She stomped off toward the house.

"That's a freebie," I said, commenting on her language under my breath. "How's Waldo?"

"He's just as whacked out as she was, I guess." He shook his head again. "No sense trying to work with him now."

"What did Kenny have to say?" I asked as Zach went back in the pen for the horse.

"You know Kenny," he replied. "I'm not exactly certain, but I think what he said was that someone had been watching to see when we left yesterday."

"Oh great," I said, exasperated. "Which is why I don't want to go to Portland tomorrow."

"I understand, but I suspect that if someone watching yesterday really wanted to do something bad, it would already have been done." He coiled the long lead up then made Waldo do two laps before he brought him to a stop and led him out the gate.

"That doesn't make me feel any better!" I complained.

He shrugged. "So go find a reason to make an arrest, Deputy." Detouring toward me for a kiss, "And drop Amber off at Savannah's on your way."

Dismissed again, I was stumped about what to do next to help with the investigation.

I went to the house and called up to ask Amber if she was ready to go to the Fordham's house now.

"I don't want to go!" she yelled.

What did I do?

As much as it was aggravating, I made my way up the stairs and to her room.

Amber wasn't a neat-freak. Her room was cluttered with memorabilia from her trips to New Mexico, horse posters, and other stuff. Usually the curtains let in ample light, but she had them drawn so the room was dreary.

"What's wrong?"

"Dad laughed at me."

"He was laughing because you were okay, despite the bloody scream that curdled the milk in the fridge."

"See? You are, too."

"I'm not laughing." At least not on the outside.

"Poor little city girl who can't handle a horse and loses her wits when she sees a snake."

"Is that supposed to mean you're feeling sorry for yourself now?" I asked.

She just shoved her hands into her jeans pockets.

"You do recall that your father ended up on his butt the other day when Rainier knocked him down," I said. "And I recall that you laughed."

Her eyes tilted up as she remembered, and she hid a slight smile.

"Being startled by something you've never seen before is not a crime," I was saying when I heard four more gunshots outside Amber's window.

CHAPTER 30

I nearly knocked Amber over getting to her window and jerking back the curtains.

Below, I saw Zach walking toward what looked like a dead animal beside the barn. I couldn't tell exactly what it was.

Zach looked up at the house and waved.

"Damn him!" I said.

My eyes met Amber's and we said together, "Freebie."

"I do wish you'd go visit," I said.

Didn't take a lot of effort to change her mind, and I went downstairs to wait while she changed clothes.

Zach came in while I thumbed through a magazine at the counter.

"And just exactly *what* did it take you four shots to kill when it only took you one to kill a snake?" I demanded.

"An opossum." He ran a glass of water. "Ugly critter. Big teeth."

"Four shots?"

"I missed once."

"More practice for you," I said. "You really missed?"

He shrugged, embarrassed. "It startled me."

From the staircase, I heard Amber laughing. "You missing trumps me screaming like a girl by a mile, Dad."

"You are a girl, though, so it hardly counts, right?" he countered.

As we said goodbye, I had to wonder if he hadn't missed on purpose.

I dropped Amber off at the Fordham's.

Savannah, the sheriff's daughter, was a year older than Amber, but they were in the same grade at school because Sav' had been home sick with mono the last half of her freshman year. While she and Amber weren't best friends, the relationship had been steady since Amber arrived and figured out she wasn't the only cop's kid in school.

Diana Fordham was outside, watering her roses, when I pulled up and let Amber out.

"Still on crutches?" she called.

"Yeah, another month, probably," I said through my rolled-down window. "I hate it."

She chuckled. "So does Wade. They need you more than ever, he says."

Nice to be missed, but I'd rather not be.

I waved and drove on to the station.

Because I'd forgotten to get the new code to the back door after Wade changed it, I went in through the front. Stephanie Potter was at the dispatch console.

"I didn't expect you here today," she said. "Things are just weird."

The youngest member of the sheriff's department, she was twenty-two, but sometimes her immaturity still shone through. Weird, however, in this instance seemed to be the perfect word.

"Wade's in his office?" I asked.

"No, they're all in the conference room."

"They who?"

"Him and some federal guys, I think."

Sooner or later, I figured the FBI would be showing up, I thought as I walked on down the hallway toward the back, hoping to evade Wade's meeting.

It's not easy to sneak around on crutches, but I made it past the conference room and into the evidence lab without attracting his attention.

We call it a lab. It's really a locked room with a wall of locked bins to hold evidence in working cases. Our deputies do very little processing of evidence – some basic fingerprinting for matches, alternate light source illuminations for blood or drugs, that sort of stuff. Still, it hadn't taken much arm-twisting to get Wade to put a computer and color printer back here when I asked, but I was pretty sure I was the only one who ever used them.

I pulled the container holding the bag and its contents Amber had found, and after I opened it up, I stood there looking down into the plastic bin, wondering how to tie all the possibilities together.

I heard voices down the hall, so the meeting must have ended, I thought. Except they continued to get louder, coming this way.

Even though I'd closed the door behind me, there was a small window. I moved out of direct view, turning my back and sitting at the computer, trying to look nonchalant in my tasks when the door opened.

"Julie?" Wade asked, obliging me to turn around.

With him stood Layne and another man I didn't recognize.

"Julie, you remember Layne Sebastian when he was with the Portland Police Bureau?" he asked. "He's now with the DEA."

I stood and nodded, but didn't hop toward them to shake hands. "Yes, I do. Nice to see you again, Layne."

"And this is one of their pilots, Michael Allen."

The pilot stood about five foot six, built like a bicyclist or a runner – lean and tanned. "Just Mike," he said with an easy smile.

Apparently Mike knows who I am and why they're really here, too.

"What brings you back out to Paradise?" I asked, playing along with not knowing.

"The DEA is doing some aerial imaging," Wade said, trying to explain what everyone apparently already knew but him. "They'd like to take a look in Skamania County to find a marijuana field they received a tip on."

"Really?" I said, almost too exuberant for my own good. "I'm sure there's stuff growing out there, but we don't have the resources to look most places."

"That's why we'd like to coordinate an air search, so we can use our infrared. Marijuana shows up as different wavelength than other plants, though I'm still learning how the system works," Layne said. "We were hoping to get a map of some possibilities."

"I was going to call you to see if maybe you could squeeze in that project," Wade said, "but Stephanie said you were here."

"Sure," I replied. "I can do that." I smiled. "Now, if they'd like."

The offer was well received by all three men, and so Wade left them with me.

"Sorry about that," Layne said. "I had no idea you'd be here."

"I'm flying a desk temporarily, but we've been working this case with the missing woman and all its complications pretty hard for being two deputies short."

"Two?" Mike asked.

"Me, and the deputy whose wife disappeared," I said. "And he is now missing in action as well, making him an even bigger suspect."

The pilot nodded.

"Actually, Zach and Amber and I worked on a map today at lunch. I don't have it with me because we were going to drop it off tomorrow when we came to Portland," I said. "But since you're here, let me see if I can remember where we want you to look."

I pulled out one of our county maps, with a topography image on one side and a roadmap on the other.

"Which map would be the most helpful to you?" I asked.

After a brief discussion, they decided to have me do the roadmap side, although the topo would be helpful to the pilot, too.

I found two highlighters and marked the areas we'd chosen at lunch. As an afterthought, I added one more. "Based on a lot of things, we came up with these."

"Looks good," Mike announced. "I can plot this into the GPS, and we should have weather suitable to fly tomorrow night."

"Night?" I asked.

"Best infrared signatures," he said. "At least for what you're wanting us to find."

It seemed like a perfect plan.

Like paradise, nothing's ever perfect.

❧

My orthopedic appointment was for a Friday morning at 9:30, which I figured would mean I would see the doctor at somewhere just before noon.

Turns out I wasn't even close.

One of his patients had been involved in a motorcycle accident, so the emergency call had taken him out of the office, likely for the rest of the day, the receptionist finally told me after I asked a third time, both of us bordering on rude.

"I have to get the sutures out of my leg today," I explained. "Can't the nurse do it?"

"Not without his supervision." She smiled and looked at a scheduling calendar on her computer screen. "I can get you in to see him on Wednesday next week."

"Well give him a note that I will *not* go another five days with sutures that need to be removed from a surgical incision today, nor will I drive back to Portland for an appointment so he can say it either looks fine or yell at me for removing them myself."

"You can't do that," she said, appalled I would even suggest such a thing.

"Removing sutures does not take a degree in mechanical engineering or nuclear physics, much less a simple medical degree," I stated. "Yes, I can. And I will." I took a step backward from the check-in window.

"Let me get the nurse."

"Really? Someone who might actually do something for me?"

She stepped away from the desk.

"Julie, you really are being a witch today," Zach observed. "It's not her fault."

"Whose fault is it?" I retorted. "These sutures need to come out today."

A door opened to my left. "Mrs. Samualson? If you'll come back here, I'll get you taken care of and on your way."

I turned back to Zach and smiled sarcastically before following the nurse down a hallway.

She apologized. I apologized. She asked if she could snap an instant picture, just so the doctor could actually see how the healing was progressing. I agreed. She then removed the sutures and placed an adhesive bandage over the wound.

"I understand your situation," she confessed. "That's actually how I ended up working for this doctor, throwing a raging fit one day when I needed to be seen."

She provided me a list of small range of motion exercises to begin twice a day, scheduled an appointment in two weeks, and we shook hands before I left.

In the parking lot, Zach scolded me for being so abrupt with the receptionist.

"I think you called it being stubborn," I reminded him, pointing at his truck. "And I seem to recall that we both got what we wanted. Oh, and you didn't have to remove my sutures."

"You're evil, you know that?"

"See? No wonder Amber thinks we argue. That sounds like a horrible fight," I said as Zach opened the door to the truck for me.

"Yes, but making up is so much fun."

We drove back home without stopping to indulge in lunch, since the appointment had run so late. Amber had stayed at Savannah's again for the day, which meant she would at least have had to do her blood sugar testing at noon. I was anxious to see how that had been for her, because she'd been so nervous about her friends freaking out about it.

"I called Layne while you were in the exam room," he told me. "They're set to fly tonight."

"That's terrific. I'm hoping we all get something useful out of this endeavor. Aren't you bothered thinking this may be a murder committed by a deputy I work with?"

"Not really. I've been there, remember?"

I hadn't even thought about it that way, but he was right. His partner in the DEA task force team had turned to dealing drugs. That had ended with Zach witnessing another team member get shot, then losing a partner who was also his best friend. Maybe worst of all, Brodenshot had kidnapped and killed Amber's mother and the young girl mistakenly thought to be Amber. Brodenshot would have killed me, given a better chance. All to make Zach suffer.

That's how Amber had come to live with us – Zach was her only living relative.

"Sorry, you're right," I said. "I try hard to forget that happened."

"Forget you risked your life to save me, twice?" he asked, then his voice softened. "I think of that every day, but I do try to forget why."

"I don't want that to change how we treat Amber," I said. "I feel bad enough she's involved in this."

He nodded, and we rode in silence for several miles before he turned to me, lowering his sunglasses. "You could quit, too."

"I could." I didn't look at him. "I might."

"But it would be for her, not for you, wouldn't it." Not a question.

I shrugged.

"Just so you know, I don't want you to quit if it's not for you," he said. "I'll protect Amber. You've proven you can take care of yourself."

"Did you quit for her?"

"No, I quit because I didn't love the job anymore. You still do."

"It's getting tougher to love it every day."

CHAPTER

31

Surprised he'd even brought it into the bedroom, Zach's cell phone rang, long after we had gone to bed.

"'Lo?"

I couldn't make out the words on the other end, but the voice was loud.

"What?" Zach said, sitting up and throwing back the covers. "Right now?"

He jerked on his pants with one hand, opened the closet door and tossed me a shotgun, which I barely saw in the dark in time to catch. "Lock the doors and call for backup," he said, taking a rifle with him and disappearing out the door. Pounding on hers as he went by, he yelled, "Do not come out of your room!"

I got up and grabbed the crutches to follow him, wondering what the hell he was talking about.

As I circled to head down the stairs, he yelled back up at me. "Sebastian says there's people on the property right now. He's got 'em on the infrared."

"It's not Kenny, is it?" I went down the steps in the dark, using the crutches to feel my way but having my left hand full with the shotgun.

"Maybe. There's two," he yelled back, and then he was gone out the front door.

From the top shelf in the foyer closet he'd left open, I got a flashlight, my duty pistol and Zach's Kimber .45 out, setting them on the kitchen counter, certain I had enough firepower to stop someone if necessary. Then I picked up the phone and dialed.

Before Bette even said her 911 answer, I told her to send me backup now. "And have responding units watch Wind River for any cars headed south on their way."

I listened as she did what I asked, sending every available unit to my address, then she asked what was wrong.

"DEA is making a night flight over Skamania County using an infrared camera. They spotted someone on our place. Zach's outside now."

"Stay on the line," she said automatically. "Sorry, you know the drill."

"Just hurry." I checked the shotgun, then each of the pistols. No one would get inside and up the stairs without a lot of holes and fatal lead poisoning.

"Julie?" I heard Amber call.

"Just stay in your room with the door locked and be quiet," I said.

Had I been able to walk, I would have gone outside, too, I thought. But I knew my job tonight was to stay with Amber, to get other help here.

When I heard Bette on the phone, I held it back up to my ear. "I have the DEA helo crew on the other line, and Zach on a third. I can hear everyone, and you all can talk to me, but you can't hear each other, got it? Okay, the helo says one suspect got in a vehicle that was parked in the ditch on the highway beside your property – looks like a pickup, maybe. It's headed south," she said, pausing. "Now it's turned east on . . . he's not sure, I'm guessing Old State Road." Another pause. "Yes, it's going south again. Two units will intercept from the south."

At least he was off the property now, I thought, and the county and state units could chase him. I was relieved.

Until I heard Zach's truck start, wheels spinning on the gravel drive as he accelerated out onto the short dirt road that ended at Wind River where he turned right onto the pavement.

"Zach's following him," I said, not knowing if he'd announced his actions. "Dark gray Suburban."

"Copy," she said, maybe to me, then there was a long moment of silence. "The helo says the suspect vehicle turned off the roadway, but they don't know where exactly, somewhere past where the road turns back south."

I heard an approaching siren from the north, going way too fast for what would be the first left off the highway necessary to follow both Zach and the pickup.

"One out of the vehicle," she said, remaining calm. "Suspect running south to southwest. The helo isn't sure they can keep tracking him through the trees."

Why was the DEA searching on our property?

Not something I needed to worry about at the moment, I realized, focusing again on the phone.

Until I heard a knock on the door to the deck.

Who the hell would be knocking?

I didn't want to use the flashlight and give away my position, but the knocking came again.

"Mrs. Zach?" a voice yelled.

Kenny?

He called again, knocking even louder.

I didn't want to stand up, but he would attract more attention outside yelling than in here, I thought, so I stood to answer the door. Still holding the phone to my ear, I heard more radio traffic, Bette relaying information from the chopper, and then a loud banging, like a cell phone dropped, then about two seconds of cursing and a loud, long, crunching sound.

"All units hold radio traffic," she stated. "Julie, you there?"

"Yes."

"Hold. Helo, are you there?"

"Roger."

"Zach, are you there?"

No answer.

"Zach, answer the phone. I still have a live connection."

Still no answer.

And then we all knew what the crashing sound had been.

"All units stand by for EMS tones." A brief pause. "Resume radio traffic," Bette said, continuing her job. "Ten-four. Responding EMS, take Wind River to Old State, follow east then south to turn right, then a slow left, looking for vehicle off the road on the right," she repeated what the helicopter crew had told her. "That will keep them away from law enforcement units intercepting," she said, maybe even just to herself, I couldn't be sure.

My heart skipped, sped up almost double.

"Mrs. Zach!" Kenny yelled again.

I went to let him in, turning on the dining room lights when I got to the switch, a pistol in one hand, the phone still cradled against my shoulder.

"Mrs. Zach," he said, almost out of breath. "Mr. Zach told me to come tell you what I saw. It was a man dragging something out that cut place in the fence to a pickup truck on the highway."

"Who was it, Kenny? Did you see who it was?"

"It looked like it was Jack Browning," he panted. "But it was really Deputy Seaver."

Seaver? Dragging something from this property to a pickup truck?

I held the phone close again. When I heard a break, I asked Bette, "Ask the helo if they identified my target."

"Your target?" she asked.

"They'll know what you mean."

"Hold," and she repeated my question. Then she gave them a different frequency.

Layne's voice came into my phone, from Bette's radio speakers into her headset. "Affirmative, Skamania. We believe that target was moved from Samualson's property."

Mitch had hidden his wife's body here all along?

"We've lost sight of the suspect running," he stated. "We'll light up the crash scene for responding units to locate, then we're bingo for fuel to PDX."

"Copy that."

"EMS ETA is sixteen – one-six."

Crap, that's a long damn time!

I heard two law enforcement responders give much shorter ETAs, and it was all I could do to make myself stay put.

"Patch me to the sheriff when you can," I said. Being the only woman she heard, I didn't need to identify who I was to Bette.

"Stand by." Clicks on the phone. "Go ahead, call isolated."

"Fordham." No chatter.

"Helo and a witness say that a pickup was used to drag a large object, likely a body, from inside our fence line. Witness is sure it was our suspect."

"No shit?"

"No, sir."

"Helo have video recording?" he asked.

"Unknown. Find Zach. I'll track the video if it exists."

"Copy. I'm here and all I see are wheels."

Zach's truck is upside down.

The sheriff disconnected, giving me no choice but to wait. Until I looked up to see Kenny still standing in the doorway.

"Anything else, Kenny?"

"No, Ma'am. I think that was everything. I'll go now."

"Kenny, you should stay here until the cops are through running around," I said. "So you aren't mistaken for a bad guy."

He thought a moment, eyes dancing all around. "I'll just wait outside at the table then, if that's okay?"

I knew better than to offer any other option, so I just nodded.

And he exited, closing the door behind him.

I went to the staircase and yelled up at Amber that she could come down now.

Her door opened. "Are you sure?"

"Yes, I'm sure." I wanted to say everything was fine, but it wasn't.

She joined me, and we sat at the counter, and I tried to explain to her what had happened in the last ten minutes.

"Why would the DEA helicopter be looking here?" she asked.

Same question I'd had. "I don't know why. They saw someone on the property and called Zach."

"Why here?" she asked. "Did they catch him?"

I didn't know that answer, either.

"And where's Dad?"

That one I knew.

"Amber, please. I don't have answers. We'll have to wait for Wade or someone to call. They're busy." Not too busy, I hoped. Well, better busier than not at all.

Please don't let me lose Zach again.

CHAPTER

32

I would have walked the floor, had it not been so difficult to do. Amber paced for me, probably unaware that was what she was doing. Nothing to say until there was news.

Finally my cell phone rang, and I snatched it up.

"Julie, I'm okay," Zach said. "But we'll have to go shopping for another truck."

"Are you sure?" I asked.

"Oh, I'm absolutely sure. It's a total loss. Airbags went off, all the windows broke, the steering column is bent, roof caved in," he said, totally serious even though he knew that wasn't what I meant. "Absolutely totaled."

"Are *you* really okay?" I repeated, not in the mood for him being funny but glad he wasn't so hurt he had no sense of humor.

"I have a few bruises and a cut on my forehead where I bumped it on the roof getting out," he said. "And I have glass everywhere."

You have no idea where everywhere is.

"Do you need to go to the emergency room for stitches?" I asked.

"No, baby, I do not. The medic checked me out and gave me a little gauze bandage to hold against my head till it stops bleeding, but it's just a scratch."

I heard background voices, then he spoke again.

"I'll have Blake bring me home in just a little bit."

"Did they catch him?" I asked, not wanting to say a name in front of Amber. "Kenny was here and said he saw him drag something out to his pickup."

"They found the truck and a body," he said. "I don't know more than that."

He assured me one more time he was all right, then we disconnected.

My chest hurt, I realized, from holding my breath for so long until the phone had rung. "He'll be here shortly," I told Amber. "Why don't you go on back to bed?"

"Are you kidding me? All that and you want me to just go to sleep?"

"That's not it. I just figured there's nothing more to be done tonight, so you could go back –"

"Not sleeping, Julie. Not." She crossed her arms in defiance.

Yeah, me, either. No time soon.

It wasn't half an hour before a car pulled into the driveway, a door opened and closed, then the car left again.

Amber ran to open the garage door, finding Zach standing in the motion sensor floodlights, looking more like he'd been hit by a truck than having just rolled one.

"Oh my God, Daddy!" she said, barreling out to him. "What happened? Julie didn't say you were hurt."

"I'm just fine, Amber," he said, hugging her against him, but I saw him wince.

"Into the house, both of you," I ordered. From the kitchen, when I looked, Kenny was still sitting at the table out on the deck, so I opened the door and invited him in to see Zach – I knew he wouldn't come in just for me.

Amber had gone into the downstairs bathroom to get Zach a wet cloth to wash the dried blood from his face.

"Okay, Kenny," Zach said, taking the rag, and dabbing at the trail of red down his nose first. "Tell me what you saw."

Our guest cleared his throat and smoothed his jacket, then took a deep breath. "I was out behind your barn, skinning that 'possum you shot earlier for some breakfast when I heard someone moving in the trees yonder toward the highway. You asked me to keep an eye out, so I listened a bit more, then I went to see who was there," he said, then inhaled again. "Wasn't hard to see 'cause it's just past a full moon and it's real bright. I didn't get too close, but I saw that man almost done digging up a big bag, like a trash bag, and then dragging it out to the road. That whirlybird was making too much racket for me to hear, but when I snuck out to the fence, I saw that blue pickup driving away with its lights still off."

"Could you tell who it was?" Zach asked him.

"Like I told Mrs. Zach," he said, nodding at me for confirmation, "it was a man who dressed like he was Jack Browning – dirty t-shirt, ratty pants – but it was really Deputy Seaver. I recognized him 'cause he's picked me up more'n a couple a times."

I heard Amber gasp.

"You can show me where he was digging?" Zach asked.

"I can do that, but maybe you ought to wait till the sun comes up."

"No, we need to get to it tonight," Zach said. "Let me call and get a deputy to come back out here."

"There's a patrol car parked right at your mailbox," Kenny told him.

"How do you know that?" I asked.

"Saw him pull up there and park, Mrs. Zach."

"Same one that dropped me off?"

Kenny nodded.

"Convenient," I muttered. "I need to call Layne and see if they got that all recorded."

Zach handed me his cell phone, took mine instead. "Let's go," he told Kenny, and dialed the sheriff's dispatcher to ask Blake to come back to the house.

The two men went outside, and I heard the car pull back up, then voices as the trio went for a walk in the dark. Once they headed toward the barn, I could see flashlight beams.

I found the number for Layne and hit send on Zach's phone.

"Layne? It's Julie." The obvious questions about Zach. "Yes, he's just a little banged up. They're out looking for where the body was dug up now."

"I'm glad he's okay," Layne said. "That looked like a hell of a rollover from above. At least two and a half times."

Not what I want to hear right now, Layne.

"The sheriff wanted to know if you caught any of this on video?"

"Sure. I'm already dubbing you a copy. I'll bring it out right now if you need it," he offered.

"I think daylight will be sufficient," I replied, looking at the clock and seeing sunrise wasn't all that far in the future.

"Not a problem. I'll bring big-city donuts."

"Maple, please," I said, feeling the exhaustion set in. "I'll need at least two, maybe three. It's gonna be a long day."

Done deal, and we disconnected.

I dialed the sheriff's cell phone. "Video will be here first thing in the morning. Any luck finding Seaver?"

"No, but we'll have a tracking dog here in an hour," he said. "Sure wish you'd think harder about being a K-9 officer for this sort of stuff."

"I wouldn't be much help tonight," I said. "And a drug dog won't hunt felons, Wade. You'd need a search dog, a drug dog, a cadaver dog, and – "

"Yeah, the answer's still no. I get it." He shuffled some papers, took a drink. "So Blake is looking for the hole with your husband?"

"Correct."

"Just be careful until we catch him," Wade said. "Right now you're the biggest threat to Seaver's freedom. And anyone who would kill his wife would do just about anything to avoid being caught."

"Not a problem, sir. I don't think any of us will be sleeping the rest of the night."

"Someone hid a body by my house, I wouldn't either. I'll see you about seven," he said. "Drop Amber off at the house. I'd like to have you and Zach both here."

"The witness is Kenny Underwood, sir," I said. "Shall we bring him, too?"

He chuckled. "If you can."

I looked outside when I saw a flash of light, just before Zach came walking out of the woods.

He was alone.

Maybe we can't bring Kenny with us after all.

Amber was still pacing when Zach came inside again.

"Is it really him?" she asked. "That deputy?"

"Don't know yet for sure," he replied, handing me my phone back. "Geo called for you, and I don't think this night is going to get any less complicated. She asked me to tell you Dana went back to her place with Jack last night. Apparently one of his buddies bailed him out, and he's been free since end of office hours yesterday."

"Oh, geez," I said, shaking my head. "At least she knows where Dana is this time."

"Once she got back to her place, Dana took her pain pills and maybe had a few beers, then she zonked out last night," Zach said, building up to nothing but more bad news, I could tell. "And she woke up to find Browning dead on the lawn."

Forgive me, but I am more than just a tad relieved he won't be able to hurt her again.

"So now there's a crime scene going on over there, too." I squeezed my temples between my palms. "Just fabulous."

"He was naked, more or less, Blake says, which explains why the man Kenny saw looked like he was wearing Jack's clothes. He was."

"Fabulouser and fabulouser," I said.

"Not a word," Zach said, raising one eyebrow, still caked with dried blood and probably dirt and glass.

"I don't even care." I inhaled sharply. "Go take a shower, then we can put some ice on your bruises."

"I'm fine," he argued.

"You think I can't see that you hurt? Quit with the BS already and go wash the blood off. We might as well throw all your clothes away – you'll never get all the glass out."

"It's not bad. I shook out my shirt before I got in the patrol car."

"Zach, you will find there is tempered glass in your socks and inside your underwear. Trust me, just throw them all out."

"It's a good pair of jeans!" he countered.

I threw my hands up in the air. "Fine. Do what you want. Just go shower now."

He did.

"Really? Glass in his underwear?" Amber asked, suppressing a giggle.

"It's sort of like losing socks in the dryer in reverse. I don't know how shards of glass get inside places with no obvious access, but they do."

She nodded in appreciation of a new trivia fact.

"Maybe," she said with grave hesitation, "I should go back and stay with Grandmom Vera until this is over."

"Maybe," I said, "if we don't find Seaver tomorrow, that's not such a bad idea."

CHAPTER

33

Arguing all the way up the stairs that she wouldn't be able to sleep for just an hour, Amber finally retired to her bedroom around four. I told her we'd have to leave the house at six.

Zach had stretched out in his recliner, an ice pack to his forehead, one on his neck, and another to a bruise on his right hip where he'd hit the console as the truck began its rollover in that direction.

"You were right, you know," he mumbled. "I found glass in my boots. I wasn't wearing socks. How on earth did I get glass in my boots?"

One of the mysteries of life I didn't bother to explain.

"I still think that cut on your head needs stitches," I told him.

"And I still think you're wrong." He sighed. "I can't believe he got away."

"How did the truck roll over?"

"Deer. I was going too fast, and this deer popped out of nowhere, and I couldn't help myself, I swerved to the right, slid right off the road and flipped." He opened an eye and peeked at me. "If I'd hit the deer, I still wouldn't have caught up with him."

"Layne says it went over two and a half times."

"Honestly, I wasn't counting."

"I'm really tired of all these catastrophes, Zach. This is crazy," I said, dropping over on the sofa. "Amber thinks she should go stay with your mother."

"Maybe she should. I never thought about something from your career being such a threat to us all," he said. "And I'm not blaming you, Julie, but I don't know how to protect you both."

"You just worry about your daughter. I think we'll have enough to bring Mitch in for questioning."

"Gotta catch him first. I bet he's back across the river into Oregon and long gone. And having a witness will be pointless once anyone finds out it's Kenny. I believe him, but most people won't." He made a circle with one ankle, the joint popping loudly.

I so much wanted to move my left ankle like that.

"Surely there's fingerprints on something in the truck, or at Dana Watson's place that will tie Seaver to the murders." I fluffed my pillow and pulled a blanket over my shoulders. "But I'm glad Browning won't be around to hurt Dana again. What he did was absolutely sadistic."

"Just out of curiosity, is it possible that he didn't actually burn her?"

"Someone did – those are not burns from a fall into a fire," I declared.

"I mean, what if Mitch was there and he did it? Dana never said that Browning did, but no one asked her specifically if someone else threw gasoline on her, right?"

"Maybe. We'll probably never know if she won't tell us. If Mitch did it, she won't accuse him, at least when there's still some chance he could do something worse."

"What's worse?"

Good point. Sometimes the worst possible outcome is not dying but wishing you would.

❖

We were running late by the time all three of us were dressed and in the Tahoe, ready to go. Amber had been cranky when she woke, and I had to ask her three times if she got her diabetes supplies.

Like it or not, she would have to do both her testing and her insulin injections at the Fordham's today.

Had Diana Fordham not been an ex-police officer herself, I'd have been reluctant to leave Amber with her. Diana had ended her career to start a family when she and Wade left Boise, Idaho, for the smaller, less stressful town in Southern Washington where her husband had been offered a job as a deputy. That had been seventeen years ago. Wade had been elected sheriff four years ago.

Diana met us at the entry to their yard, enclosed by the proverbial white picket fence and arched trellis over the gate, surrounding a childhood-fantasy two-story cottage painted white with blue shutters and trim. She appeared to be a fairytale good queen, standing against the evil of the world, as she shooed Amber inside, waving to us as Zach drove away.

"She'll be fine there," Zach reassured me.

"Funny, I was about to tell you the very same thing."

We arrived at the station about ten minutes after seven.

As promised, Layne was there with two dozen fresh donuts. The men shook hands. I dug into the food, took two, and poured myself a cup of coffee.

At a quarter after, Wade got everyone seated in the cramped conference room, then he began a summary of the previous night's events.

"Going chronologically last night, Dana Watson states Jack Browning picked her up from Georgia McCall's house and drove her to her home west of White Salmon. Apparently she consumed alcohol along with her pain medication, so Ms. Watson slept through the murder of Jack Browning outside on the lawn. The perpetrator took Browning's clothes off him to wear himself, and then he proceeded to the Samualson's place on Wind River to move the body of Rachelle Seaver." He sipped his coffee, making a face at its wicked strong taste. "DEA was making a night flight over the county, looking for drugs and for potential burial spots, thanks to a combination goal coordinated by Deputy Samualson. Just before they were done, Agent Sebastian said he wanted to fly over the Samualson place for no reason other than his own curiosity. That's when he spotted activity on the edge of the property, two living subjects, one dragging what was discovered to be a decomposing body, from inside the fence to the ditch and into a pickup truck, which also happens to belong to Jack Browning."

No comment from the dozen people crowded together.

"Sebastian called Zach Samualson, who attempted to follow the pickup with directions from the helicopter, but he had a vehicular incident," Wade had to pause to let the chortles in the room subside, "and was unable to continue pursuit. The driver of the pickup, identified as Mitchell Seaver by Kenny Underwood, left the truck and ran into the forested area where the helo lost sight of him, even with the infrared. Search dogs on scene within the hour have so far failed to locate him."

He indicated the television monitor. "Agent Sebastian was kind enough to bring both the video of the incident and this morning's caloric input," he said, holding up a donut, again with a few laughs. He pushed a button on a remote, and the tape played.

"First of all, I have to say I'm astonished at the quality of the image provided. I've already watched a couple of times, and about here," he said, pausing the video, "is the best shot for identification. Does anyone not agree this is, within a reasonable doubt, Mitchell Seaver?"

No one spoke.

"Very well. As of now, we will issue an arrest warrant for Seaver for the murders of Rachelle Seaver and Jack Browning, trespassing, tampering with a body, impeding a criminal investigation, auto theft, and anything else we can add to the list to make sure something sticks long enough to keep him in jail while the details on prosecution are sewn up. The first big evidence we have – besides the video – are his fingerprints on the bag holding the remains presumably of Rachelle Seaver and those from inside that pickup."

I glanced at Zach, who nodded he'd already heard that news.

"We are handling the county search," the sheriff continued. "The FBI will coordinate regional and national efforts."

There was a groan from someone.

"I expect every one of you to work with other agencies on this. Doesn't matter who catches him – now our highest priority is getting Seaver behind bars. I don't have to tell you how embarrassing it is for us to be chasing one of our own. The media has already begun circling like sharks."

"How do we find him?" Blake Erwin asked. "Seaver's probably left the country by now."

"That's true, and he knows he's at the top of our list. We'll go over plans at the end of this meeting to catch him. Meanwhile, because of these crimes, he is also the primary suspect in the solicitation of Eddy Anderson to injure or kill Zach Samualson or his daughter Amber during the search for the boy last week, which didn't end well for Anderson," Wade said, again to a few chuckles. "He also is believed to be responsible for the bombing of Julie's personal vehicle, detonating it at their residence. With this in mind, increased security will be provided to the Samualsons for the interim."

"That's not necessary," I said, thumbing off the maple frosting from the third donut from my lip. "While he may have attempted to stop me from participating in the investigation involving Dana Watson, probably so we wouldn't discover he'd let Browning go, he's obviously left too much evidence for intimidation of just one deputy."

"He bombs your car, and I certainly feel threatened," Richard Langston said.

"We're all at risk now," Wade replied. "And we all need to react accordingly."

"And how's that?" Langston prodded. "He only needs to catch one of us to make the threat credible to us all."

"We catch him before he can do anything else. With that, let's discuss how to catch him."

❈

After the meeting, I found Zach and Layne standing outside, talking.

Neither of them had any actual jurisdiction to the case, which in my mind made their opinions less restricted.

"So how do you propose we find him?" I asked when their conversation about football or racing cars or some other sport had ceased.

"Stake out his kids," Zach offered.

Layne shook his head. "A man who'd kill his wife won't care much about his kids," he said. "But, you mentioned that he has a new mistress. You should stake out his boat."

"Spectacular idea, Layne," I replied. "Now all we need to do is find *it*."

"You said it was a big Bayliner, new, right?" Layne asked. "Boats have to be registered. And knowing where it came from might lead you to where it got put into the water. Plus, there aren't nearly as many places to keep a thirty-five-foot boat as something smaller."

"But it was new, so who knows if it is in the water. Or if it's even still in Portland?"

"Where else would he take it?"

"Up river, down river. On a trailer to who-knows-where," I replied. "Or maybe he just left it when he ran."

Both men disagreed. "A guy who drops seventy five grand on it won't just leave a boat like you're talking about," Layne said. "Like a hunter won't leave his favorite gun. This guy might run, but he'll take that boat somehow."

"Okay, then. I'll have someone start checking dealers and docks."

On our way back home, Zach yawned as he drove.

"I can't believe you just took off after someone last night," I said, trying to sound mad, but lacking energy for the enthusiasm required. "And then, for the record, I had to listen to your crash."

Just like I listened to you get shot one night.

"Sorry. It's not like I planned to park upside-down in a ditch and bleed on my favorite shirt."

"I suspected you didn't like that gray SUV nearly as much as you let on," I teased. "Or maybe you just want to torture the guy into finding another one?"

"Guess we do have to do that again," he said, and then yawned again. "But that part was kinda fun."

"Sadist," I muttered.

"I told you about that a long time ago," he replied.

"You said hell is where the sadist has to be nice to the masochist."

"See? You remembered." The smile beneath his mirrored sunglasses was brilliant in the sunshine.

"That statement didn't indicate you were a sadist," I replied.

He shrugged. "Turns out I'm not, am I?"

I ignored the question for one of my own. "So why me?"

"I told you that a long time ago, too. Once I saw you all grown up, I just knew."

"Knew what?" I didn't mean to sound perplexed, but I still didn't fully understand.

"That you would be the one woman who'd make my life mean something. That I could love you without hesitation or limitation as long as I lived." He lowered his sunglasses to peek at me, then slid them back into place. "Not many other men talk about being so in love with a woman, but I'm not ashamed of the way I feel about you, nor am I afraid to show you or tell you. If you doubt me, maybe I need to spend more time proving it."

CHAPTER
34

The next twenty-four hours passed like the landscape to a passenger on a bullet train. Everything's a blur, and there's no way to get off.

I tried to nap after we got home from the briefing, but that was short-lived when Amber called to ask if I could come get her.

When I got to the Fordham's house, Diana was sitting outside on the porch, and she waved me on inside.

"I know all the deputies are working hard to solve this case," she said, offering me a glass of tea.

A Blood Mary sounds better.

"Even you, still on crutches."

Although I didn't feel I'd done much to contribute to the whole case, I accepted the tea, and we chatted.

Diana didn't ask about specifics, but she did echo her husband's surprise that one of his deputies was the target of our now increased manhunt.

"Creepy," she said. "Makes you doubt everyone you meet."

I wonder if she doubts me. She probably would if she knew anything about my past.

Upstairs, I heard Savannah and Amber laughing about something.

"She's welcome to stay as long as necessary," Diana told me. "In fact, I was thinking of taking a trip over to The Dalles to my sister's for a couple of days. I don't know if you've thought about Amber leaving, or whether she would be comfortable going with us, but I thought I'd throw that out."

"Honestly, she's been a little withdrawn about this diabetes thing, and I'm not sure she would want to go right now," I replied. "I appreciate you caring about her safety, though."

"I'm in no hurry, so we'll hold off a few days," she said, "but if you change your mind, just let us know."

Why hadn't I thought about taking Amber somewhere else for her safety?

"I suspect Seaver left the area," I said. "He got caught moving his wife's body, so now I have to believe he's in the wind. Nothing good can come of him staying here where everyone's looking for him."

Diana stated the obvious truth. "Honey, if he were that smart or logical, he wouldn't have buried his wife on your property."

"Had Dana Watson not ended up in the hospital, none of this would have come to our attention. No matter who actually caused her burns."

But that didn't ring true in my mind for some reason.

Amber and Savannah came down, and we said our goodbyes and thank-you's.

In the truck, Amber leaned back and sighed, eyes closed. "She can be so exhausting," she told me.

"Who, Savannah?"

"No," she said, her face twisting to exaggerated shock. "Not her. Mrs. Fordham! She served breakfast at eight, lunch straight up at noon, a snack at three. She made sure I was testing and taking my insulin before I ate, and what she fixed for lunch was just horrible!"

I tried not to laugh. "What did you have?"

"A salad with little orange slices and cottage cheese."

"And you didn't like it?"

"Maybe if it had some grilled chicken or something on it," she complained. "Breakfast didn't have any meat, either. It was buckwheat pancakes with yogurt and blueberries."

"Meat. You mean no bacon or sausage?" I tried to sound appalled.

"Yeah. Or leftover chicken fried steak. I grew up where you have meat with every meal."

"You know that nutritionists say you only need about four ounces of animal protein a day," I proposed.

"That's crazy! Maybe with just breakfast, but what about a burger or steak for supper? There's always more than a measly four ounces in our meals, isn't it?"

"Ours, yes." In fact, I typically chose steaks that ran about seven to twelve ounces each with nice marbling, trimming fat from the edges only when it was excessive. And I made burgers that ran over a third of a pound. "I agree that we eat lots more meat than that."

"All these diets around, I don't get it. No carbs, all meat. Or no meat and all veggies. Or just cabbage soup." She shook her head in disgust. "And people try to follow them? It's bizarre."

I agreed, but I wondered where she'd learned that.

"I guess you haven't caught the bad guy yet," she said, changing the subject.

"No, not yet."

"He's not going to come back again, is he?" Genuine fear made her voice quiver.

"My gut says no, since he'd only risk getting caught now that we've positively identified him and his crimes."

"And Dad's really okay?"

"Yes, he was just tossed around a little when the truck rolled."

"Rolled?" she exclaimed.

Oops, I forgot she didn't know that.

"The truck slid off the road when he tried to avoid hitting a deer."

"He didn't kill it, though, did he?" Her voice just kept getting higher and louder.

"No, Bambi's just fine," I said, the sarcasm lost on her. Then I yawned.

"So we're down to just one car again while his in the shop?"

"Shopping again," I told her. "His brand new truck isn't in much better shape than the last one he replaced."

"Really? But he's okay?"

That's the beauty of seatbelts and airbags, I thought. But our insurance agent must have begun to hate us.

❦

"I called the dealership and asked the salesman to find me another truck," Zach told us over supper that evening. "I also called to get a new hot tub delivered, but it might be a week or so. I'm disappointed. A long soak sounds good. And we're still waiting on the shower to be repaired."

Amber had offered to do the preparations for fajitas, including a marinade for the meat, then slicing onions and Anaheim peppers to brown, as well as making fresh guacamole and pico de gallo. All Zach had to do when it was time for supper was grill the skirt steak because she'd done the rest.

"Can they find another truck like you want?" I asked, taking a bite of the contents inside a rolled flour tortilla.

"I told them a week was fine this time," he said, swiping a chip through the pico with its tomatoes, onions, jalapeño peppers and cilantro with other things. "This is really terrific. What's your secret?"

She hefted her shoulders in pride. "I use lime juice."

He nodded appreciatively and took another bite.

For fajitas, one of our favorite meals, the three of us took turns creating the marinade, so the meal turned out different each time. I liked the meat to have more sauce, so I sliced the steak up to marinade it, then cooked it in a skillet with the onions and peppers. Zach's marinade was similar, but he used the large griddle on the grill to slow cook the skirt steak whole, letting the marinade evaporate, giving the meat a rich smoky flavor. Amber's choice was to season the beef with a dry rub and have Zach grill it whole, so it tasted more like a steak.

"Mrs. Fordham mentioned going to see her sister," Amber said. "I got the feeling that she wanted to take me out of town."

"No different than considering sending you to my mom's," Zach told her. "I think we'll be okay, but it's always a possibility."

"I agree with Julie," she said. "This guy won't come back if he knows everyone here is gunning for him."

After two fajitas, I quit. Amber had two, but Zach had four, which finished off the meat. He swiped a few more chips through the guacamole before letting Amber take his plate as she cleared the table.

Over in the corner by the fireplace, Laser's head popped up and his ears radared forward as he sniffed then barked once.

When I looked out the dining room doors, I saw Kenny Underwood coming toward the house from the woods beyond the barn and pens.

"Don't forget to pay him," I said, nodding that direction to get Zach's attention.

"Oh, yeah!" Zach hopped up from his chair and hurried outside, meeting Kenny halfway to the barn.

I crutched to the kitchen, more aware than ever how sore I'd become. The injuries were healing, but the devices and instructions to recover faster were almost worse.

Through the window over the sink, I watched the two men talking, Kenny pointing back behind him, making digging motions, then other gestures I didn't understand.

I don't have to get it, so long as Zach does.

I wanted a glass of wine, but I didn't think I had the energy to open a bottle, much less to try carrying it to my recliner. So I sighed and just headed to the living room without it.

Not time for the news. Not interested in the evening choice of cop shows that only irritated me for their gross lack of reality or the latest seasonal selection of what was supposed to be sit-coms, few of which I thought were funny.

I picked up the book Zach had been reading a few nights before, finding he was halfway through *Comanche Moon* by Larry McMurtry. That didn't surprise me. I knew he'd read and watched the mini-series *Lonesome Dove*. He'd told me it made him a little homesick, reading about the cattle drive and open range.

Zach came inside from the deck door, locking it behind him.

"So what's new with Kenny?" I asked when Zach came to the living room and dropped into his chair with far less excitement than he'd rushed outside.

"The good news, I guess, is that Kenny saw Seaver bury the body out there two weeks ago or whenever it actually was. He's not sure he can pick a day, but he watched him do it. That backs up the fingerprints they found on the bag and inside the pickup."

"Do you mean Kenny's on this property that often?" I asked, avoiding the discussion of Seaver.

"I told Kenny a year or so ago that he could make himself a little camp over in the far northeastern portion in the trees if he wanted," my husband said. "I stayed over there with him several days before Gordon was arrested."

"Really?"

Zach looked at me as if I'd lost my mind even to question his seriousness. "Of course. He doesn't want to live in a shelter around other people who think he's dangerous, and I can't say I blame him. I've spent enough time with him to know he's not."

"He might not be dangerous, but he really is mentally ill," I replied.

"We have a deal that he can live out there if he takes his medication, which I've been buying for him. When he needs money, I find him some odd job he can do, so he's actually earning something, not just taking a handout. That's really all he's ever wanted."

"He's loyal to you," I said. "But I get the feeling he doesn't know what to think about me."

"He saw you with Gordon," Zach said without accusation or innuendo. "He didn't comprehend that you thought I was dead because he knew I wasn't."

That made sense, I guessed.

"What about Amber?" I asked.

"He won't come around her because too many people in his past have accused him of malicious intent with children," Zach answered, "but he wouldn't ever hurt her."

I nodded. "So if that was the good news, what was the bad?"

"Kenny won't tell anyone else but me what he saw. I'm hoping none of that is actually necessary in the long run."

"Why wouldn't he have told you when he saw it?" I asked, perplexed.

"He told me he didn't know what was in the bag," Zach replied. "And he knew it was the deputy, and because it was on our property, he didn't think what Seaver was doing could have been illegal." He motioned to me. "It's been a long, long day. Let's go to bed and try again for a full night's sleep."

❧

Sure enough, all three of us slept in the next morning.

However, sleeping in to Zach means something completely different than to the rest of the world. To me, the perfect morning starts at 11:59 a.m. with breakfast in bed. To Zach, it means watching the sunrise, coffee in hand.

When I woke just before eight, Zach was downstairs, making breakfast, so I knew the horses had already been fed – they always came before the humans.

I grabbed clean clothes and made my way downstairs in hopes of grabbing a quick shower before he was done.

"Good morning," he said, leaning over to kiss me. "Sleep okay?"

"Apparently like a rock," I replied. "Doesn't look like I even turned over."

I didn't feel like it, either, all slow and achy as I moved around.

"You can take a shower after we eat," he told me. "Amber talked me into taking her to a roping north of Vancouver this afternoon, if you'll let us use your truck."

I lifted an eyebrow at him, faking an *Are you joking?* look.

"We're hoping you'll come along," he added.

"And why is that?"

"I don't know for sure," Zach answered, dumping his concoction into a skillet. He held up a finger to me, then yelled up at the ceiling, "Amber? It's almost ready!" He smiled at me. "She was the one who wanted to know if you'd go."

Really?

"I think it would be good for us all to go and get away from this place for a day."

So after breakfast, that's what we did.

Although Zach and Amber didn't win anything as a team in the heading and heeling event, he did get a fourth place finish in the calf roping. This I thought was quite admirable, since neither of them had had much practice roping live animals since she got out of school, and even before that, their training had been limited to livestock over at Del Clinton's place.

We stopped on the way home and ate pizza in Vancouver.

After we'd ordered, Amber picked up her oversized hobo purse and announced that we were going to the ladies' room, which was a little out of character for her to include me, I thought.

Once inside, though, she dumped her diabetes testing stuff onto the small counter. "I just feel exhausted," she confessed. "I'm not sure whether I think my blood sugar is high because of the stuff I ate, or low because of the exercise. But I wanted you to be with me, just in case."

I nodded and let her stick her finger for the glucose testing. Her result was 75.

"So I don't need insulin before I eat this time," she said. "But I don't feel like it's too low."

"Because the fluctuations are so new to your body, that reading isn't so far below the levels where you've been living that it seems critical. If you were forty and your sugar levels stayed above 300 all the time, then 75 would feel low," I said. "The idea is to balance your activity and your diet so that you use the least insulin necessary to stay in the range you want."

She nodded and began packing her stuff up.

"We should find you a smaller test unit for your bag," I said when she was done.

The glucometer she'd been using was larger than some of those I'd seen at pharmacies. I thought a smaller one might make her less embarrassed to use it at school or other events she attended.

"That might be nice, so I don't have to keep moving it from my bag to my bathroom all the time," she said, straightening up and looking at our reflections in the small mirror. "Thanks for coming with us today. I felt a lot better knowing you were there in case something went wrong."

"My pleasure," I said, giving her a shoulder hug. "I'm glad you got out to try something new."

By the time we returned to the table, Zach had made his trip through the salad bar and was waiting on us.

I sat while Amber went to make her own salad.

"Everything okay?" he asked in a low voice.

"Yes, it's all very okay."

❧

Monday morning, I put on a uniform and went to the sheriff's department, with no intention of actually working unless there was some specific task that needed my attention. My goal was to catch up on the attempts to find Mitchell Seaver. I found very little had been positive so far. Finding the boat had not been fruitful. Yes, we found the dealer that sold it, but the Bayliner had been on a trailer. After a dozen tries, a Multnomah County deputy found the marina where the boat had been put in the water a two weeks prior, but it had been hoisted back to its trailer just two days ago. The best we got from any of the marina employees was that it had been a white guy in a dark big Ford truck. "Really big," said one. "Brand new," said another. But they couldn't even agree on a color.

Deputies had tried to find the sale of a new truck to Seaver, but dealerships were closed on Sundays. So far today, they'd concluded that he'd either just bought the truck so paperwork for ownership had not been processed by Oregon DMV or he'd borrowed it. It made no sense he would have stolen the truck – the dockhand said he'd been very protective of it.

Geo had left me a note, thanking me for giving her moral support and defending Dana against Browning when he'd shown up the first time; however her sister had elected to stay where she was instead of going back to Geo's house.

That gave me an idea.

I drove to Dana's house. Grabbing my crutches and hobbling to her porch, I had to knock a second time before she barely cracked the door, squinting at the sunlight.

"Dana? It's Julie Samualson," I said. "I just wanted to check and see how that burn on your leg was doing."

The door opened a bit more, revealing a drawn, pale face. "I'm taking antibiotics Dr. Bishop gave me," she said, almost so quietly I didn't hear. "But it still hurts."

"Can I come in?" I asked. "I'm not here in any official capacity."

She shrugged, allowing the door to swing open as she walked away, letting me let myself inside to the darkened room.

"Did Geo talk you into going back to the burn specialist in Portland?" I asked, closing the door most of the way, except that the light from the crack was the only illumination I had as I followed her into a small living area.

"Didn't want to go," she said, dropping into a chair, making no motion for me to do so.

"I understand, Dana. I like Boyd Bishop, but I'm not sure he can give you the specialty care that you need," I said. "If the antibiotic you're taking isn't going to cure the infection completely, you're only making it more dangerous."

She gave another half-shrug.

"Can I ask you a question?" I said. "Completely off the record."

She neither nodded nor shook her head, so I continued.

"Jack Browning can no longer hurt you." I tried to choose my words carefully. "But your burns appear to be the result of someone throwing gasoline on you, and, even though Jack might have hurt you before, I'm concerned that he didn't do this."

Her sallow eyes met mine and held, without blinking, for almost a minute before she shook her head. "I loved Jack."

"Dana, I would never question that. But we're looking for the man who killed him, right here on your place," I said, pointing out the front door. "And I have to wonder if you weren't injured by that man, too. All I want to do is make sure the right person is held accountable for this crime as well as all the others."

I let the silence float between us almost five minutes before she finally shook her head and told me.

CHAPTER
35

Like Kenny's statement about witnessing the burial of Rachelle's body, I wasn't sure Dana Watson would be able tell her story of such brutal injury to strangers. Her grief for Jack Browning was an invisible fog that hung in the dark rooms of her house, weighing down her already weak shoulders.

She told me she hadn't let Geo in to help her with the bandages in several days, and I feared the sickly sweet odor I detected once or twice might be from the infected wounds, possibly even indicating gangrene.

I begged her to go to Portland. I even offered to drive her there myself. "And I promise you don't have to stay, but this is so serious."

Dana just shook her head, though it was barely perceptible in the darkness of her home.

"Geo would be devastated if you died because she couldn't help take care of you," I argued. "And think of your parents. Do you want them to believe you sat here and committed suicide over the next few days or weeks?"

She lifted her chin. "Suicide?"

"You're just killing yourself. Isn't that suicide?" I asked.

Again, silence became my only tool, and I'd almost given up on it and any response from her when she finally whispered, "You'll take me?"

"Absolutely."

"Can we not go in your patrol car?" she asked.

"Let me go home and I'll even change into civilian clothes. Is an hour okay?"

She nodded.

I let myself out the front door, relieved to be back in the sunshine.

On my drive back to the station to swap vehicles, I called Geo. "I am going to take Dana to the burn unit," I explained. "I sort of feel bad goading her into going, but if thinking she's sitting there dying is what it takes, she can hate me later."

"Bless you for whatever it was you told her if she'll just go," Geo told me. "Maybe just getting out for a bit will change her mind enough to let me help her."

"I was thinking maybe you should just meet us back at her house after your shift," I suggested. "And I think it's time you told her about being a nurse."

❧

I had been right, unfortunately, about the specialist wanting to admit Dana for in-patient treatment of her infection. About Dana refusing to stay. About the two sisters not wanting to cross that line toward an emotional connection they'd apparently avoided for years.

Dana was angry when I pulled the Tahoe into her driveway where Geo's little car already sat. Geo sat on the porch in a rocking chair, but the look on her face lacked congeniality and cheer as well.

"Both of you, inside," I said, herding them like kindergartners into the house, following and turning on the lights so one didn't need night-vision goggles to navigate. "Sit."

I went to the kitchen and poured us all a tumbler of some cheap tequila I found in the cupboard, then asked Geo to come get them and take them into where they were sitting. I managed to carry the bottle.

"Now, I intend to referee any derogatory remarks about each other that may surface, but the two of you need to share, because there's no one else either of you has who will ever be closer than a sister," I said, raising my glass for a sip, then pulling out a coin.

"Otherwise, I have nothing to say. Geo, you're the older, so you call heads or tails to go first."

I flipped the coin into the air, caught it, and flipped it over onto the back of my left hand, waiting for her call.

"Tails, go last."

"Heads it is, so you go first." I held up a finger. "And what is said here stays here."

So Geo did, but she tossed back the liquid in her glass first.

"You were still in school," Geo began, talking to Dana. "I left home, wanting to be anywhere else but here. This little town had become the epitome of oppression, or so I thought. That wild freedom of being done with high school, having a whole world to explore, was too much, so I left."

She continued, explaining how she and a friend who had moved away a few years before graduation had met up in Portland, hitched rides here and there up and down the West Coast, finally settling for a while in San Francisco. "In 1968, there were lots of protests against the military efforts in Vietnam, and I was offended that people couldn't see the difference between hating a war and hating a soldier."

Dana nodded. "I remember how, even here, there were a lot of hateful words about everything. When that boy from your class came home, missing a leg, people actually booed him in the streets. I never understood."

"Me, either," Geo said. "So when Marsha and I couldn't agree on disagreeing about the war, I went to nursing school and then joined the Army. After boot camp, they scooted a dozen of us on a plane full of young men going off to Viet Nam."

I knew from our previous brief conversation, Geo's time overseas was anything but enjoyable. They say war is hell, but I would not stoop to even believing it was that good in most cases, given the conditions there and those to which many of the survivors came home. I listened.

"My second hospital was in Chu Lai with the 312th Evac," she said, then stopped to fill her tumbler again, had a swallow, then continued. "In June of 1969, a rocket hit one of the wards, killing a nurse, several prisoners of war and an older child, injuring a dozen or more. The whole wing was unusable, but once the bodies were removed and the injured treated, we were expected to go on working as if little more than a breakfast tray had been dropped. And the wounded soldiers kept coming, day after day. We adjusted our routines, business as usual. None of the nurses had time to grieve the loss of one of our own – we didn't have time to have feelings at all."

We all took a drink in the pause.

"You know, it's odd. I'd gone to basic training in Texas with that nurse who was killed. Now I don't even remember her name," Geo said, shaking her head. "I don't want to remember anything at all about those months. When I came home, I got a job at the hospital in Vancouver for a short while, but I couldn't do it. I don't know if I couldn't stand the memories or I hated how mundane it seemed, but I decided I'd rather be waiting tables than working as a nurse."

I interjected, though I'd said I wouldn't. "Her nursing career was a secret all these years, Geo recently told me. She is happy to help you with your dressings, but that she wouldn't do that for anyone else."

"Why didn't you tell any of us where you'd been?" Dana asked. "You never wrote, never called. I thought it was because of something Mom or Dad had done. Just last year, Dad blamed me for you leaving."

"I'm sorry," Geo said. "Once I got out, I didn't want to face any more confrontations and hatred than I'd already witnessed. Not telling anyone seemed to be the best way to escape. I swear I never knew they blamed you."

"That you would take care of me like this," Dana said, tears in her eyes. "I can't imagine how much it must bother you."

Geo raised a shoulder in dismissal.

"No, you don't get to shrug off her appreciation of your efforts, Geo. It is something special," I said.

"No, it doesn't bother me," she said. "I would do it whether I had been a nurse or not. You're my baby sister."

"Now for you, Dana. Share with Geo what you told me about Jack."

The two women stared at me.

"Dana? I think Geo deserves to know, don't you?"

Her eyes flashed from me to the bottle, which I suspected had been how she hid from so much of the pain before, both mental and physical. She didn't reach for it, hadn't even taken a sip from her glass, but she was silent a long time before she began.

"Julie thought maybe Seaver did this," she said, pointing in a circle to herself to indicate the burns. "He didn't. But he was talking to Jack about something to do with his wife a couple of nights before this happened. I was taking them each a bottle of beer when that deputy thought I'd overhead something. Jack promised him I wouldn't say a word." She shook her head. "Then a few nights later, I kidded Jack about having a new buddy at the sheriff's department, you know, just joking. Jack lost his temper. He tried to make me tell him what I'd heard Seaver say, but I kept saying that I hadn't heard anything. Finally, Jack knocked me down, then he threw gas on me. When I stood up, he threw a cigarette at me."

She didn't continue. She didn't have to.

"Were Seaver and Jack were talking about how to kill Rachelle or to hide her body?" I asked, prompting Dana to continue.

She nodded. "I'd heard, but I wasn't about to let on." She hung her head. "If I had, Jack'd have killed me, just like he killed that woman."

Dana had been peeking out the bedroom window when Jack crawled out of Seaver's patrol car. She watched, horrified when Seaver opened his trunk and dragged Rachelle out and dropped her onto the gravel. The woman had been alive until Jack stepped behind her and pulled a plastic bag over her head, suffocating her.

"I'll never forgive myself, letting him kill her like that," Dana said, her voice hoarse. "When I close my eyes, I can still see her face shape in that bag, see how hard she clawed at Jack to get free. It seemed like it lasted forever."

I left the two sisters in a hug, crying.

On our way back from Portland, Dana had also told me that she watched Seaver kill Jack Browning. I wasn't sure what I could do about it. If she didn't tell her story officially, that she really had been awake, I didn't know how to proceed or if it really mattered anymore, either.

But I figured that could wait, because apparently Seaver had made it clear that if Dana talked, Geo would die next.

CHAPTER 36

How do I propose to protect Georgia McAdams and Dana Watson from the deputy who was now the subject of a manhunt?

That was the big question that pinged around in my brain while I drove home.

Protection by law enforcement officers would be obvious and only indicate to Seaver that Dana had talked, giving him more motive to retaliate.

Sure, he might have been bluffing about the threat to kill Geo. Why hadn't Seaver killed Rachelle himself?

That idea brought even more confusion as I wondered about the possible victims before Rachelle – had Seaver had them killed instead of doing it himself?

All in all, I decided Geo, knowing about the threat, could probably take care of herself as well as an assigned guard. Maybe Dana would go back to Geo's house, which would make it easier to address that issue if it came up.

The hardest part of the investigation now, however, would be tying Seaver to other crimes, including whether he was involved in the disappearance or death of Catherine Bishop, and finding whether he'd been married before Teresa Lopez.

I dialed Wade Fordham's cell phone, figuring he was home for supper by now.

"Wade, we need to focus on that tattoo and library card," I said, explaining what I'd learned from Dana. "Without her testimony, we need to establish his behavior is part of a pattern."

"Do you really think he would have killed a previous wife, too?" the sheriff asked, unsure of the premise.

"We have one missing woman with a definite tattoo matching the style and location of his, one ex-wife with one, and an unsubstantiated theory about at least one wife before his marriage to Teresa Lopez. Then we have one piece of human skin with a very similar tattoo on it," I offered. "It's about the only lead we haven't chased to a conclusion, sir."

"Then follow it," he told me. "I know I gave you a go-ahead before, but if you're right, that might be the only real evidence we already have."

I knew that if I returned to the station, I'd be there all night, skipping supper, so I continued home.

Zach had everything ready to start cooking his version of stir-fry when I came into the kitchen. "You look like you've had a tough day," he said, wrapping his arms around me. "I take it you finally got Dana Watson to go to Portland?"

I nodded. "She wouldn't stay, though. Then I made her and Geo sit down and talk."

"That's not a good thing?" he asked, letting go of me. He pointed at a wine bottle, but I shook my head.

"Legally, I don't think so. Dana told me and Geo – so I heard it twice today – that Seaver didn't actually kill Rachelle. Browning did." I stole a piece of sliced carrot from his prep dish. "But Seaver told Dana after he killed Browning that if she talked, he'd come back for Geo."

Zach gave the 'ah-ha' nod. "That explains all the silence about what happened when she got burned. Did Seaver do that?"

"No, but it was because she had overheard Seaver and Browning talking about Rachelle."

"You do know how to find messes, don't you?" he said with a wink.

He dumped the slices of beef into the hot skillet to brown first, then he stirred the rice in another pan, artfully conducting each like sections in a symphony.

I grabbed a glass and poured myself some tea.

The beef gave off a powerful spicy aroma as it began cooking, onions, red peppers, curry. Once it was partially done, he turned down the burner and added the veggies – baby corn, broccoli, carrots, snow peas, summer squash, and water chestnuts.

"Amber, it's almost ready!" he called.

I washed up, set the condiments on the table, and poured tea into the other two glasses.

"So how is your foot," Zach asked, continuing to stir his creations.

"Seems to be healing. I began the small exercises this week," I said, trying to remember what the nurse had told me when she removed the sutures. "Take off the boot and just do a little movement, about an inch each way."

"It's a start. You'll be back to running marathons in no time," he teased.

I can't even say marathon without getting short of breath.

When his stir-fry was done, he dumped it out into a heavy ceramic bowl that had been warming in the oven, and brought that and the pan of rice to the table.

"Amber?"

"I'm starving," I said, ready to dig into the food when I pulled out my chair.

Again, there was no response from upstairs.

"Maybe she's asleep," he said. "Go on and start. I'll get her."

Not needing to be asked twice, I spooned myself a helping of rice then covered it with the stir-fry mixture, and I'd taken one bite when Zach knocked on Amber's bedroom door. Then again when he called her name, louder.

I'd just swallowed when I heard him jiggle the doorknob and knock again. I took another bite, then heard him call her name one more time.

Then there was no question when he busted through her door.

I had barely gotten to my feet when Zach yelled.

"Julie! Call an ambulance!"

❈

Zach paced in the small waiting room, the heavy clomp of his boots echoing two of the three steps his bulky frame managed each direction.

I sat out of his way.

He'd found Amber unconscious on her bed, a syringe and two bottles of insulin at her side. A note saying how sorry she was that she couldn't deal with being a diabetic, that she hated being a freak to even her best friends. She blamed me for making her test all the time, for lecturing her about how she would die anyway if she didn't take care of herself. The note hadn't been finished, but it said enough.

I was devastated she'd felt that way. And now Zach directed his anger at me as well.

Not speaking to me. He wouldn't even look at me, which I found unnerving.

My hands and feet were cold because I was so upset. My head pounded. The two bites of dinner I'd managed sat like a rock in my stomach, but I was far past being hungry.

Zach had carried Amber out to the ambulance as it stopped in the driveway, not wanting to have the debate again about getting her down the stairs. Her unconscious body had hung limp in his arms, then like a blob of hot putty when he put her on the gurney.

I'd stood at the back of the ambulance, watching both medics inside working on getting an IV, hooking her up to the EKG, getting a blood glucose then administering dextrose. Zach sat out of the way, then moved closer to her, holding her hand, when the EMT climbed out the back and closed the doors, then hurried to the driver's side, leaving me standing alone as the truck pulled away.

Now I sat in the waiting room, more or less alone, having had no choice but to drive here by myself. I didn't even know if I should call Zach's mother, and when I'd tried to ask him, the look on his face clearly told me he didn't want to acknowledge my presence in the room with him.

I wanted to be mad that he couldn't see past Amber's accusations. And part of me wanted to get in the Tahoe and drive back to the cabin without him, leaving him without a ride. I'd even gone out to the parking lot to sit in the truck, debating that very idea, but in the end, I couldn't do it.

So I sat in the corner, away from the hulking man who paced, awaiting some word about his daughter's condition.

Finally, Dr. Sanderson came to the doorway and motioned Zach to follow. When Zach walked past him, the doctor saw me, hesitated for a moment to see if I got up, then disappeared behind the entry with Zach.

If Zach wants me, he can come get me.

So I waited alone. An hour passed, then another.

I decided that Amber either had been admitted to ICU or would be transferred to a larger facility by ambulance, and I doubted anyone would be letting me know, regardless of the plan. Gathering my bag and crutches, I went back outside to my truck, only to find Zach leaning against it, arms crossed.

"Figured you'd come out here eventually," he said, his voice flat and low.

"I might as well go home," I replied. "No one wants me here."

"She needs you."

"I doubt that," I said, shaking my head. "And you don't want me here."

He inhaled, held it a long time, then let it out slowly through his nose. "Actually," he said, pausing again. "I do."

"Thanks for letting me know that four hours ago."

"I didn't four hours ago." He pressed his forehead with the heel of one hand. "But sitting up there with her in intensive care, I realized there was no one I wanted to be with me more than you. That you were the part of me that was missing. The part that would get me through this."

"I don't think I've ever seen you so mad, Zach," I said, ignoring the confession of his change of heart.

He shook his head. "No, you wouldn't have seen it, but I have been. Every time you've been hurt, it's been all I could do not to tear down the walls or pound some idiot to dust."

"I see." Words failed me.

I had seen him that mad once, just before Donny Bowers went halfway out a hotel window.

"Now Amber's up there, where they're undoing the damage she's intentionally done to herself. I just needed to blame someone else for a while because I couldn't blame her when I thought she was dying." He uncrossed his arms and took a step toward me. "I'm sorry, Julie. I hope you can forgive me. I really do need you now, but more than that, I want you."

When I stepped into his arms, I felt his body sag as the fear and anxiety he'd bottled up the last few hours flooded out of him in tears. "I can't lose her, J'," he said. "I don't know how to fix this, but I can't lose her."

CHAPTER

37

We sat again together in the intensive care room the rest of the night, watching the nurses and fluids and monitors.

When the paramedic had tested it before leaving the house, Amber's blood sugar was too low to measure this time, meaning below 40, but the hospital lab testing on that same sample showed a reading of 32. Very, very low, yes, but not zero. And with IV administration of dextrose starting in the ambulance, the readings had begun to come up steadily to her current level of 108. The nurse was still sticking her finger for a reading every hour because it was possible that the duration of the insulin would outlast the available sugar in Amber's bloodstream.

"None of this makes any sense to me," Zach said. "She doesn't look any different when her sugar is dangerously low than when it was dangerously high."

"You can't see it, but it's very different," I explained. "And I'd tell you, but you wouldn't remember it now anyway. Trust me that she's stable and being monitored for any changes."

Amber had opened her eyes and looked around a couple of times between visits from nurses or lab techs. She hadn't tried to speak to Zach, even when he took her hand and told her we were there.

"Is she mad that I found her?" he asked, sitting back down beside me. "You know, that she's still alive?"

"I don't have an answer for you."

At shift change, we left the unit and went to the cafeteria. Zach looked worn out in the fluorescent lights.

I'm sure I don't look any better.

We sat, waiting, nibbling on a shared muffin, drinking an average cup of coffee.

Almost done with our break, we heard the overhead page.

"Code Blue, ICU. Code Blue, ICU. Code Blue, ICU."

The operator hadn't said "code" the second time before Zach was on his feet and headed out the door without me.

No, I was certain that the cardiac arrest wasn't Amber. Whether Zach realized or not – and I'm sure he'd had tunnel vision all night – there were other, far more critical patients in that unit than his teenage daughter.

Nonetheless, I began to stack the tray with our cups and shared breakfast when a young man stepped over and offered to take care of it for me, since I was on crutches. Or maybe since my husband had responded to the code faster than any of the staff had.

I thanked him and crutched on toward the ICU, where I showed up minutes behind everyone else. However, there was no running for me, regardless what the emergency might have been.

I peeked through the door into the department, seeing that indeed, all the activity was two doors away from Amber's. Trying to be as inconspicuous as possible, I snuck around to her room, finding Zach breathing hard at the foot of her bed.

None of the commotion had woken Amber, which made me think the doctor had written orders for a drug to reduce her anxiety.

Zach could use one of those at the moment.

Embarrassed, Zach said nothing when I came in. We just went back to our chairs and waited some more.

"Sorry," he finally said. "I just couldn't help myself."

"I understand. I'd have hurried more if I could."

He nodded.

Around nine, Amber finally stirred, yawned, and turned to look at us.

Zach went to the bedside and took her hand. "I was so scared," he said in a low voice. "When I thought you were dead, everything inside me shattered."

"I'm sorry, Daddy." Amber began to cry. "I hate this. Cody, Savannah, even her mom – they all thought I was a freak before. Now everyone will think I'm crazy, too."

"Honey, you're a teenager facing a huge life-changing disease. Until you figure out how to deal with it, the rest of us don't know how to treat you. But that doesn't make you crazy," he said. "It means you need help coping with this, just like we do."

She leaned forward to look around him at me. "I wrote awful things about you, Julie, but I didn't mean them."

I struggled to my feet and hopped to the bed, not using my crutches. "Amber, I've never wanted anything but for you to be the best you can be. Sometimes I push too hard, and I'm sorry."

We cried, all three of us.

❧

When the lab tech came to draw blood just before noon, Zach and I left ICU to go outside for some fresh air.

"We'll get through this," I promised him.

"Amber and I will. You need to go catch a real crazy man and put him away before he hurts anyone else."

"I don't want to leave you –" I began.

"Stop. Both of us don't need to sit and watch the IVs run. I can do that alone. It's more important – to me, to her," he said, pointing at the building, "to a lot of other people that Mitchell Seaver goes to jail, or whatever else might happen to remove him from being a threat to society. I don't need a vehicle. I don't need to go home to sleep. I don't need clean clothes." He smiled. "Well, maybe that's not true, but this is okay for now. You need to go do what you're so very good at doing. Solve this case and find him. And be safe doing it." He kissed me. "I don't want you both in here, understand?"

I would have argued more, but he physically turned me around and pointed to my truck.

"Call when you can," he said, then nudged me forward.

Getting into the truck, I looked back to see him wave.

Against my better judgment, I left and drove to the sheriff's department. But on the way, I had an idea about a lead to follow.

Wade was in his office on the phone when I glanced in, but he waved me in to a chair, where I sat while he ended the call.

"How's Amber?" he asked after he crashed the receiver into its cradle.

"Oh, I think physically she's fine, though had she been alone, things could have been much different an hour later," I said. "Emotionally, she thinks everyone sees her and her diabetes as some freakish abnormality in humanity."

"Teens are just so sensitive about everything," he said. "Like pimples and new loves of their lives every week – it's mostly temporary. I can see how a permanent disease would change everything. You know you can have whatever time you need to be with her, right?

I nodded. Obviously I wasn't taking any of it at the moment.

"So what's up? I certainly didn't expect to see you today, regardless of that."

"Me, either, but Zach insisted I come in," I said, giving a shrug of confusion. "I have an idea. Teresa Lopez said she believed Mitch was married before they met, but we haven't been able to find any sort of record, right?"

Wade shook his head.

"I'd like to poke around in the vicinities of where he was in the military in Texas. If he was married before Teresa, maybe there are records there."

"Okay," he said, sounding less than hopeful.

"And to come up with a smaller date range, I'd like to contact law enforcement departments near where he was stationed for any cases where a piece of skin had been removed from a murder victim. It's a slim shot, but I think it's worth asking. I wish that sort of information was in the FBI database for violent crimes as far back as we're looking, but it's still possible we can find a match to one or the other, given the unusual circumstances."

Wade reached behind him to a credenza with half a dozen stacks of papers averaging a foot in height and handed me a file folder almost an inch thick. "Seaver's county employment records and everything else we've found so far, with references to his military background. Follow your nose," he said.

So I did.

From the file, I put together a timeline of Seaver's life events as we knew them, from high school on. His parents both died a decade or more ago of disease-related causes. He had no siblings. Army time from 1974 to 1978, mostly at Fort Hood, Texas, in Killeen.

Pulling out a map, I measured the distance from Killeen to Cross Plains, which was about 140 miles.

That brought to mind a whole new set of questions. Had Catherine had followed him to Texas, lived in Killeen for a while, even married him, then somehow ended up in Cross Plains? Given his apparent temper, if she left him, had he tracked her down there and killed her, and if so, would anyone have found her? Then, did he get remarried to someone else when he was still enlisted and, if so, was he technically still married to Catherine?

I needed more information about Catherine Bishop and Cross Plains. Given the date the card was issued from the library, and the last time she used the facility, we had a tighter window of opportunity when Seaver might have crossed paths with her, and possibly the next woman, if there really was one.

With the time difference of two hours, I needed to make contact before businesses closed, so I began looking up phone numbers, starting with the Cross Plains Library.

Giving the woman who answered a brief explanation of who I was and why I was calling, she gave me someone else, which meant I had to start all over. Fortunately, the next woman had been with the library since it had opened, so I crossed my fingers she would have a good memory. She looked up the number from the metal band on the library card, noting that this sort of card was used in the mid-seventies.

Yes, she confirmed the card had been issued to Catherine Bishop in June of 1976. "We had to put her maiden name on it because her driver's license hadn't been updated yet when she came in, the note says," the woman told me, "but the application says Catherine Seaver."

BINGO!

No, she couldn't tell me a specific date when Catherine quit using the library, but the last books she'd checked out – in December of that same year – had never been returned.

Exactly the information I'd wanted.

Next, I called the Callahan County Sheriff's Office to cross-reference Catherine Seaver to any criminal cases. Not nearly as helpful, I learned most of the records from solved cases were filed away without any hope of ever being computerized.

"That's just small town budgets for you, Ma'am," the deputy told me. "But I'll pass your number on to John Senior tomorrow. He's worked here for the better part of three decades and might remember something about what you're asking for. I'd say it'd be memorable if someone was found with a hunk of skin missing."

Not such good luck there, at least yet. Whoever John Senior was, I was hoping he'd call me back.

Next, I turned back to the possibilities of Seaver getting married in Bell County where Fort Hood was.

Some of the counties in Texas are bigger than whole countries overseas.

I called the county office main number to find out which department would record marriage licenses, even if the ceremony might have been on base.

Many cases of identity theft are successful because birth records and death records are not matched. In most cases, a person doesn't die in the same county where he or she was born, so creating such a link for each citizen is not likely to happen in the coming decades, even as fast as computerization and technology are booming. Marriage license records have also always been totally separate from birth and death records.

Because Bell County had been home to a military institution for decades, its records were in better shape than Callahan County's. Still, having a wide window of about two years, getting someone there to flip through what could be hundreds of pages looking for marriage license names was going to take some major bribery, best not even attempted at such a late hour.

I gave up on that, hoping the sheriff's department in that county might have a lead to make it worth their while to review the documents.

A knock on the door interrupted me.

"Geo?" I was surprised.

"I just dropped by to sign some papers for the county so I can take time off for Dana," she explained. "She doesn't feel safe here, so we're going –"

Holding up my hand, I stopped her. "I don't need or want to know where. You be safe. Call if you need something. I'll drop you an email when it's okay to return. If it doesn't have the word 'purple' in it, it's not from me."

"You," she said, shaking her head. "You think of everything. But thanks."

When I turned back, the clock read 4:10. I was famished.

All in all, though, I had made more progress on this case than I'd have guessed. I needed to see if Zach wanted dinner. Least I could do would be to meet him in the cafeteria, but I was hoping to go grab a burger instead.

When I peeked into Amber's ICU room, I found it empty.

"She was moved to a regular room," a nurse called from behind me, perhaps having had family members crack under the absence of a patient, thinking the worst. She gave me a room number, so despite the pain walking caused, I gimped on to the new room.

Zach was standing outside the door, and when he saw me coming, walked to meet me halfway.

"She's talking to a counselor," he told me. "What she told me is she didn't want to die but she didn't want to live." He tilted his head, considering his own words as if they were a foreign language he'd only repeated by sound but not understood. "Does that make sense?"

I waved my hand in a so-so manner. "We've both been in a far worse state of mind."

"Maybe so, but neither of us actually acted on those feelings," he replied. "Honestly, it's so hard to wrap my head around this."

"This might be a good time to go eat," I suggested. "I suspect you haven't."

He shook his head.

"Tell her nurse we'll be in the cafeteria, then let's go. I'll catch you up on my afternoon's progress."

Forty minutes later, I'd done just that, punctuated only by the pauses to bite and chew.

"That," he said about the news the library card had been issued to Catherine Bishop, though on the application she'd used the last name Seaver – the first evidence they'd been married, "is probably the most damning news to come along against him since this began."

I nodded, crunching a stale tortilla chip. "Finding her may still be next to impossible, but still it's now more than a theory." I paused. "Should I tell Amber?"

He didn't answer immediately, chewing as he thought. "Yeah," he finally said. "I think that case has been a motivation all along. Making progress now by tying the two investigations together is directly a result of something she did. Without that bag, where would you be?"

Where would we be? Why did Mitch identify the tattooed skin found in the wallet to begin with if he had something to do with the crime that created it?

"I'm sure he never thought we would get this far, especially because Amber had found it," I said. "We need to prove conclusively that the tattoo was or was not Catherine's."

"Wouldn't the easiest way be to eliminate a match be differing blood types?" he asked. "It might not, but knowing it came from someone else immediately could alter your direction."

"We're still trying to find a lab to do those tests. And I need a dental expert to obtain specimens from the baby teeth for the DNA if the blood type is the same."

And it took so little to get me wound back into the investigation with a new goal.

Without going to see Amber, I returned to the station.

The next time I looked at the clock, it was almost midnight, but I had found Catherine's blood type in the files, saving me from having to sample a baby tooth just for that. Then I coerced a lab tech at the Portland forensic lab to run the human skin for basic blood type and mitochondrial DNA sampling. We would have to keep looking for a lab to perform the more detailed PCR DNA testing, but I was beginning to think we should just submit the sample and wait our turn. Either way, we were waiting.

Hopefully, since Catherine's blood type was a much rarer B-negative, the results would be conclusive whether the skin was hers or not.

Although predicting the outcome of an evidence test was poor judgment usually, I had to wonder what step to take next if the sample was definitely not Catherine's. Wouldn't that indicate that there *was* another woman between Catherine and Teresa? The DNA would not give us an identity, but wouldn't it indicate there was another person to search for?

Is that good or bad? We already couldn't find Catherine Bishop.

Knowing Catherine obtained the library card in June of 1976, I didn't know if her driver's license was ever changed to her married name. Did the lack of names like on Teresa Lopez's tattoo indicate a lack of children from another wife after Catherine? Had the child in the photo in the wallet been Mitch's and Catherine's? Did her tattoo have a name?

If the child in the photo were still living, how old would he or she be today? Given that the image seemed to be just older than a toddler, and circus tickets might indicate about a six-year-old, that math didn't add up. Catherine disappeared from Washington in 1975, stopped using the library card at the end of 1976. There's no way a six-year-old child could be hers unless the photo was taken in 1980 or later. And Mitch Seaver was already out of the army by 1978.

But a child who was around six in 1980 would be eighteen now, give or take.

Now I really had to get that photo enhanced.

Tomorrow.

I packed up everything I'd been working on, locked up the lab, and went to see if I could talk Zach into going home for the rest of the night.

Amber was asleep, so I didn't have to twist his arm too hard when I reminded him he could sleep in a bed, take a real shower in the morning, and change clothes.

CHAPTER
38

At home, I let Zach take a shower first, expecting him to use twenty minutes of hot water. He was out and dressed in a pair of cut off sweats, hair still dripping, in ten.

"Would have been a good night for the hot tub," he commented. "Wish the new one would get here."

"Me, too," I said, leaning up to kiss him. "I cleaned up the kitchen. Sorry about your stir-fry, but the two bites of it I had were really good."

In the last day and then some, however, the sauce had congealed, and the rice hardened into a solid block, both of which I threw into the garbage.

"It smelled pretty good," he admitted. "We'll have to try it again some time."

I unfastened my walking boot and took his place in the small bathroom built downstairs, probably with the idea he could clean up without tracking all the way through the house, but I'd never asked.

The layout of the cabin had seemed perfect for the two of us, but with Amber, sometimes what would have been extra space just barely seemed enough, even though she had a bedroom and bathroom for herself. But she was already fifteen, so college and her future didn't seem all that far away.

I washed up and shampooed my hair, just now passing shoulder length with what I pretended not to notice were occasional gray hairs.

Probably have a few more of them these last few weeks.

When I came out, wearing sweats and an old t-shirt of Zach's, he offered me a glass of wine, and I nodded.

"It's sangria," he told me, and poured me a glass. "Needs a squeeze of orange."

I sipped, then he took my glass to carry out onto the deck, setting them down on the table between us.

"Hot tub, soon, I promise."

"You just wanted to crawl into it tonight naked," I teased.

"And you didn't?"

"Good point."

He asked how my detective work had gone for the rest of the day, and I summarized it for him.

"Okay, so if you don't think Catherine could have had a child who would have been old enough to be in that photo by the time she no longer used the library card, whose kid is it? Seaver's?"

"I don't know. I haven't even proven Catherine was one of the people in the photo."

"Say for the moment it is, but it was taken at whatever time it would be for the child to be the proper age," Zach said. "The image *was* in a man's wallet, right? What if she escaped him, and he only found a couple of pieces of evidence when he looked for her? He was tied up in the army to start with, but then he came back here to become a deputy. Maybe he just lost her completely after she left Killeen."

"Where would you run with a small child to escape Seaver?" I asked, taking a drink.

"I'd go to Alaska," he replied. "But she might not."

"That means I'm back to locating someone who has spent the last twenty years not wanting to be found?" I shook my head in wild sarcasm, "That should be easy."

"No, but consider this," Zach said. "If he had been looking all these years for the woman who got away, wouldn't he still be obsessed with finding her now, even when he's on the run?"

"Which helps me how?"

"Doesn't help, Julie, but you gotta find her first."

❋

The next morning, I visited with Amber for a short while, then left her and Zach at the hospital.

All night, Zach's suggestion that finding Catherine could help catch Seaver had pinged around in my head like a pachinko ball, too fast for me to track the possibilities or consequences of each bounce. In daylight, the task still seemed impossible, but I had thought of my next lead.

In the lab, I dialed back the Cross Plains library number, asking again for the woman who'd given me the information about the card yesterday.

"One other question crossed my mind," I said. "Do you remember ever seeing her?"

"I don't recall," the woman told me, then hesitated.

"How about a small child with her?"

"I handled the children's section at that time," she said. "Maybe. There was a wee boy, I think. Perhaps three or four? We encourage parents to let their kids have a library card of their own after they get to about eight, but not any younger. I remember him because she got him a card anyway."

"I hate to ask, but could you look for a child named Seaver from the time Catherine got her card forward for about a year?"

"Sure, but I can't do it right now. I have a reading group that just assembled. Can I call you back?"

Wasn't any point in telling her lives were at stake. I agreed and made sure she had the number.

Next, I called back to the sheriff's office in Callahan County and asked for John Senior, still unsure why I didn't get a real name before. The person who answered happily told me to "hold a sec'," and hit a button that transferred me.

"'s John," the man answered.

I took a breath and started my story again, and I'd gotten to the part where we were searching for Mitchell Seaver.

"Yeah, I got all that from my deputy," John said with slight impatience, but the statement told me he was the sheriff. "What exactly is it you need?"

I decided the words "I have him in custody" was too much to ask.

"We suspect that Seaver was married to at least two women while at Fort Hood –" I began only to be interrupted.

"Fort Hood's in Bell County, Ma'am," he corrected me.

"Yes, but I have evidence that one of those women had lived in Cross Plains because she had a library card, but she stopped checking out books suddenly in December 1976."

"And?"

"I was wondering if you might remember any unsolved cases during that time where a young adult female was killed," I said, then threw out the last card, "and had a piece of skin missing from her left shoulder area."

There was an ominous silence, and I began to suspect the call had dropped when he said in a slow drawl, "Well, I'll be damned. Hang on a minute."

Wonder what that means?

CHAPTER

39

Took about two minutes before he came crashing back onto the line. "Yep, just like you said, Detective," he announced, but I didn't bother correcting him on my title, after all, I was detecting. "In early 1975, we found a woman who'd been beaten, it looked like, tossed out on the south side of Highway 36 west of town in a thick stand of trees. Didn't look like she'd been dead but a month or so, but the wildlife had been snacking on her. But now that you mentioned it, I do remember her having this square piece missing from her shoulder."

A chill went through me. "Any leads on who she was?"

"Nope, not a one. I can send you the case notes if that would help."

"Do you have the particulars on what she looked like, any medical history?" I asked, flipping the page of my yellow legal tablet.

"Dark hair. About five feet six. Autopsy said she had blue eyes. Had delivered a baby by C-section, the doctor wrote," he said, then continued, but my mind had come to a screeching halt.

Maybe I interrupted him, I don't remember. "Any idea how long before she died she'd had the baby?"

"Ah, the coroner wasn't sure, but well over a year."

Possibilities went wild in my head. *What if what if what if!* I couldn't think fast enough to make sense of it all.

I asked him to forward me the notes, and I hid my surprise when he offered to email them.

"What's got you so wound up, if you don't mind me asking," he said before we hung up.

"I don't know who she is, but I believe she might have been connected to Mitchell Seaver, who is now wanted in connection to several murders here. He was based at Fort Hood starting in 1974, and so far, every woman we've associated to him has had a similar tattoo to his in that same left shoulder area."

"Well, you keep me posted. If there's anything else I can do to help you, let me know."

"Actually, there is. Might there have been any tissue saved so we could do a DNA comparison?"

"I can't imagine there would have been, but I'll let you know when I send you that email."

When we hung up, I found I was almost panting.

"That good?" Zach said from the lab door. "What's his secret?"

I jumped to my feet, forgetting my crutches until I put weight on my left foot. "Ouch! Crap!" I sat back down. "The sheriff in the small Texas town where Catherine's library card was issued remembered a case where a woman was found missing a piece of skin. And she'd had a baby."

His eyebrows went up. "So was it Catherine?"

"No, I don't think so," I said, motioning him inside to sit. "I think the dead woman was involved with Seaver *before* Catherine got there, but I think the baby is the child shown in that picture."

"Wow, that's bizarre."

"I need to tell Wade," I said, reaching behind me for the crutches this time.

"No need," a voice called down the hall. "Be right there."

Was I really that loud?

A minute later, the sheriff entered the room. "Sorry, I was grabbing a ream of paper and overheard your news." He plopped the pack of printer paper on the counter and pulled up a stool.

"Yeah, it was really amazing," I explained. "And now I need to find out who this woman was, starting by matching her DNA to that skin."

"So do you think that maybe," he said, hesitating, "Catherine Bishop is still alive?"

I shrugged. "There's a possibility, yes. Boyd was already pretty sure the tattoo we had wasn't hers. She had been married to Seaver, but then she ended up in Cross Plains, Texas, for some reason, which is where the other woman's body was found."

"Suppose this other woman is the mother to the child," Zach ventured. "And for some reason, whether they were married or not, he killed her. Then he invited Catherine down to Texas and presented her with a baby and a marriage proposal. Or vice versa."

Wade and I both nodded.

"At what point would she have had enough and left him," Zach continued, "ending up back in that little town. The next question is, why there – the same town as the last woman? Maybe because the kid's family was there or something else to do with the child she took with her."

That was one of the theories I'd had in mind when I hung up with the sheriff of Callahan County.

"Did Mitch find them and kill Catherine, and possibly the child," Wade asked, "or is she alive for us to find?"

"Or did he kill her and abandon the kid?" Zach concluded.

Gee, first I needed to find a killer, but now I have to find out what had happened to three people twenty-some years ago.

"Zach, you want to help? I'll pay you as a consultant, get you on the phone," Wade offered.

"Thanks, Sheriff, but I have enough problems of my own right now with Amber," my husband deferred. "If something comes up where I can help in a day or so, I'll do it and we can make it official later."

"Fair enough," Wade said, standing up again. "Let me know what you need, or just do it. I trust you to spend the county's money sensibly." He walked out the lab door.

"Wow, that's two things no one has ever said to me," Zach said. "Spend all the money you want, and welcome to Internal Affairs, here's your promotion."

"Not likely to happen any time in your future, now, either," I replied. "And I still don't think you getting Eric Rader to give me my job back was funny."

"I did," he said, ducking when I threw my pen at him. "And again for the record, giving you the job back, with the promotion, wasn't my idea."

Eric Rader, now the commanding officer over New Mexico State Police Internal Affairs had reactivated my credentials to give me back my job and legal authority while I was there to protect Amber, but the position had required me be of a certain higher rank than I'd been when I left my job, so he'd also promoted me. It was all very temporary but useful, nonetheless.

"I didn't even get to sleep with anyone in IA," Zach said, continuing the joke.

"Keep on and you won't be sleeping with someone who used to be in IA, either." I gave him a sarcastic smile. "Meanwhile back to solving this crime," I said, trying to get him to focus on something else. "Let's follow this out. She escaped from Seaver at Fort Hood, taking the toddler with her, lived in Cross Plains for part of the year, then had to leave again when he got close. So where would she go?"

"What kind of skills did she have?" Zach asked.

"None that I know of, but at least originally she would have had to make money that was untraceable, like waiting tables."

"That would make keeping the child difficult," he said. "But you're right, the income would need to be cash until she could steal identification for herself."

And then it hit me. "I'm betting she stole one, all right, but one that makes everything so much easier for the child. What if she took the boy's mother's identity after she ended up dead?"

"Oh, wow," Zach said. "Now you just have to identify a dead woman."

The phone rang, and it was the Cross Plains librarian who'd promised to call me back. "I can't find a single name for a Seaver in the next few years," she said. "But I did find one card for a boy that stood out, not so much because I knew his mom. I mean, I knew almost all these kids and their parents through the years. I recognized his name because he wasn't even in preschool, but he could read."

"Go on," I said, pen poised. "What was his name?"

When she told me, I was so stunned, I couldn't even write it down.

CHAPTER
40

After I hung up, I felt my face flush, then go pale as my heart rate nearly doubled. When the room began to tilt, I feared I'd simply faint, so I hung my head between my knees and tried to breathe.

"Julie?" Zach had said several times, though I couldn't seem to answer. His voice sounded tinny and far away, like the old AM radio stations I could only pick up in the middle of the night when I was a kid. "Julie?"

Maybe he was afraid I'd pass out again, like I had in the emergency room, so I inhaled deeply and sat up.

"I know who it is," I said. "I don't know everything, but I know enough to solve this part of the case. Trouble is, we still need to find Catherine Bishop."

His eyes met mine.

"I was right. She did steal the identity of the child's real mother," I said, reaching for the phone.

Zach squinted as he tried to make a connection like I had, but failed.

Wade answered my call. "You need to come hear this," I said. "Right now."

I looked up a number and dialed the Callahan County Sheriff's Department and asked again for John, Senior.

"He's not in the office right now. Could I take a message?" the woman asked.

I explained who I was. "Tell him I know the identity of the body," I said. "He'll know what I'm talking about."

She might have said something else, but I was already hanging up as Wade walked in.

"I don't know how all the pieces of this fit together a quarter of a century ago," I told them both, "but the woman in the photo is Catherine Bishop, after she was no longer with Mitch Seaver. And the boy?" The excitement had left me almost breathless again. "The librarian knew him as Bear Langston."

"Any kin to . . ." the sheriff's voice trailed off. "Oh shit."

"Yep, our very own deputy Richard Barrett Langston. That's where his nickname came from – Bear from Barrett," I said. "So now we have to find out where Catherine is, only she's been using his mother's identity all this time."

Didn't take long for the sheriff's order to get Langston returned to the station followed, but we still sat in stunned silence, waiting for him.

"I doubt he knows any of this," I cautioned. "Probably doesn't even know who Catherine Bishop is, because she's been using his mother's name all along."

"And I'm only a little lost as to how this helps us find Mitch," the sheriff was saying when we heard on the portable radio that Langston checked out at the station.

Zach answered for me. "Under all this stress, I think Mitch is going to resort to the one thing that he never completed when he was younger, which is to find Catherine and the boy."

Langston poked his head around the doorframe, shy as a boy in trouble at the principal's office.

"Come," Wade said, motioning to a chair. "Sit. We have something to tell you."

Seeing how nervous that invitation made Richard, I waved him on in. "You're not in trouble, but we have a few questions you may have answers to."

Still reluctant, he did sit, but I felt his knees bouncing underneath the table.

"While trying to find Mitch Seaver, I've been doing a lot of digging about a woman who disappeared from this area in the mid-1970's," I began. "From what I can surmise, she went to Texas to meet up with him when he was stationed at Fort Hood. My theory is that he had custody of the little boy of a woman he'd been involved with earlier, though the math says he was probably already walking by the time Mitch met the boy's mother."

So far, the story didn't ring any alarm bells for Richard.

"I believe Mitch killed the child's mother, whose body was found outside a small town over a hundred miles away, but he kept the boy and needed a new mother for him. When Catherine Bishop arrived, having all but disappeared here, Mitch presented her with this child to take care of. And, so goes this theory, when Mitch became abusive, Catherine took the boy and left, going at first to the small town where the boy's real mother had been raised," I said. "In Cross Plains, Texas."

Richard's eyes opened wide.

"From there, I don't know what happened, but I do know that a young boy named was given a library card there in 1976," I continued. "He was not quite four years old, but I'm told he could already read. His name was Richard Barrett Langston."

His skin lost its color, and I imagined I could see right through to Richard's skull.

"No," he squeaked, the cleared his throat and tried again. "No. My mother's name is – was – Dorothy Langston. She died five years ago of breast cancer in Tacoma."

"She had a tattoo, didn't she?" I pointed to an area on Zach's massive shoulder as an example.

The look of confusion on his face deepened the creases as his mind zipped through a million memories. "I never saw her in a swim suit or shirt that would have shown it. She had a scar, so I suspected she'd had something removed there." He told the truth, but he kept shaking his head in denial.

"Do you know why she would have gone back to Cross Plains with you?" I asked.

Almost a minute passed before finally he focused on me and said, "My grandmother lived there. We stayed with her for a little while, but then my mother up and moved us to Tacoma. She told me my grandmother died in her sleep."

"After you moved?"

He nodded.

"Wonder if that involved Seaver," Zach said aloud.

"I'm sorry she's no longer with us," Wade said, clapping a hand on Richard's shoulder. "But now we really do need to protect you from Mitchell Seaver."

"You don't think he knows about me, about this, do you?" he asked, eyes jumping wildly from Wade to me to Zach and back. "I mean, hell, I didn't know!"

"All we can do is try to get in front of him," I said. "If he figures this out like we did, I think he'll come looking for you."

The sheriff took a flustered Richard Langston, who was now in no shape to go back to work, to his office.

"I need to get back to the hospital," Zach said. "Amber is supposed to be released this afternoon."

"Today?"

"She has a followup appointment with a shrink tomorrow morning," he said, rolling his eyes. "I'm not sure what talking to someone four times her age is supposed to accomplish, but that's the plan."

"Sixty isn't so old," I said, feeling it was much closer to around the corner than ever.

"Okay, five times her age," he corrected. "I don't think I could garner much enthusiasm for seeing him, but it's his job to assess her emotional stability now," he said, making quotation marks in the air with his fingers.

Zach left me to my digging, though I'd exhausted my eagerness to make any more connections.

I'd almost given up for the day when the phone rang again. With a feeling of dread, I answered, worried I'd used up all my good news mojo.

"Detective Samualson? John Senior in Cross Plains," he told me.

"Sheriff, I gotta ask," I said. "Is there a John Junior who works there?"

He laughed. "Well, there is another John, but he's not a junior to me. Senior is actually my last name."

"All right, then," I said. "I bet you've had to explain that a hundred times. What did you find?"

"Me? I was only pulling the case file for you," he said. "You called me."

Oh yeah, I forgot.

"Yeah, well, I think I know who your Jane Doe was," I said. "But now I'm more concerned with something a bit different first. I need to know the cause of death for Mrs. Leona Copeland, sometime around 1977."

"Her?" he asked. "I don't recall which of her ailments got to her, but it wasn't homicide."

"Okay," I conceded. "The Jane Doe would have been her daughter Dorothy."

"No, Dee and her boy lived here with Leona until just before she died," he told me. "Heard she'd just started a new job out west somewhere and couldn't come back for a funeral. The ladies in Leona's church had a small service at the graveside, but that's all."

So I explained how we'd come to the conclusion about who she was and how Catherine had taken over her identity. And who the boy was.

"Son of a buck," he said when I was through. "So now you're looking for this Seaver, who probably killed the real Dorothy, and his current wife?"

"Actually, according to a very reluctant witness, Seaver let another man kill his wife, then he killed that man." I shook my head. "I know, it's all very complicated."

"No kidding. I'll find Leona's death certificate and see what was listed as her cause of death, but I can't imagine it was foul play."

"I'd appreciate it."

"You get any more surprise twists, you give a shout, okay?"

I don't know about your county, but I'm not sure mine can stand any more twists like this.

I gathered up my things to go home, unsure what had security measures might have been put into place for Richard.

Poor kid, I thought. What a way to find out that your whole past was fabricated, and then not to be able to even confront the woman who'd been your mother for two decades.

At the cabin, I found Zach's Mustang sitting in the driveway, a gleaming black with a silver strip over the hood and roof.

Crap! I'd forgotten again that he didn't have a vehicle when he left the station.

He and Amber were sitting on the deck in the shade.

"Car looks fabulous, Z', but it's not red," I said. "Sorry I forgot you needed a ride. It didn't even occur to me how you got to the station today."

"No worries. They called this morning to say it was ready, so I asked them to deliver it to the hospital. Worked out perfectly."

"It even smells new," Amber observed.

I sat down between them, dropping my crutches to the deck. "It's been a crazy day. We've found out what happened to Catherine, thanks to you," I said to Amber.

"Really?" she asked. "Is she still alive? I knew it!"

I put my hand on her knee, trying to hold her down. "She was alive," I explained. "Until about five years ago when she died of cancer."

"That's so sad!" Amber said, deflating from her excitement.

"Apparently Catherine went to Texas in 1975 to be with Seaver, and it looks like they got married, but we think Seaver already had the child in the photograph from a previous relationship. Calculating his age, the boy must have been about two when Seaver met his mother, and then for some reason, he killed her – it's most likely her skin we found in that wallet," I explained. "We think that when he abused Catherine, she moved the boy back to Cross Plains, where his grandmother still lived. Seems Catherine took over his mother's identity, that of Dorothy Langston, maybe to hide from Seaver.

Eventually they ended up in Tacoma."

"So they were close to where she grew up, but she couldn't return home after Seaver came back up here, too."

I nodded. "More or less true, though we can't prove most of the reasoning she had for the things she chose to do."

"How'd you figure all this out?"

"The librarian in Cross Plains. She remembered a very young boy because he could read. His mother got him his own library card."

"I can't believe I missed all that," she said, frowning.

"You're the one who found the bag, or we wouldn't have been trying to put this all together, Amber."

Where would we be without that bag? Without any connection between Mitchell Seaver and Catherine Bishop. Without any theories regarding the similar tattoos.

CHAPTER
41

No sleep for me tonight, I thought, sharing at the ceiling. Insomnia had plagued me for the better part of the week. Beside me, Zach stretched out on his stomach, snoring softly.

So much had happened, not just in our lives in the last two months, but all around us. And yet so many of our problems had gone unresolved, such as Amber's diabetes, or an arrest that put Seaver behind bars.

Still less than a month since my surgery, but ready to escape anyway, we'd packed to leave the next morning, stopping on the way for my orthopedic appointment in Portland, to drive to Cannon Beach and along the Oregon coast. Six days of getting away from home, from work, from a case that had gone nowhere, despite some great evidence.

The blood typing did not match the teeth to the skin from the wallet, which we knew for sure now. Without any way to prove it, we presumed Dorothy's tattoo did not have a name beneath it because the child had not been Seaver's. It was even possible, though I doubted we'd ever find out, that Seaver had intended to kill the boy, but Dorothy had stood in his way, so he killed her instead.

The photograph in the wallet could not be salvaged, but Richard recalled it was of him, his grandmother Leona, and the woman he'd known most of his life as his mother. We learned that Leona had been wealthy, so she provided enough money Catherine did not have to work until she left Texas.

The photo of the tire print was finally matched to the patrol car Seaver had been driving, so we presumed that he met Rachelle at her van, then drove away with her, maybe not even against her will, to Dana Watson's property, where Jack Browning killed her. Some expert in burials estimated that her body had been placed on our land within a day or so of her death.

That was a subject I really didn't want to learn more about.

I turned over and fluffed my pillow, wishing my mind would stop repeating these details.

Out in the hall, I heard Amber open her door to sneak down the stairs. She might have believed no one could hear her, but she had not inherited her father's silent mode. However, I did appreciate that she was trying not to wake us because it was three in the morning.

I yawned.

She'd been doing really well, managing her diabetes. Although I knew she sometimes snacked in the middle of the night, she usually got an apple or banana. She must have grabbed something from the counter instead of the fridge, I thought, when I didn't hear the door open, but then I didn't hear her come back up the stairs, either.

I know, because she always makes the fourth riser from the top squeak.

Although it was dark in our bedroom, just enough light shone through from the new moon to illuminate Zach's silhouette. His broad back, now imperfect with the scars from surgery and injuries, was still tanned and defined, the muscles in statuesque relief.

I reached to touch his shoulder, and his muscles quivered like those of a horse. Waking him would not make him angry, I knew. He would roll, wrap his arm around me and tuck me close to his body, which might lead to other physical pursuits. But the night was too hot for sleeping so close to his overly-warm body.

Thinking about our first night in this bed, I smiled. Almost Christmas, two years ago now, we'd left the balcony doors open but had the gas fireplace lit just for its ambiance. Tonight the doors were open for the breeze, only now beginning to be too cool. I pulled the sheet and a lightweight blanket up over my shoulder.

Downstairs, I heard a thud. I didn't recognize the sound. Maybe Amber had dropped something on the counter or bumped into a wall in the dark.

At least I didn't have to be this tired because of Amber's sleepless nights as a baby.

Thinking of babies, I wondered again why Nolan hadn't passed along Olivia's news about the baby, if what she'd really meant was that she was pregnant. And of course, I'd forgotten all about Nolan's invitation to Las Vegas for their wedding. I'd need to call him.

And my mother.

Crap.

My last call to her had been more than two weeks ago, and fortunately she was getting ready for work so we didn't talk long. There was just so much it would take hours to explain to her that I didn't want to talk about.

I closed my eyes again, still hoping to get a few hours of sleep. I did not want to interrupt our getaway because I couldn't stay awake. Zach would be cooking breakfast at dawn.

Turning away from him, I rearranged my pillow and tried to relax. Muscles in my neck and back ached from being still.

Below I heard another noise, then careful footsteps on the stairs, including that tiny squeak on the fourth riser. At least Amber was going back to bed, I thought.

Beside me, Zach rolled from his stomach back to his side, facing away from me. The soft snoring sound he'd made quit. While his breathing seldom bothered me when I was sleeping, when I couldn't, it might as well have been a jet plane, echoing in my head.

I inhaled, letting the air out slowly in an attempt to blow out the tension.

Amber turned at the top of the stairs and took a few steps past her door, maybe going to her in the bathroom before going back to bed.

Light switch. Hint of a squeak of the door hinges.

Ugh, will the noises never end?

And then something I didn't expect.

The whisper of the bolt sliding as the knob turned. In *our* bedroom door.

I opened my eyes, willing my heart to stop pounding in my ears.

Beside me, though nothing else I'd heard had disturbed Zach, I felt him tense as his head turned slightly so he could hear better, then as he moved his left arm off the side of the bed.

For his gun.

The door slammed open, all the way around to the wall, revealing a man with both arms clasped in front of him. In the dim moonlight, I saw he held a gun.

"Don't move," he growled at Zach, who froze, hand still empty when he'd jerked around at the sound of the door smashing open. "Just couldn't let it go, could you, Julie?"

"Let go of what?" I asked, pulling the sheet up without thinking.

"That damned bag. Should'a never been found," the voice replied, clearer now I knew it was Mitchell Seaver. "Now I'll just have to kill you all," he said, "but maybe I'll have a little fun with that yummy teenage daughter of yours first."

"You didn't find the boy, did you?" I asked in hateful defiance.

"What boy?" He raised the gun.

Did he really not know about Richard Langston? Did he not care?

Three shots rang out, almost too fast to be counted.

Shock spread over Seaver's face, his arms dropped. A dark stain blossomed on his light colored shirt, then he fell, first to his knees, then facedown into the room.

I hadn't moved. Zach hadn't.

"Dad?" Amber yelled, swinging around the top of the stairs toward our bedroom door. "Are you okay?"

We exchanged a glance as Amber came barreling through the door where Seaver had just stood.

"Is he dead?" she asked, my Glock 9x19 in her hands, now lowered to the floor.

Zach slid off the bed, taking two steps to reach the footboard, another to where Seaver lay. He knelt down, extended his arm to feel for a pulse, then turned back to me.

I was already on the phone.

"Julie? What's wrong?" Bette asked, knowing from the caller ID who she'd answered.

"Seaver. He broke into my house, Bette. He's dead."

When I looked up again, Zach had taken the weapon from Amber, and they stood together in a tight hug.

After I hung up, Amber swiveled to see me. "I remembered what Nolan told me about pointing a gun," she said, recalling her first lesson at the gun range. She nodded at the body. "He said he was going to kill us all, and he had a gun pointed at you, so I shot him."

"Yes, you did, Amber," Zach said. "He was clearly a threat to us all. And I'm very proud of you."

CHAPTER 42

Richard Barrett Langston paced in the conference room, waiting for our other guests.

I understood that he was nervous, given the circumstances of the meeting. The woman who had taught him to read, who had worked two jobs sometimes so he could have school supplies and healthy meals, who had helped pay for him to go to college, and who had stood proudly when he graduated at the top of his police academy class in Seattle, had not been his biological mother. She was, by his accounts, a wonderful mother, nonetheless.

The real Dorothy Copeland-Langston's story was a bit more convoluted as we began unraveling it. The only daughter of a fairly well-to-do family in Cross Plains, she had married at a young age a soldier, Barrett Langston. She had gotten pregnant in their first few weeks of marriage, before he went off to the army and was killed. Their son, Richard Barrett Langston, started life missing one parent already. His mother, then a single mom, more or less left the boy with her own mother, Leona Copeland, while she went off in search of someone else to make her happy or whole or whatever it was she thought was missing from her life. Though Mitchell Seaver was not her first encounter, he proved to be her last.

Although neither Dorothy nor her mother were still alive to explain, I spent hours with Richard trying to piece together how his biological mother might have met and moved in with Seaver, finally marrying him in some JP's office near Fort Worth. We only found this because a friend of Dorothy's mother had saved all the letters found at the Copeland home, hoping some day that sweet little boy would grow up to come looking for the truth. It had taken a quarter of a century before that happened. That friend's grandson, now in his forties, had kept the letters as his mother and the grandmother before had done.

I found it amazing how this family friend had seen the importance of such letters and made sure that the next generations had kept them. Even more amazing, the existence of these letters had been noted by the funeral director who handled Leona Copeland's graveside services. When I contacted him, he read me that notation, scribbled onto the files regarding her last wishes and location of her grave, and one added line about who currently held the letters.

Worried such a valuable piece of his history could be lost in the mail, Richard had flown to Dallas-Fort Worth, rented a car, and then driven to Cross Plains, Texas, to meet this grandson and receive the letters in person. Turned out that the grandson was actually Richard's second cousin, the only living relative left from his father's side of the family. The pair had spent a week untying their pasts and becoming friends.

Now with more answers to how Catherine had become his mother, and why she'd taken Dorothy's identity – which had been at Mrs. Copeland's request, as described in the letters – Richard was ready to look at Catherine's past, too.

So here we sat in the tiny conference room of the sheriff's office in Washington.

While we'd waited, I'd emailed Geo a note: *All is well. The kingdom is right again, and the prince will be dressed in purple for his coronation. Come home soon. Julie.*

Wade sat in the corner. Zach, Amber and I stood out of Richard's way as he walked back and forth.

When the couple came in, everyone who'd been seated rose.

"Mrs. Bishop, Dr. Bishop? I'd like you to meet the boy Catherine raised after Seaver killed his mother, Richard Barrett Langston. Rich, meet Catherine's parents, Esmeralda and Dr. Boyd Bishop."

I introduced the couple not to the deputy they'd known over the last few years, but to the grandson they'd never known because of their daughter's commitment to his safety, knowing that Seaver had also come back to Skamania County to work as a deputy.

Might be true that they were not related by blood, but then again, Catherine had been adopted, so the Bishops' relationship to her was not genetic, either.

I suspected that would make no difference.

Boyd had wanted closure by finding out what had happened Catherine. Esmeralda had been afraid of the truth, fearing the young girl she remembered had fallen prey to evil ways and died a drug addict or worse. The truth – that their daughter had taken in a toddler to protect and to raise as her own after his mother had been murdered – would be a conclusion to make them both proud.

Yes, all was right in the kingdom.

I walked out into the bright sunshine, got in the Mustang with Zach and Amber, and we headed west to the coast.

EPILOGUE

Given the circumstances, the investigation of the shooting death of Mitchell Seaver was mostly ceremonial. Because she was still a minor, Amber had stood before Judge Harry Harrison in his chambers a week ago to explain what had happened that night, how she'd been in the downstairs bathroom when Seaver came through the patio doors, having picked the lock. He passed within feet of where she stood behind a closed door, sneaking up the stairs.

"I told the judge that I opened the foyer closet and got your gun," she told me later. "I had to explain why you and Nolan showed me about shooting, but he understood."

Maybe she had learned a little about how Zach moves without a sound, because she had come up the steps behind Seaver, stepping over the squeaky riser but remaining low on the last two stairs as he was threatening to kill us.

"So I stood, aimed at his back, and fired."

"And you saved our lives, Amber," Zach told her.

"But I killed a man," she stated. "I understand now what you meant about doing whatever is necessary to protect your family."

"Not easy to live with, is it?" Zach asked, putting his arm around her shoulder as we'd left the courthouse.

"Hey, I have diabetes. I can live with most anything," she said with a wide smile.

After discussing the situation with Zach, we thought it best to leave out the whole criminal element to our updates regarding his resignation when we talked with our mothers.

As I suspected, the medical news was the higher concern for both, with dozens of questions regarding Amber's diabetes, its onset, the current treatments and so on. We left it up to Amber whether to tell either or both about her insulin overdose, and she elected not to share that news.

Vera Samualson was a little curious about what had made Zach decide to quit working for the government, but she'd known about the conspiracy to catch Gordon, so it wasn't hard for her to understand how Zach hated how it had played me for months, letting me believe he was dead and then using me as bait.

My mother didn't ask any questions about that at all.

I invited both moms to Las Vegas for Nolan's and Olivia's wedding, hoping we could make another family get-away of it.

Vera didn't know Nolan, but my mother also declined the invitation.

So in October, the three of us flew to Las Vegas and spent a four-day weekend with the newlyweds, who looked happy together. Olivia had elected not to bring her son Brian, citing their winter trip to Orlando with him to celebrate instead.

"How's retirement settling with you?" Nolan asked Zach the second evening as we sat around a table after a huge dinner.

"It may take a while to get used to this," Zach replied, "but I'm working on it. There're lots of projects to go around the place, and we're still working on rodeo events." He put his arm around Amber's shoulders. "But no one has shot at me in at least," he paused to look at his watch, "four hours."

"Dad!" Amber chided. "That's not even funny."

"Now you just have to get Julie a job counting horseshoes, and you can both skip out on the knife-and-gun club events."

"I might just do that," I said. "But not this week."

"Now that Nolan will be around more," Olivia chimed in, "I started back to school this fall to finish my master's degree."

She wouldn't become a physician as she'd set out to do a decade ago, but I'd seen her in the lab at the hospital, and she was very skilled.

"And the baby ought to be here during semester break in January," Nolan said, beaming proudly. "It's a girl."

We toasted the newest Forresters.

"Olivia wanted me to tell you the evening I called to invite you here, but I wanted it to be a surprise."

"I heard her, but I didn't understand at the time why you didn't tell me," I said.

"What about you, Amber?" Nolan asked. "You've got college coming up in a few years. Any ideas what you want to do?"

She smiled. "Oh, I have lots of ideas, but I'm not committing to anything just yet."

Thank you so much for reading one of
Val Conrad's *A Julie Madigan Thrillers.*
If you enjoyed the experience, please check out
the next book in the series!

Dreams of Like Souls by Val Conrad

COMING IN 2020